To: Dorothy

The Murder Prospect

Lee Mossel

With my best regards!

Lee Mossel

December, 2012

ISBN: 0-6156-5237-9
ISBN-13: 9780615652375
Library of Congress Control Number: 2012910433
The Crude Detective
Parker, CO

chapter

ONE

I got a thrill looking at my name on the office door: <u>Crude Investigations, Cortlandt Scott, Geologist.</u> The ornate gold script with bronze underlines didn't reveal much about the company's business and left plenty to the imagination. I liked it. Too bad the pretty sign hadn't brought in some clients though—- four months had passed since the lettering went on.

It'd taken a leap of faith to hang out a shingle as a private investigator after fifteen years as a petroleum geologist. My four year stint as an Army Ranger after college had also given me some decent self-defense skills so I felt confident I could take care of myself if need be. I started talking about doing oil field investigations with my long-time girlfriend, Gerri German, during a canal barge trip through Burgundy. At first, she'd scoffed at the idea but had come around when she realized I could do something related to the oil business without being a geologist. She also knew my "retirement" at thirty-nine had left me bored and needing something to do.

I'd taken over the office space on the sixth floor of the Equitable Building in downtown Denver from Sid Bonner, a geologist friend, who had to retire at sixty-three when he'd started slipping into Alzheimer's. That was a shame because Sid was one of the good guys. He'd spent a lot of money decorating and furnishing the roomy three office suite.

***

I was sitting in the inner office reading drilling reports when I heard the outer door to the reception area open and close. I strolled out and found a young man, maybe eighteen or twenty, standing at the desk. He was tall, slim, and well dressed in ranch style clothes. Something about him looked familiar, but I couldn't place it.

"Morning, what can I do for you?" I asked.

"Hello, sir. Are you Mr. Scott?" He had a hint of southwestern accent.

"I'm Cort Scott. You don't have to call me sir." Actually, I liked being called sir.

He stuck out his hand, "You probably don't recognize me although I've met you—- probably ten years ago. I was just a kid. My name's Evan Linfield. I live out by Byers."

I certainly knew the name. The Linfields ranched and farmed south of Byers thirty miles east of Denver on the Colorado plains. The Crude Company, an oil and gas outfit I'd founded, made its biggest field discovery on their ranch. The family had become wealthy from their lease royalties. The last time I'd checked production records, the field was producing almost five hundred barrels a day from twenty-two wells. At that rate, their royalties were worth over a hundred thousand dollars a month.

I shook his hand and noted the firm grip. "Are you Randy's son?"

"Yes, I am." The kid looked away for a second. "My dad died July last year. He had a heart attack while he was cutting hay up on Byers Flat."

That was a shock. I hadn't heard or read anything about it. Randy Linfield and I had spent lots of time together watching some of the early wells come in. He was a straight-shooter, a gentleman, and a man of his word. We'd become friends and I felt ashamed I hadn't made more of an effort to keep in touch over the years. "I'm really sorry to hear that," I said. And I meant it. "I liked your dad—- I considered him a friend." I couldn't believe I didn't know of his death.

"He considered you a friend too. In fact, that's why I'm in Denver. My dad used to say if we ever had a problem with the oil, we should talk to you and you'd help us. My mom read the notice in the newspaper about your new company and had me read it too. Mr. Scott, we've got some real problems and mom and I would like to get your opinion on some things. If you don't mind, before we talk, may I ask what you charge to do an investigation?"

"Your mom's name is Julie, isn't it?" I remembered Randy's wife as a pretty woman and a good ranch hand.

"Yes, that's right."

"Well, Evan, I plan to charge about the same as geological consulting, which is six hundred dollars a day plus expenses. To tell you the truth though, I haven't done any investigating yet. I don't know how long things take. Why don't you explain your problem and I'll give you a day rate that will cover it?"

"That sounds fair. The oil production has meant a lot of money to us and that's part of the problem. My mom and I talked and decided we'd pay you ourselves. We didn't want to stir up the rest of the family until we know more and you tell us if you can help."

"Come in, Evan. It's a lot more comfortable in my office. Can I get you something to drink—- coffee or a soda or anything?"

"Thanks. Maybe just some water for now."

I led the way into my office from the reception area and pointed at one of the club chairs. I got Evan a bottle of water from the mini-fridge, poured a cup of coffee for myself, and went behind my desk. I thought better of it, picked up a legal pad, and came back around to sit beside Evan in the other guest chair. He was obviously nervous and I wanted to put him at ease.

"What kind of trouble do you have? Start anywhere—- I'll keep anything you say strictly between us. I'm not a lawyer or a doctor so that isn't guaranteed by law, however it's my intention."

"Thanks, Mr. Scott. This is important to me and my family."

***

Evan Linfield told me the story of what had happened to his family and what was concerning him now. After my discovery of oil on the ranch, the four Linfields formed a corporation to divide their royalty income equally. They made the arrangement because the three boys, Randy, Bob, and Jeff, and their sister, Mary, had each received an equal amount of land from their folks who'd who'd passed on years ago. Before they'd inherited, it'd all been one ranch and they decided it wouldn't be fair to not share the oil royalties equally regardless of whose land the oil field fell on. They formed Linfield Family Royalty and organized as a corporation. The men each had families but Mary had never married. She lived in the original ranch house and concentrated on raising and showing horses. Randy, the eldest, had been the original CEO and chairman of the corporation. He'd also stayed on the ranch and built a house on his land. Randy and Julie had wanted to continue ranching even after the oil made them rich. The other brothers, Bob and Jeff, had left before oil was discovered. Bob was a veterinarian and had a large animal clinic in Greeley. He was married with three almost grown kids.

Evan said his folks and Aunt Mary didn't discuss Jeff much. Jeff, the youngest, had attended Colorado University for several years, though never graduating. Between stints in Boulder, he'd lived with Mary. When he was on the ranch, he worked for Mary and Randy, spending most of his time complaining about being stuck out in the sticks. He allowed them to manage his part of the land as they wished, sharing the expenses and profits. Jeff had been a late-in-life child and was fifteen years younger than Randy and twelve younger than Bob. Ten years separated Jeff from his sister, Mary. He'd been in his mid-twenties when the oil checks started to arrive. Within a few months, he left Byers and now only came to the ranch once a year, around Thanksgiving, when the corporation held an annual meeting. He lived on the Nevada side of Lake Tahoe with a wife no one had ever met. Evan didn't know what his uncle Jeff did although he'd mentioned real estate investments.

Following last year's meeting, Julie told Evan about the terrible row they'd had over deciding who should succeed Randy as head of the corporation. Bob was the natural choice as next oldest, however he was busy with his vet clinic and was considering making a run for the Colorado House of Representatives next year. Julie, as Randy's widow, had a vote but, according to the corporation's by-laws, would be replaced on the board when Evan turned twenty-five and only a direct heir could serve as CEO. Julie thought Mary should take it since she lived on the ranch. Mary had agreed—- Jeff objected. He wanted to take over, however he wasn't willing to move back to Colorado to run the corporation. The corporate by-laws also said the CEO must maintain a primary residence in the state. When Mary pointed it out, Jeff had erupted and stomped out of the meeting for several minutes. After he returned, Bob nominated Mary, Julie seconded, and Mary, Bob, and Julie voted for her as CEO. Jeff voted no.

Evan gave me an excellent summation of the corporation's by-laws concerning investments and the disposition of funds. When I asked him how he'd gained such a deep understanding, he said his mother and Aunt Mary had explained everything to him in great detail after Randy died.

He told me investment decisions were subject to a vote and, in the past, most votes had been unanimous. The by-laws said any tie votes could be broken by the CEO although that hadn't been necessary.

Royalty income was paid into the corporation and fifty percent of the gross was distributed quarterly to the families in equal amounts. Another thirty percent was placed in an interest-bearing account and used for estimated tax payments while five percent was donated to various charities.

The remaining fifteen percent went into an investment account at Merrill Lynch. While Randy was alive, he'd worked with a Merrill Lynch investment advisor and they jointly made recommendations to the family.

Evan shifted in his chair, lowered his gaze, and his tone. "Mr. Scott, I had no idea there was so much money in the investment account. Mom said during the first few years when new wells were coming on and production was flush, Merrill Lynch was taking in over seventy-five thousand dollars a month. Mom told me there's almost *sixteen million dollars* in that account. She said we've never made a disbursement and everybody's been happy with Merrill Lynch until Uncle Jeff started complaining this time."

I'd calculated the Linfields' income several times over the years because each time crude oil prices shot up, shares in The Crude Company also skyrocketed. My share holdings climbed so far that three years after the discovery on Linfield Ranch, I sold my twelve percent interest in the company for seven million dollars. Still, I was surprised at the amount the Linfields had accumulated. I agreed with Evan. "That's a lot of money."

He continued with his story of the Thanksgiving board meeting that had spun out of control. "Mom said they voted Aunt Mary in as CEO and reaffirmed the charity support so the question of retaining Merrill Lynch was the next order of business. She said Uncle Jeff introduced a motion to fire Merrill Lynch and have the corporation manage its investments directly. Mom said she and Aunt Mary and Uncle Bob just sat there in stone silence for several moments and then they had a big argument about how no one had the time or knowledge to manage that much money. Jeff said he wanted to manage 'his' share himself and didn't care what the rest of them did. He argued they should agree to disburse if one family wanted to manage its own share. Mom said tempers were flaring because that would mean liquefying about four million dollars of the investment account to disburse an individual share."

Evan said the next day, over breakfast, Julie had wondered if Jeff had money troubles because he seemed anxious to get his hands on the investment account money. She said they'd taken a whole bunch of votes and finally agreed to sell some holdings and, in the future, keep twenty-five percent in cash. An individual family, by giving three months' notice, could withdraw twenty-five percent of their share of the cash each year.

Evan said he'd asked her, "How much money are we talking about, Mom?"

He didn't look away this time. "That's when I found out about the sixteen million. Mom did the math and told me any one of the families could draw two hundred and fifty thousand dollars by giving ninety days' notice."

Evan told me he'd been stunned when he asked, "So, what's your share of the total, Mom?"

He told me, "She kinda hesitated before she said, 'Twenty-five percent of the sixteen million, I guess. And, it's not mine, it's *ours* Evan.'"

I asked him, "So what'd you say then?"

"I asked if Uncle Bob, Uncle Jeff, and Aunt Mary all had four million and she said, 'Yes, and don't forget each family also receives forty to fifty thousand every quarter. How do you think we've been able to buy all the new equipment and animals and pay for you and your cousins' college? Even buy the wheat ranch over in Kansas? It was all purchased with the quarterly payments. That's why everything got so heated up in the meeting. Your Uncle Jeff wants to get his share out plus have the corporation make different kinds of investments.'"

I thought about that for a moment and asked Evan what he thought would happen.

He said he'd asked his Mom the same question. "Is Uncle Jeff going to get his way?"

"What'd she say?"

"She said, 'Not entirely, but we've got to consider his proposals. Jeff's trying to convince Mary to make changes.'"

"Will your aunt change her mind, Evan?"

"I think it's going to be a big fight."

That got my attention and I asked, "What's happened since the meeting? Has Jeff met with your aunt and, more importantly, what brings you here?"

Evan shifted position, drank some water, and faced me. "It's sort of all wrapped together. Uncle Jeff stayed at Aunt Mary's house for a couple days after the meeting, went back to Nevada, came back in April, and stayed a week. Mom and I knew he was at her house—he never came to ours. Aunt Mary came over a couple times and said he was putting a lot of pressure on her to invest in an oil drilling deal and that's what made us think of you. When we saw your announcement about doing oil business investigations, Mom and I decided I should talk to you. We haven't mentioned it to the rest of the family yet."

I'd placed announcements in the business sections of the <u>Rocky Mountain News</u> and the <u>Oil Journal of the Rockies</u> when I decided to try investigating. A few friends had spotted them and inquired although no one had responded with any jobs. It was nice to know "someone" had seen them.

"What exactly do you want me to do, Evan?"

"Mom and I want you to check out the company Uncle Jeff's pushing us to invest in. He told Aunt Mary their drilling deal is in Wyoming, someplace called the Mosquito Basin. I don't know where that is…you probably do. Jeff wants us to buy a twenty-five percent interest in a well and a bunch of leases. He also wants us to buy stock in the company. We're not sure how everything is supposed to work. Mom said the company is private, but they told Uncle Jeff if they raise enough money, they'll go public and our stock will be worth a lot more. Does any of that make sense to you? Would you be willing to check out their deal for us?"

I'd already decided I was going to do whatever he asked and this made my decision feel even better. I wouldn't be doing some after-the-fact forensic examination of a sham deal. I'd be involved up front in evaluating an oil deal and trying to prevent some good people from being taken. I hated to think an oil and gas company might be crooked. Unfortunately, I also knew it was way too common. I wouldn't mind flushing the crooks out of the business.

I stared intently at Evan. "First of all, what you've described is a common way to get a small company off the ground. I used the same basic plan for The Crude Company. As far as looking into it for you, yes, I'd like to."

"Good, I'm glad. When can you get started?"

"Immediately. I'll start today and call you next Monday with a report. What's the name of the company you're interested in?"

"Black Blizzard Petroleum."

That name rang a bell, but I couldn't place it. In the first place, it was a crappy name for an oil company and, secondly, for some reason I didn't like the vibe I got when I heard it. The ringing bell was carrying a sour note.

chapter

TWO

I walked Evan Linfield to the door. "Evan, thank you for coming to see me. Would you ask your mom if I can meet with her and your Aunt Mary? I'll drive out to Byers if they'd like. It'll be easier for everyone if your aunt knows what's going on. If they agree, give me a call and I'll come out early next week if the timing works for everyone."

"I'll ask. Mom and Aunt Mary are pretty close so I think it'll work. Thanks, again, Mr. Scott."

Maybe my plan to change from oil prospecting to investigating wasn't so off-the-wall after all. The Linfields were asking me to do something I knew how to do and it would be good dealing with them again. I had met them all, except for Jeff, although the only ones I knew well were Randy and Julie.

I remembered how Jeff had tried to get better lease terms from the leasing agents I'd sent. He'd wanted more up-front bonus money and a higher royalty percentage for leases on his part of the ranch. Luckily, the others had already signed so he didn't have much leverage. We told him if he didn't sign a lease, we wouldn't drill the prospect. That'd been a bluff, of course, but it caused the others to pressure him and, ultimately, it worked.

***

Evan's mention of Black Blizzard Petroleum jogged my memory back to the week I'd opened my office. I'd wandered down to the Mandarin for lunch and a couple beers. The Mandarin's bar served as an unofficial petroleum club. It catered more to oilfield service hands and salesmen than to oil company executives who lunched at "the" Denver Petroleum Club on top of the Anaconda Building.

I'd grabbed a place next to Mark Mathey, a retired landman, who held court daily from the middle of the bar. "Hey, Mark, long time, no see. What in the world's going on?"

"Well, well—- Cortlandt Scott. It's been a while. What did I read about you doing something weird? Crude Investigations? What the hell is that?"

"Oh, I thought I'd try something different. I wanted to keep a toe in the oil biz, though. I got tired of beating my brains out trying to sell prospects."

"I hear you. It's tough out there."

I motioned to the bartender for a round of beers, "You heard about any new players or big deals floating around?"

Mark took a long pull on his beer as he considered my question. "Do you remember Jerome Biggs? He worked for your alma mater, Shell, back in the eighties. That was probably before your time."

"It *was* before my time. I've heard about him and met him once at a convention. I heard Shell fired him because he was tipping somebody off about filing on federal leases around their plays. Why do you mention Biggs?"

"Because he's back in Denver as exploration manager for some outfit called Black Blizzard Petroleum. He opened up some expensive office space in the new Petroleum Building and says he's looking for drilling prospects. Word on the street is the money's coming out of New Orleans and LA, which aren't the first places you think of for Denver based oil companies."

"That's a fact. Anybody we know sell anything to 'em?"

"Not that I've heard. I figure anyone who remembers Biggs wouldn't trust him with the time of day let alone a bona fide drilling prospect."

***

I recalled the conversation and began thinking of ways to get a look inside Black Blizzard. I could probably get a feel by showing them a drilling prospect. The quickest read would come by showing something I knew *wouldn't* work. If they spent time doing a proper evaluation and turned it down, they might be legit. On the other hand, if they snapped up a guaranteed dry hole, no questions asked, and tried to resell it at a marked up price, they were probably running a scam.

I booted up my computer, opened the Colorado Secretary of State's website, and clicked on the corporation's link to see what kind of paperwork Black Blizzard had filed. That turned out to be interesting. The original papers had been filed a year ago December. The corporate offices were listed in-care-of Renoir and Mondragon, a law firm in New Orleans. The company founders were Maurice DiPaulo, James Davidoff, John Marcello and Myron Metropolit. An amended filing changed their headquarters to Denver and listed Jerome A. Biggs as general manager. Something about the founders' names struck a chord, but I couldn't make the association.

It was almost noon. I grabbed my jacket and headed for Sounds of the South, a Cajun restaurant and another place where oil-field types hung out. I lucked into a seat at the far end of the bar. My friend, Andy Thibodeaux, who owned the place, was busy mixing and pouring so I pointed at him, signaled for a beer, and mouthed, "I need to talk to you." He nodded, slid the beer down the bar, and held up three fingers. I sipped the beer, turned on the stool, and looked over the room. I noticed five guys wearing suits in a booth in the far corner. They caught my eye because suits were unusual in Sounds of the South.

Andy finished filling an order, dried his hands, and strolled over, "How you been, *Mon Ami?*" Andy's accent was thick as ever and he was so typically Louisiana French, I'd always thought his picture should be in the dictionary next to "Cajun." He was fairly tall with a small pot gut, sloping chin, large nose, and a receding hairline. He proudly traced his family all the way back to the Nova Scotia Acadians who'd arrived in New Orleans in 1765.

"I've been good, Andy. Listen pards, I need to ask you about some names from New Orleans. You have a minute?"

"Yeah, I got one minute, mon. I'm beaucoup busy, t'ank da gud lord. Who you need to know 'bout?"

"You ever hear of a law firm named Renoir and Mondragon?"

"Hoo, mon. Dat some heavy name droppin' dat you do. Dat outfit been in N'Awlins for hundred years. Dey handle da big time crooks, ya know. When da mob got organized down dere, dat Renoir and Mondragon bunch be dere mout'piece."

"That's interesting. Here are some more names for you. You ever hear of Maurice DiPaulo, James Davidoff, John Marcello, or Myron Metropolit?"

"Who-oo, Jesus Christ!" You doan wan' to know any of dem guys. Dat's a 'Who's Who' of da mob in N'Awlins, yes. DiPaulo and Marcello are second go-round pure wop. Dere fathers were capo regimes for da Abodando fambly till dey got too old and den dese two took over. Used to be said dat Marcello killed Sock Capriati who was da big boss after ol' man Abodando got capped. Davidoff, he da consigliore. I t'ink Metropolit is da money changer guy. He came to N'Awlins right when I was leavin'. I t'ink he from New York. Dese be some bad guys. Wha' you wan' to know 'bout dem for?"

"I'm running traps for some friends of mine. Renoir and Mondragon filed the papers in Colorado for Black Blizzard Petroleum and the other guys are listed as founders."

"Dat ain' no good, Cort. Dat outfit gotta be crooked if Renoir and Mondragon is mixed up wid dem."

I knew the names had sounded familiar. Anybody who'd spent time in New Orleans had seen them in the _Times-Picayune._ They were usually mentioned in the context of organized crime figures. It sounded like Biggs had made some bad choices in business associates.

I was having trouble figuring out how they could form a company if they're known crooks. "How could that bunch found a legit company in Colorado? Don't all of them have records?"

"Mon, I don't know if any of dem have been convicted of anyt'ing. I tole you dat Renoir and Mondragon are good. Mebbe dey got dem crooks off. I doan remember ever seein' where dey did any time."

"How can that be? I remember reading about them years ago. They were always being picked up or questioned for something"

"You know dat, I know dat, ever 'body know dat. Mebbe da DA been happy just givin' 'em parking tickets and such. T'ings are different in Colorado. Dey prob'ly gets away wid stuff in N'Awlins dat dey can't here."

Andy glanced around, leaned over the bar, and said, "See dat guy wid da brown suit sittin' in da chair at da end of dat boot'?"

I slowly turned on the barstool and glanced at the five men I had spotted earlier. The guy at the end of the booth was medium height, stout, and looked strong. He had dark curly hair cut short and a deep tan that he hadn't got in Denver. "I see him. What about him?"

"He start comin' in 'bout two weeks ago. He say dat he work for Jerome Biggs over to Black Blizzard. He nevair say what he do. He ain' no geologist or engineer."

I took a drink. "What's his name?"

"He say his name is Mike Landry. He say he a coon-ass, but he doan talk lak no coon-ass. We talk 'bout N'Awlins though, and he fo' sure been dere, yes."

"Listen, Andy, I'm going to make a point of coming in every afternoon for a few days. I'll look for an opportunity when there's an open stool next to Landry. When I see it, I'll sit down. I need you to introduce me."

"Why you wanta do dat? It think you askin' for some kinda bad troubles, ma fren."

"It's just something I'm working on. I'll be seeing you soon, buddy."

I walked past the Black Blizzard booth and saw Jerome Biggs sitting on the inside. He'd gained some weight and lost some hair since the last time I'd seen him although that'd been ten years ago. There was a flicker of recognition in his eyes, however he didn't acknowledge me and I quickly looked away. The others were wearing clothes more suited to summer in the South than fall in the Rockies. I knew what oil and gas investors were supposed to look like. These guys didn't fit the bill.

chapter

THREE

Evan Linfield's mention of the Mosquito Basin stirred up some other memories. Sid Bonner, the former occupant of my office, had worked the area. Each time crude oil prices spiked, he would dust off his old prospects and start flogging them around Denver. They never quite qualified as flavor-of-the-day because the basin had been a graveyard for wildcatters. Sid had made a fortune in other areas where success rates were greater although he kept going back to the Mosquito because leases were cheap.

Back in my office, I opened the Wyoming Oil & Gas Commission website and kept hitting links until I found a drilling permit report for the Mosquito Basin. Not much help there. The commission hadn't issued a permit in two years.

I caught a break in the State of Wyoming lease records and found Black Blizzard had recently taken several thousand acres of state owned oil and gas leases. The bonuses had been modest by current standards at ten dollars per acre. The going price in the Big Horn Basin to the north was more like a hundred dollars an acre. Next, I accessed the Bureau of Land Management records and found more Black Blizzard leases on federal lands. Altogether, they'd amassed over ten thousand acres. I needed to find out if they'd also been leasing private land owners. That could wait until tomorrow.

With the low bonuses, there was plenty of margin to mark up the cost to investors. That didn't make it a crooked deal. In fact, it was a common approach to the business. How much they marked it up and the story they were telling potential buyers would be the deciding factors.

Now that I knew where their leases were, I started looking for old wells. It wasn't a surprise to find Black Blizzard's leases covered with dry holes. Unless they were targeting a deeper formation or had some reason to think all the dry holes were actually mistakenly plugged producers, the company "had" to be conducting a scam. I couldn't prove it yet, but it was sure as hell suspicious. I printed out several pages of lease and well records, shut down the computer, and headed for home.

***

My house in Parker, a rapidly expanding suburb twenty-five miles south of Denver, had taken a substantial chunk of the money I'd made from The Crude Company. It was way too much house, but I loved living on the edge of open rangeland and the Black Forest. I walked straight through the house to the deck and saw a huge five-point buck standing in my back lawn. He was contentedly munching the mums that separated the mown grass from the wild area behind it. No wonder I never had any fall flowers. My thoughts drifted to my father and the place deer played in my memories of him. I saluted the buck and went back inside.

I poured a glass of Nobilo sauvignon blanc and walked to the deck on the west side to check out the sunset. I sat in the glider thinking through what needed to be done before seeing the Linfields. I started a list although I hated making lists.

***

The next morning I set up the coffee maker and went for a run on the open space trails behind my house. When I returned, the message light was blinking—- Evan Linfield had called and asked me to call him back. I poured a cup of coffee, went into my office, and pushed redial. "Good morning, Evan."

"Hi, thanks for calling back so quickly. I thought I should tell you Uncle Jeff is here. I mean, he's on the ranch at Aunt Mary's. You said you wanted to come out and visit with Mom and Aunt Mary but we didn't know if you'd want to come while he's here. He stopped by our house last night and said he'd be here for three or four days."

I thought about it for a bit. If I could get the things on my list done today, it might be worth talking to all of them. "Has your mom had a chance to talk to your aunt about me coming out?"

"Yes. Aunt Mary said it was fine and she'd look forward to meeting with you."

"Okay. Let's plan on my coming to Byers on Wednesday. I should have enough information about Black Blizzard to have a good idea of what's going on. If you'd pass that on to your mom and aunt and ask them to tell your uncle, I'd appreciate it. I'll plan on being there after lunch, say about 1:30."

"I can do all that. Thanks, Mr. Scott."

"Thanks for the call. This may speed things up for everybody. I'll see you Wednesday." So much for reading the paper, I had things to do.

I called the Yellow Knife County, Wyoming, clerk and recorder's office to check on leases recorded in the last year and found Black Blizzard Petroleum had taken thousands of acres. I couldn't get the exact descriptions although I felt certain they were inter-mixed with the state and federal leases. By my rough calculations, they'd assembled nearly twenty-five thousand acres in the Mosquito Basin. Their lease block was heavily populated with dry holes, not the most encouraging sign for an oil and gas drilling program.

Next, I called Sid Bonner's wife. After talking about how Sid was doing, which turned out to be a good day/bad day thing, I asked if he'd been showing his Mosquito Basin ideas to anyone in the last year or so. She wasn't certain—- told me he'd been rummaging around in his old files in their basement and had taken some maps downtown. I asked if she remembered when, but she didn't know for sure.

"You know, Cort, I told you Sid has his days. I actually think he's doing quite well. His doctor put him on an Alzheimer's drug and I think his memory has improved some. At least it's not getting any worse. If you're interested in visiting, I think there's a good chance he could help you. He's been recognizing people for the past few weeks. Would you like to see him? He enjoys visitors even if he doesn't know exactly who they are and he still has a great sense of humor."

That was far better news than I'd expected. If Sid remembered showing his Mosquito Basin geology in the last couple years, it might explain how Black Blizzard had gotten wind of it. I told her I'd drop in on him this afternoon.

When I hung up, I was surprised it was already 11:00. It would take an hour to drive to Lakewood so I planned to leave at 2:30. That left three hours to do more investigating. I'd come to like the term. I felt like I was making good progress.

I called my best friend, Tom Montgomery, at the Denver Police Department to see if he had any ideas about the detail that continued to bother me: How could four mopes from New Orleans, listed as founders of Black Blizzard Petroleum, qualify for ownership of a company?

Tom hadn't been a voice of encouragement when I'd explained my plan to change career paths. His exact comment, "you're fucking nuts," had seemed harsh at the time. If I hadn't thought it through and had several discussions with my girlfriend, Gerri, I might have taken offense.

"Hey, Tommy, how's it hanging?" I said when he picked up.

"Like a drum. You wanta beat it?" Tom was a funny guy—-not very original, funny none the less. Plus, he had a really dirty mind and a potty mouth. "What do you want?"

"I was wondering if you could check something out for me about some guys in New Orleans who might be mobbed-up. You know anybody in the PD down there?"

"I asked you *not* to get me involved in *your* PI business, but who do you come running to the first time you need something? Who're the bad guys you need to find in New Orleans?" Tom pronounced it New OR-Leans.

"I haven't met any bad guys yet, Tommy. I think they're all in jail because you're so damn good at your job. Seriously, I could use a little help if you have the time to inquire."

"All right, I'll quit giving you a hard time about playing detective. I know it's something you want to do so I'll help you if I can. One thing though, if you do get in over your head, let me know."

"I will, Tom. Thanks."

"Who're you trying to check out?"

"A company called Black Blizzard Petroleum filed incorporation papers in Colorado. The registered agent is a law firm in New Orleans named Renoir & Mondragon. I talked to Andy and he said they're a real old time firm and they represent mostly mob connected guys going back to the thirties. The registration statement lists four guys as founders and stock holders in Black Blizzard Petroleum. Andy says he knows of them and they're real bad characters."

I walked around my desk and looked out the front window. The leaves were changing on the sugar maple in the front lawn. "Their names are Maurice DiPaulo, James Davidoff, John Marcello, and Myron Metropolit. I'd like to know if they have any felony convictions that would prevent them from being shareholders in a company in Colorado. I've heard they're planning an IPO soon and they're trying to find investors for a drilling prospect in Wyoming. I've done a little geology and think it's probably a hoax—- maybe even fraud. My first clients are being pushed to invest in the prospect *and* the company so I'm looking into it. As soon as Andy told me about these guys, I decided I'd better learn all I could about them."

Tom exhaled loudly. "Sounds like you've been busy. As it turns out, I know a woman cop in New Orleans. She can probably find out anything there is to find. I'll make a call, give her the names, and see what she turns up. Fax those names over. From the sound of them, they might have some interesting spellings. If you do it right away, I can still get them to her today. Isn't New Orleans two hours ahead of us?"

"I think it's only one. They're on Central Time."

"Yeah, you're right, still—- the sooner the better."

"I'll do it soon as we hang up. I really appreciate the help. I'll keep you up to speed on what's going on. Who knows? If Black Blizzard turns out to be crooked, there might be some guys here in Denver you can slap the cuffs on."

"That would be good for everybody. I'll let you know when I've got something."

I printed out the names in block letters, faxed them to Tom, and checked the clock—- another hour was gone. I decided I'd better keep a record of everything, so I opened a folder, titled it Linfield: Case 001 and put everything in chronological order from the time Evan had walked into my office. I was surprised when my notes filled nearly three pages. The investigative business might kill more trees than geologic reports. I decided to store everything electronically until a case was closed. Then a final report could be printed and put in a file cabinet.

I finished up around two p.m., changed into slacks and a golf shirt, slugged down a protein shake and a power bar, and got the mail. More good news—- mailbox money, and this was the big one—- a check from Williams Natural Gas for my royalty interest in Barn Burner gas field. Barn Burner was one of the largest natural gas fields in Wyoming and although my override percentage was small, the checks were usually several thousand bucks a month. The income was the main reason I could try out this new line of work. I'd purchased my override from a good friend who'd done the geology leading to the field. My buddy's percentage was five times mine so he was really logging in the dough.

***

I pulled into the parking lot of the Alpine Village care center at 3:35, parked my Corvette in the open, away from the flowering plum trees lining the lot. They were shedding like crazy and, even though the top was up, I didn't want leaves all over the car. I entered a reception area which resembled the entry to a safe deposit vault. There were reinforced glass doors on both sides of the receptionist's desk and I could see an open atrium area in the center of the building. The receptionist was early thirties, attractive, and perky. She may have been five or ten pounds over her fighting weight, however I wasn't looking to fight her, so I appreciated the way the extra poundage filled out her sweater.

"Good afternoon, name's Cort Scott and I'd like to see Sid Bonner."

"Yes sir, Mr. Scott. Mrs. Bonner called earlier and said you'd be visiting. Mr. Bonner's in the courtyard enjoying the sun and fresh air. I'll buzz you through. One of the attendants will meet you inside and take you to him."

"Thanks."

She pushed a button under her desktop, the door to my left buzzed and slid open and I stepped inside. A pimply faced kid in green scrubs stood by French doors opening out to the courtyard. I could see Sid sitting on a bench across the well-tended garden area. The kid swiped a card through a reader, opened the door, and pointed. He never said anything.

Sid raised his head at the sound of the door, smiled, and waved. I was pretty sure he recognized me. I walked diagonally across the garden toward him and when I was about six feet away, Sid stood and extended his hand. I was pleased to find his grip was still firm. I tried to make mine firm and not too hard. His hand felt a little frail.

"How are you, young fella'? It's nice of you to come see an old fart like me." Sid's voice was husky and phlegmy. It sounded like he needed to clear his throat. I remembered the same voice timbre from my Dad. Sid had always called everyone by their name for as long as I had known him, so calling me 'young fella' made me wonder if he did recognize me.

"I am doing just dandy, Sid. Cort Scott," I said. That was a trick I'd learned dealing with my mother who'd also suffered from Alzheimer's disease. Near the end, Mom only recognized my sister who saw her almost daily. I only saw her a couple times a year in her last five years. My sister told me to use my first name early in a conversation and Mom would usually pick up on it. I saw a spark in Sid's eyes as soon as I said my name and waited for his next words.

"Of course, Cort. I have to admit you look familiar as hell. Frankly, I couldn't put a name to the face until you said it. Cortlandt Scott, right? My wife tells me you took over my old office in the Equitable Building. It's nice to know there're still a few independent geologists around."

We stepped over to the bench. "I'm just trying to keep the seat warm, which is why I wanted to talk to you. Do you remember how you used to break out your old Mosquito Basin prospects every time the oil price went up five bucks?"

Sid laughed which was good to hear. "Sure, I always figured every ten years or so there'd be a new flock of people who hadn't seen some of those deals and I could turn 'em again. Hell, I musta sold some of that acreage four or five different times. I got a lot of wells drilled too. None of 'em ever worked out."

"When was the last time you gave a show-and-tell?"

"Christ, I don't know for sure. My memory isn't what it should be, that's why I'm locked up in this joint." Sid laughed again. It didn't sound as good as the earlier one. "I seem to recollect some guy called me a few years back inquiring about the Mosquito Basin and whether I still had any maps or prospects in the area. I'm pretty sure

I pulled some old maps to show him, but I'll be damned if I can remember who it was."

"Do you remember a guy named Jerome Biggs?"

"Hell, yes. I remember that shitheel. What's he got to do with this?"

"I thought it might have been him who called."

"I wouldn't have given Biggs the time of day. That son-of-a-bitch busted one of my plays twenty years ago. I showed a North Dakota deal to Shell, which they turned down, and about three weeks later I got a call from a friend who worked for the BLM. He told me some outfit from Billings, Montana, had filed on a bunch of federal leases all over my prospect. I called the State Land Board in Grand Forks and found out the same company nominated state leases for auction in the area. I couldn't prove anything at the time. I heard Biggs got run off from Shell for bullshit like that. The Billings outfit turned out to be a distant cousin or his wife's cousin. I never trusted him after that and I never showed him another deal."

Damn it! I'd been sure it was Biggs. "You can't remember who called you about the Mosquito Basin?"

"Not at the moment—- my memory comes and goes. Leave me a telephone number and if I remember who it was, I'll call you."

"Thanks. Can I ask you another question?"

"Sure, what is it?"

"Did you ever get to a point where you thought the Mosquito Basin wasn't going to work?"

Sid didn't hesitate. "Hell, yes. After I got four or five prospects drilled, I figured out something was wrong although I couldn't identify what it was. The funny thing was, every few years here would come a whole new crop of companies I could show it to and they'd get all excited about the possibilities. I made money every time I revived it. Mostly, I just sold the ideas for cash and an override. Sometimes, I bought leases if they were cheap enough, marked them up, resold them, and kept an override. Hell, you should give it a try—-it doesn't take much seed money and you can always get it back one way or another."

"I think it's happening again, Sid. I don't think the company doing it "wants" to find any oil. I think it's being used to promote a share float and maybe to cheat some people."

"Jesus, I hate to hear that. I may've been selling deals I wasn't a hundred percent sure would work, but I was selling to legit oil people every damn time. I never tried to cheat anybody. I always showed all the dry holes and how they either condemned some areas or set up other ones."

"I know that, Sid. Hey, do they let you out of here now and then?"

"Oh, hell yeah. My wife and kids take me out to dinner and over to the house sometimes. I was kidding about being locked up."

"That's good. Maybe I can take you out and we'll have a drink sometime?"

"Goddamn, that sounds terrific...I'll have to pass, though. The doc has me on some medication, and it seems to be helping, but I can't have any alcohol. I'm not sure I want to remember everything if I can't have a drink or two to make it worth remembering." This time the laugh was full and real.

"That's a shame. Tell you what though, I'll give you call soon and we'll go out to Bear Lake, drink some sodas, and watch the birds and sailboats."

"You do that, Cort. I'd be grateful. It feels good just to cuss a little. My family doesn't do much of that and this place frowns on cussing. Goddamn 'em!" Another good laugh followed his little outburst.

We stood and shook hands again. "Great seeing you, Sid, I'll be in touch."

"I intend to hold you to it."

I walked to the French doors and into the hallway. The security door opened from this side without being activated.

I asked the receptionist, "What's the procedure for taking one of the patients on a day trip?"

She pulled a form, handed it to me, and said, "You need to register with us and get approval from the family. It takes about a week."

I took the form, thanked her, and walked out to the late afternoon sunshine. This had been a busy day and wasn't showing signs of letting up. I wondered what the rest of it would bring.

chapter

FOUR

From Lakewood, I made it to the parking garage at Fifteenth and Champa in twenty-five minutes. I hoofed it over to the Equitable Building. The wind had picked up and the temperature had dropped several degrees. I ran up the six flights to my office; my morning runs were doing some good. The message light was blinking and I found a call from Tom Montgomery. I hit the return button, it rang through, and Tom picked up immediately.

"Hey, Tom, I just got back to the office. You called?"

"Yeah, I did. I got some info for you from New Orleans. Before I tell you, I'm going to say one more time you should rethink this whole PI bit." Tom sounded serious. He almost always sounded serious, except when he was being funny.

"Why's that? Is this gratis data gathering wearing you out already?"

"I knew you'd have some wiseass answer. I think you may be in way over your head already. You're just a dumbfuck geologist, not a "real" private detective, and you're sure as hell not ready to be hired muscle. I don't give a shit what the army taught you."

"Thanks for the vote of confidence. That wouldn't be in the playbook anyway. I'm a big boy, so why don't you let me have what you got. I'll see what I think."

"It's your funeral, pal. Andy wasn't shittin' you. The names you gave me are some real treats. DiPaulo and Marcello have each been arrested about twenty times. Almost all the charges have been dropped for lack of evidence within twenty-four hours. They've been picked up for everything from petty mischief to murder but, get this, the only convictions either one have are for misdemeanor obstruction of justice or interfering with a lawful order. They either have the best lawyers in the country or, more likely, they've got someone in the DA's office on the pad. Davidoff is pretty much the same except he doesn't have any violent crime arrests beyond an assault charge about twenty years ago. Even that was reduced to menacing and he got probation." I could hear Tom pacing and the phone cord rubbing against his desk.

"Metropolit is a different story. He's never been charged with anything in New Orleans although he's got a long rap sheet from New York and Los Angeles. He's been charged with all kinds of paper and accounting crimes, everything from fraud to counterfeiting to forgery.

"His old man was in the rackets in New York. He was some kind of child prodigy, math whiz and got pretty high up in the numbers biz and loan sharking right after World War Two. Myron started working for his old man as a teenager, went to school for a while, and studied accounting. He never finished. His story gets kind of hazy during the seventies...he was probably doing something for one of the five families in New York 'cause he was living on Long Island." I heard Tom's chair creak as he sat down.

"He spent three years, total, in a couple of New York jails. He did five hard at Vacaville out in California. That was for running a money laundering scheme for Mexican dopers. Metropolit got caught with almost half a million in cash he was putting in about fifty different banks. He kept each deposit under the ten thousand dollar limit that triggers automatic reporting to the feds. The local cop shop set up a sting, used bills with recorded serial numbers, and made several small buys from street pushers. Every one of those bills, every single fucking dollar, turned up in Metropolit's apartment and briefcase. The interesting thing was he never said a word about anything to the DA's office. He didn't try for a plea deal. He did the whole five so he wasn't on parole when he got out. That was three years ago."

"What's all that mean?"

"My best guess is Metropolit was probably well paid to take a fall for the Mexicans. Not the real high ups in Tijuana, the guys in LA. I figure he did the whole stretch so he wouldn't have any travel restrictions after he got out. He probably used some of his old New York connections to hook up with DiPaulo and Marcello in New Orleans. I can guarantee you that whatever he's doing, it isn't legit."

"How old are these assholes? Did you get that?"

"Yeah, DiPaulo is sixty-two, Marcello is sixty, Davidoff is sixty-five, and Metropolit is seventy-two. Pretty old to be doing this kind of shit, don't you think?" I could sense a smile on Tom's face.

"Seems like it. Are they married?"

"Hang on." After a moment, he said, "All of 'em except Metropolit. I don't see any record of him ever being married. DiPaulo and Marcello go through wives like shit through a goose. DiPaulo's been married three times and Marcello twice.

"Davidoff's a lifer, still married to his first wife. What the hell difference does that make?"

"I don't know. I just thought I'd ask. How'd you get all this stuff in five hours?"

"The wonder of computers, my boy. My friend in New Orleans had everything on DiPaulo, Marcello and Davidoff...nothing on Metropolit. After I got her started, I tapped into the NCIC for him and about filled my machine's memory. It took a little while to sort him out from his old man because they have the same name. About the time I was finishing, my friend emailed me the New Orleans stuff."

"I owe you big time, buddy."

"You're goddamn right you do. What are you going to do with all this?"

"I need to organize my notes and think it through. I'm meeting my clients on Wednesday. I figure if I let them know the background on these mopes, they'll stay away from the deal and that will be that. I can collect my fee and move on to the next case. There's nothing to this PI gig."

"I hope you're right. If that's all it takes, you might be on to something. Lord knows you don't want to do anything that resembles work. I'll warn you one more time though, try not to push it too hard, and for Christ sake, don't get involved with these New Orleans guys. You'll end up with your nuts in a vise."

***

My girlfriend, Gerri, was back from a geologists' convention in Dallas so I gave her a call to see if she was interested in driving to Louisville for dinner at the Blue Parrot. In Colorado, Louisville is pronounced Lewis-Ville, not Lou-ee-Ville as in Kentucky. It's a little town outside of Boulder settled mostly by Italians in the early 1900s. Several "tavernas" had opened during the 1920s. During Prohibition, the government let people make wine for family consumption and religious sacraments so all the Italian families made wine and said they had big families who went to Mass several times a week. That part was true. The families had stretched to include all the taverna's customers and anybody else who wandered in. Between the churches and the tavernas, it was pretty easy to get a drink in Louisville.

Most of the old places were closed, but the Blue Parrot had survived and was thriving. Two of the reasons were the margaritas and daiquiris made totally from scratch right behind the bar.

Gerri agreed to a night out. "Why don't you pick me up on the street right outside my office? I don't have a whole lot going on at the moment, we could leave a little early and beat the rush if you want. How does 4:30 sound?"

"Great. I especially like the part about picking you up on the street. You must be reverting to your old ways."

"Really funny, I'll be the one in the crotch-length skirt and six-inch platforms. You can't miss me." Gerri's laugh came through the phone like a tinkling mountain brook. It sounded like she was in a great mood and I knew I was. It'd been a productive day.

"Okay, you slut, I'll see you at 4:30."

I picked her up as planned and was disappointed—- she'd lied about her clothes. She had on a tailored, brown and gray, herring-bone jacket with brown slacks and medium heeled pumps. I almost missed her disguised as a business woman.

We headed south on Broadway to Colfax and then west to I-25. Unfortunately, it was too cool to take the top down.

I glanced across at her. "How come you're in such a good mood and why don't you have work to do?"

"Because I'm with you, lover. We sold a big deal today, and I don't feel like working. I want to celebrate instead. We only had to show our Green River Basin prospect twice. Wyoming Gas Exploration called this morning and said they'd take the whole damn thing. The *really* good news is they have a drilling rig up by Pinedale and can move down to drill our location within ninety days if we can get all the paperwork done."

"That is a big deal, congratulations! What kind of a business arrangement did you make? Did you get your seed money back?"

"In spades, baby. We've got about fifteen thousand acres in our block, averaging twenty-five bucks an acre for lease bonuses, land-man fees, title...the whole ball of wax. WGE is paying us FIFTY an acre plus, they're going to carry us for a twenty-five percent interest in the first well."

I whistled. "I think I'd better get back in the business. If you can turn a dog like that for that kind of money, think what an experienced, successful guy like me could do."

She punched me in the arm. "You're a career screw-up who couldn't find oil and gas if you fell in it. Besides, I thought you were intent on embarking on this new career investigating big oil and bad guys."

"There is that...though your deal sounds like easy money to me."

"Think again, jerk! We worked damn hard putting everything together, but enough about my successes. How's the crime fighting going?"

"I found out a bunch about the guys who own Black Blizzard Petroleum and it tells me the Linfields should be running in the opposite direction as hard as they can run. The good news is what I found out should convince them of that. I probably won't have to go toe-to-toe with any of the scumbags promoting the scam. The other good news is I went to see Sid Bonner today and he's in a lot better shape than I thought."

"I'm happy for you on both fronts. When are you going to talk to the Linfields?"

"On Wednesday. I'm going out to see Evan's mom, Julie, and his aunt who runs the family corporation now. There's a chance that Jeff, the younger brother who's pushing Black Blizzard, will be there too."

"How's he going to take the bad news if he's the chief advocate?"

"Don't know, don't care. Mary Linfield runs the show so what she says is all that matters."

We pulled into the lot, parked, and went in to an aroma of garlic, basil, and oregano. As planned, we were early. Only three of the twenty-five or thirty tables scattered around were occupied.

The girl at the door said, "Seat yourselves anyplace you like. We just opened for dinner and some of the servers aren't here yet. I hope you're not in a hurry." That was an inside joke because service at the Blue Parrot had never been fast. It wasn't a place you wanted to go if you were in a hurry…just the way I liked it. At the Blue Parrot you didn't "eat," you dined.

She handed us menus, stepped from behind the hostess podium, and made a sweeping arm gesture indicating we could go anywhere. She looked Italian although her attire was strictly CU coed chic. She had on UGG boots with a denim micro miniskirt starting a good four inches below her navel, which was pierced with a dangling pearl pendant. Her long-sleeved, clingy spandex top came to just below her breasts with several inches of exposed skin between it and her skirt. Gerri grabbed both menus and headed inside. I checked the view and followed.

We took a table away from the kitchen entrance and I sat in the corner, sort of post Wild Bill Hickok style. One couldn't be too careful in the Wild West.

"Did you get a good look there, Lothario?" Gerri laughed. "Don't think I don't notice you when you're checking the goods."

"I thought I got away with it. Interesting outfit, you'll have to admit."

"Yeah, it looks like she just threw something on and almost missed. Why don't you buy me something like that?"

"You don't have that much distance from top to bottom. You have a more mature figure. Not that it's a bad thing."

"Mature figure, huh? That's what my father used to call a woman with a big ass—- a mature figure."

That got a laugh out of me. "Good one. Mind if I use it sometime?"

"Be my guest just don't apply it to me."

Miss Bare Belly hadn't been kidding about the service. I asked Gerri if she wanted to try one of the fresh-made margaritas, which she did, so I went around the corner and gave an order to the bartender. He said the cocktail waitress had just come on shift and would deliver the drinks. The margaritas arrived a minute after I returned to the table.

A waiter finally showed and we ordered dinner with a good Barolo. I asked the waiter to open it as soon as possible.

As we sipped the drinks, I told Gerri most of the stuff about Black Blizzard and its founders. I concentrated on Metropolit, skipping over the violent backgrounds of the New Orleans mobsters. I didn't think telling her about possible murderers was a good idea. She agreed with my assessment that running over the background should be enough to warn off the Linfields.

We finished dinner, paid the tab, and I took another glance at the hostess to Gerri's amusement. Outside, the wind had started blowing again. The sky was clear and with hardly any traffic on the road, we made it to my house in twenty-seven minutes. When we walked in, Gerri said, "Good dinner. Too bad we left our doggie bags on the table."

I raided the wine cellar for another bottle of Barolo and we headed for the hot tub. As we settled into the water, Gerri said, "I don't know why, but there's something about Jerome Biggs or Black Blizzard setting off an alarm for me. I think Martin may have mentioned something about Biggs calling him soliciting deals. We didn't have the Green River Basin prospect ready, still Martin might have told him we'd show him something." Martin Gear was Gerri's partner and a cofounder of her company.

I sat up straight and glared at her. "Tell Martin to keep the hell away from them. They're bad news. And you do the same. There're some other things I haven't told you about. Take my word for it—you don't want to get mixed up with those guys."

chapter

FIVE

The next morning, Gerri showered and dressed in one of the outfits she kept in my closet. I made coffee and drove her to the light rail station. The train would drop her off in front of her office building door. As I kissed her goodbye, I repeated what I'd said last night. "Remember what I said, babe—- stay away from Biggs or anyone else with Black Blizzard."

She nodded without saying anything. As she turned for the platform, she said, "I hear you, Cort, but I'm a big girl and can take care of myself." It wasn't what I needed to hear.

I spent the rest of the day organizing my notes and writing a report summarizing everything for the Linfields. I was still full from the Blue Parrott the night before, so had a small salad for dinner and went to bed early. The investigator life-style must be taking its toll. I never used to go to bed before midnight.

***

Wednesday morning, over coffee and oatmeal at the kitchen table, I watched two does and a spike buck behind my house while deciding what a successful oilman/PI should wear. I settled on gray slacks and a wine-red, long sleeved, mock turtleneck, stuffed my report and notes in a briefcase, grabbed a jacket, and backed the Corvette out of the garage.

It was another magnificent fall day in Colorado. The sky was deep purple-blue with the mountains etched in high relief. The only things missing were snowcaps on Mt. Evans and Longs Peak—- we hadn't had an early snowfall yet.

I-70 to Byers is an hour's worth of nothing drive so it was a relief to turn on the two-lane farm road going south out of town. It would have been a great place to open up the throttle because it's straight as an arrow for several miles—- the Arapahoe County sheriffs knew that too. The rolling hills provided great places to hide—- something I learned through experience.

The entrance to the Linfields' ranch was four miles south of town. Their rustic pole-and-iron gateway arch displayed a big 'L' with legs, which stood for the Run-Like-L ranch. It was also the registered brand for their livestock.

The gates were open and I slowed to a crawl across the cattle guard. Everything looked new. The fences, posts, gates, and arch were either new or freshly painted. I remembered the first time I had come here with my landman to try and lease them. Everything had been well maintained although it was old and worn. Even though the ranch was successful as far as ranches go, the family lived season to season. They were dependent on weather and cattle prices. It produced a living, though not much more, if they played it close to the vest. The oil had changed everything except the Linfields. I was glad to see how the place looked. The old gravel ranch road had been replaced with pavement which was better maintained than the county road.

I crested a small hill and started down into the headwater drainage of West Bijou Creek. The descent seemed steep because everything else was flat. I saw the main ranch house and out-buildings on a flat terrace fifty feet above the creek bed. Half-way down, I was driving through nice outcrops of flat lying sandstones. The view was like something out of a John Wayne movie with the big ranch house down in the river valley framed by rim rocks. I almost expected to see an Indian war party up on the rim.

Several vehicles were parked in front of the house. Three Ford pickups with the ranch's brand logo on the doors, two GMC SUVs and a Cadillac Escalade with Nevada plates made up the fleet. I felt a little self-conscious in the Corvette—- I should have driven my Bronco.

I climbed the rough-hewn plank steps onto the long, covered porch and knocked. The glass oval in the door gave a distorted view of whoever was approaching, although I could tell it was a woman and she had blonde hair.

Julie Linfield opened the door and smiled. "Hi, Cort. We were expecting you and here you are, right on time." She was an attractive woman in her mid-fifties. She had a classic westerner's tanned face with smile lines around the eyes. It'd been ten years since I'd seen her and she'd aged well.

"Mrs. Linfield. It's been a long time. It's nice to see you again."

"Oh, please call me Julie. And it has been far too long."

I stared at my feet for a moment. "I was so sorry to hear about Randy. It was quite a shock when Evan told me. I can't believe I didn't see anything in the papers or even on the news. He was pretty well known."

She stepped back from the door and gestured me in with a wave of her arm. "There was just a small obit in the _News_ so unless you read the obituaries every day, you probably wouldn't have noticed."

I nodded as I brought my eyes back to her face. "I was surprised to see Evan in my office and was really pleased you would think of me. Evan's grown into a fine young man. You must be proud of him."

"I *am* proud of him. He looks a lot like his dad, don't you think? He's a lot more serious than Randy was though. Sometimes I wonder if he ever has any fun."

We strolled through an entryway toward the back of the house which had been completely remodeled. Outside, it was still an old ranch house; inside it was western modern. The ceilings had been raised and lofts added. Most of the walls had been removed so it was open and light compared to the small, dark rooms I remembered.

"You've certainly changed the old place, Julie. It's great."

"Thank you. Mary and I worked together on the renovation. We've got an office and meeting room downstairs now. Mary and Jeff are waiting for us there."

"Where's Evan? I thought he'd be here."

"He's down at the horse barn mucking out stalls. We talked it over and decided it wasn't appropriate for him to attend just yet. We'll start having him sit in on meetings a couple years before he turns twenty-five. I'll catch him up on everything when we're done."

We walked through an extensive great room dominated by a river rock fireplace I remembered. I couldn't tell if it was in the same place since it was beautifully framed by new floor-to-ceiling windows displaying the West Bijou Creek canyon. I could see Julie's house farther down the valley. One end of the great room was the kitchen with a huge granite-topped counter island separating it from the living room. Julie led the way through a doorway on the right. The kitchen wall was actually a blind. Behind it was an open stairway going down. Above that, and accessible from the left, was another stairway going up.

"Nice design," I said and followed Julie down.

The wide stairway opened out into a recreation room. The ceilings were lower on this level although the floor must have been dug out to give some added height. At the far end, they'd created a walkout to a patio. Double doors to the right led to the office and meeting room Julie had described. A man and a woman were seated at a wooden conference table covered with file folders. They rose as we entered.

Mary Linfield was also mid-fifties and a strikingly beautiful woman. She was tall, athletically built, with dark curly hair cut short. Her piercing jade-green eyes brought my attention to her face. She was wearing Lady Wranglers with a lime-green polo shirt and low-heeled Roper boots. She smiled and extended her hand. "Mr. Cortlandt Scott. It's nice to see you again." She shook hands like a man. "It's kind of you to come all the way out here to visit. We 'all' appreciate it." She shot a glance at Jeff as she spoke.

"Likewise, Mary, and please call me Cort. Randy and Bob always did and I seem to remember you doing the same the few times we've met."

"I suppose I did. After all, I am your elder. " She laughed. Her laugh was that of a strong woman who knew her strengths. "I'm sure you remember my brother, Jeff. He's staying here for a few days. He's been presenting some new ideas about how we should invest our money. I know Evan's told you about one of them, an oil drilling project and an investment in an oil company. Since you're in the business, we'd like to hear your opinion."

Jeff Linfield had to be around forty but looked older. He didn't resemble his siblings except for skin coloring and dark hair. Where they were all tall and slim, he was medium height and running to fat, although "strong" fat, the kind weight lifters and body builders get when they quit working out. He nodded and said, "Scott." He didn't offer to shake hands. There wasn't much warmth in his voice or his one word greeting. Obviously, he wasn't thrilled with my being there. Julie or Mary must have told him why I was involved and he didn't like it.

"Hello, Jeff. I don't believe we've ever met. I understand you've left the farm so to speak. You live in Nevada now?" I phrased it as a question.

"That's right. I don't have a whole lot of time. Can we get down to business?" Jeff was already pissed and I hadn't said anything yet.

"Sure. Evan told me the drilling prospect is in the Mosquito Basin. Why don't you tell me what Black Blizzard has presented. I've done a background check on them and I'll tell you what I've found."

Jeff moved abruptly to the other side of the table. Mary went to the end and Julie sat next to me. It wasn't a big table so we were close together. Julie asked if anyone needed anything to drink and everyone declined. Mary jerked her chin toward Jeff. "Explain the whole thing to us, Jeff. All you've told me is this Black Blizzard outfit *wants* us to do two things. The first is a drilling deal in Wyoming and the second is buying shares in their company. Is that right?" Mary had emphasized "wants" and it hadn't been in a good tone.

Jeff leaned back, stared at Mary, and slowly shifted his gaze to me. His voice was hard. "That about sums it up. I've got to say, I don't think Scott ought to be here putting his nose into our family business. I don't see how what he has to say has anything to do with us."

Mary inhaled sharply. "Julie and Evan asked him to look into Black Blizzard because Randy said if we ever had any questions about our wells or the oil business we could go to Cort Scott and trust what he says. I've got to admit though---she glanced at Julie---I wish you and Evan had run this by me before you went directly to him. I'm not saying you shouldn't have, and I'm glad to get his input, however we should have talked about it first. I know Jeff isn't happy about it."

Jeff continued to stare at me. "You've got that right. I don't think we should involve outsiders in family business."

"That's water under the bridge and since we've already begun changing the way we invest, it's not strictly a family business anymore, is it? Let's get on with it. What do these guys want to sell us?" Mary ran a tight ship.

"The first thing is the drilling prospect. Since our wells are declining pretty fast, I thought it would be a good time to find some new ones." Jeff spoke fast and with a lot of tension in his voice. He sat ramrod straight as he talked.

"I met a guy by the name of Metropolit in Tahoe. We got to talking and I told him we had some oil wells in Colorado that weren't pumping as much as they used to. I said *I* would like to find some new wells. He told me about an oil company he and his friends were starting in Denver and how they have some deals that would interest us. That's when I told him about our family company and how we relied on investment advisors to help us. I said we hadn't invested in oil properties and how we all had to agree on investments. Anyway, he said I should meet with their Denver geologist and look at their prospects. If I liked what I saw, I could present it to the family and we could buy in."

Mary pushed back from the table and glared at Jeff. "For someone who's complaining about the rest of us, it sounds to me like you told a total stranger an awful lot about our business."

Jeff slumped and mumbled, "Mostly, I was talking about me. You know I've wanted to change the way we do things for a long time." He straightened up and stared at Julie. "I don't think Randy and the rest of you ever thought enough about the future or what happens when our oil runs out. We're going to need to do things differently."

"Maybe so, however, you shouldn't be trying to do it on your own. Our family company has worked pretty damned well for a long time. Everything has been a mutual decision and, as a result, we have a hell of a pile of money to show for it." Mary spoke slowly but forcefully. Her face had reddened and her eyes were even more piercing. I could tell she was really mad.

"That's bullshit, Mary. I've been complaining about how we invest for years." Jeff was hot too.

Mary didn't back down. "Believe me, I know you've complained plenty—- that's why we have a corporation and votes. We even changed the rules last year and you can take a lot more money out of the investment account now. Isn't that good enough for you?"

His face and neck red, Jeff slapped the table, "Randy kept saying we were all getting plenty of money from our share and the trust account was building an inheritance for our kids. Goddamn it, I don't have any kids! I don't think I've been getting 'plenty' of money! I want access to more of my share and not just what the rest of you want me to have."

"Cool down, Jeff, and do it right now. If you don't, we're not going to bother listening to anything else from you." Mary didn't raise her voice, however I could tell she was serious. I thought the meeting might be over before I could say anything about Black Blizzard—- or how many dry holes were in the Mosquito Basin.

Jeff choked back his anger and made an effort. "Let me tell you the rest. I called the guy in Denver who Metropolit told me about. His name is Jerome Biggs. He flew out to Reno about a month ago and drove out to my place with a bunch of maps and reports to show me their prospect. I know I'm not a geologist, but the maps looked pretty good and it sounded all right to me. It's a big area and they've got the leases tied up so if we find something, we'd have lots of room to expand. It could bring our production right back up again and with today's oil prices, we'd be making a ton."

"How much would all of this cost?" Mary asked.

"With the deal they're offering, we'd pay forty percent of the cost of drilling the first well, plus the cost of leases, and Black Blizzard's overhead. We'd get twenty-five percent of the oil. He said it was a standard deal oil companies make. If they sell a deal like that three times, they end up with twenty-five percent for free and get back the money they spent for leases and for doing all the work. When a well finds oil, they pay their twenty-five percent share of what it costs to put the pipe in the ground and put a pump on it. They would operate the well and handle the paper work and we'd pay them a set fee every month."

Mary turned to me, "What about all that, Cort? Does it sound like a good deal?"

I stared straight across the table at Jeff, "No. First of all, the Mosquito Basin is a graveyard for drilling. The area has nothing but dry holes. It's not a place for people like you to make an entry into the oil and gas business. Second, Biggs is taking a lot of liberty in saying their deal is 'standard.' If you do the numbers, they have more incentive to drill a dry hole than a producer. Three times forty percent is a hundred and twenty percent and you have no way of knowing how much they may have marked up the price of the leases, or prospect fees, or overhead. They'll furnish you invoices for the drilling, however, if it's a dry hole, they pocket a nice profit on the leases and fees without having spent any money."

I watched each of the others carefully as they listened. Jeff wasn't interested, he rolled his eyes once. Mary was leaning forward and listening intently. Julie was expressionless although she kept nodding as if she agreed.

"There's no such thing as a standard deal. Legit companies like to sell fifty percent interest in a prospect for sixty-six and two thirds percent. That way they have a half interest if it works, and they've also got skin in the game by paying a third of the costs. If it doesn't work they're out some money the same as their investors, if it does work they're equal partners. You see, the incentive has to be success and not to drill dry holes. If a company is strapped for money, they may sell three-quarters of the deal for a hundred percent of the cost. That way they don't have any costs unless the well is completed—- they're not making money on a dry hole."

Jeff stood, put his hands on the table, and leaned across close to me. "You talk way too fast for my liking. What the hell is in this for you, anyway? Are you romancing Julie or something? Are you trying to get more out of us than our oil?"

I stood, backed off a step, and stared at him. Julie jumped like she'd been slapped. In a low, steady voice, she said, "How could you say such a thing? I haven't laid eyes on Cort Scott in over ten years. He only came here because Evan and I didn't feel like we knew enough to make an intelligent decision. Oh, Jeff, that's such a hurtful thing to say." Her voice broke and tears welled into her eyes.

"That's it, Jeff. I don't want to hear anything else from you." Mary's face was a red mask of anger. "We're not even going to bring this to a vote. I know how Bob would feel, I know how I feel, and Julie also has a vote. That makes it three to one against whatever you want to do."

Mary started stacking file folders and gathering papers. "Bob and Randy and I used to talk about what you were up to, why you always seemed to be short on money. You never told any of us what was going on with you." Mary started around the table towards Jeff. Her hands were waving in frustration. "You told us one day you had gotten married, for God's sake. You didn't invite us to your wedding and we've never met your wife. You say you don't have kids...how're we supposed to know? How do you spend your time? What kind of house do you live in? We don't know anything about you."

Jeff stepped back from his infuriated sister. I thought he was afraid she was going to slap him, and I wasn't sure she wouldn't.

Mary was up in his face now. "If there was a way to do it, I think the rest of us would vote to just cut off your money entirely! Don't worry, you *are* our brother and we won't do that. You'd better get a few things straight though. Don't try to involve us in any more schemes or deals. Don't tell other people about our business affairs or what kind of resources we have. Don't come to us if you run out of money and expect us to bail you out because that's not going to happen. And last, I want you out of my house. If you need a place for tonight, you can sleep in the tack room or go into Denver and get a motel but, by God, I want you out of this house!"

Jeff scraped the papers into a pile and stuffed them in a briefcase. "This isn't the end of it, Mary. Twenty-five percent of everything in the investment account is mine and I want it. *All of it!* Do you understand? And as for you, Scott, *stay the fuck out of my business! You hear me?"*

I stepped away from the end of the table to make sure I wouldn't be blocking his way out and said in the calmest voice I could muster, "I haven't been in your business, Jeff. I was hired to do some things for Julie and Evan and that's all I've done. I'll tell you, though, if I'd given the rest of my report today, you wouldn't have liked it. Black

Blizzard is a completely bogus outfit. Biggs has a shady reputation and his partners, including Metropolit, are a bunch of New Orleans thugs. They're probably mobbed up—- as in organized crime. You don't want to be involved with them. From what I hear, these guys play rough and if you complain you get hurt. You might even get dead."

Jeff sucked in a lot of air. "I'm a grown man, Scott. I'm not the snot-nosed kid you cheated when you leased the ranch. I can deal with whoever I want and I don't need you sticking your nose in where it doesn't belong. I can play rough too, if I have to. Don't forget that." He stomped out of the room and moments later, we heard him climb the stairs to the guest rooms.

Mary sighed, sat down, and looked at Julie and me. "That was ugly. I've seen this coming ever since Randy died. It would probably have happened even if he was around. Julie, I'm really sorry about what Jeff said. He was completely out of line. Cort, I should probably apologize to you too."

"That's not necessary."

Julie held a tissue to her nose and blew into it. Her eyes still glistened although her face was back to normal. "I don't believe Jeff meant anything by it and we all know it's not true. Maybe 'I' should apologize to you, Cort, for involving you in a family feud kind of thing."

Mary cleared her throat, "Cort, I assume we owe you some money? How much? I'll write you a check right now."

I didn't know what to say. I wanted Crude Investigations to get started on the right foot, still I felt sorry for the Linfields and for witnessing the blowup. "You can just send me a check in the mail. I haven't figured up my time and expenses yet and you didn't even get my report."

"We got the gist of it, am I right? You were kidding, though, about some of those guys being in the Mafia?"

"I wasn't. I know at least three out of the four are mixed up with organized crime in New Orleans and this Metropolit guy Jeff mentioned is connected to the other three. Plus, he has a long rap sheet all the way from New York to California. He even did some hard time in prison for drug money crimes."

Mary shuddered and her voice quavered when she said, "My little brother is tied up with these guys? Oh, God, this scares me to death. Jeff has always been different, but organized crime and drugs and who knows what? Where do we go from here?"

"I can't answer that. Maybe today will be a wakeup call for Jeff and he'll think twice about what he's doing to the family. I hope so. If anything else comes up and you think I can help, don't hesitate to call. I'll send you a copy of my report."

We heard footsteps along the upper hallway and the front door banged shut. "You might want to wait a few minutes before you take off," Mary sighed. "Jeff doesn't cool down very quickly and he's as mad as I've ever seen him. How about taking the time to have a drink with us?"

"Sure, I can do that. What's for cocktails?" I tried to lighten it up. There was no reason to be a catalyst for more trouble with Jeff.

Julie led the way into the recreation room and to a bar tucked under the stairs. She went behind the bar, opened a refrigerator, and said, "We have Coors, Bud, Bud Light, and Corona as far as beer. She peered through the glass of an under-the-counter wine cooler, "We've got a Washington State pinot grigio and a Spanish tempranillo. Or, we have lots of hard liquor if you'd prefer. What sounds good?"

Mary said, "Pour me a glass of the white wine, please, Julie."

I smiled at them both and said, "A full service bar—- I guess just a glass of the same, if there's enough."

Julie held the bottle up to the light. "There's plenty. I think I'll have it too." She took three wine glasses from an overhead rack and poured equal servings in each. "Here's to you, Cort. Thanks for helping out. It's nice to see you after all these years even under the circumstances." She raised her glass toward Mary and me.

"I'll echo that," Mary said.

We touched glasses in a toast, "It's good to be back out here. Your oilfield made me in the oil business. It was my first big discovery and ended up having more wells than any field I found before or after. I'm sorry it seems to be causing you some trouble now."

"That's not your fault," they said together.

Mary led the way to the overstuffed chairs. "What made you want to be an investigator? That seems like a huge change of direction."

"It's hard to pinpoint one reason. Probably burnout more than anything. I got tired of constantly having to adapt to new technology and showing prospects to investors who couldn't understand the geology. They wanted to be in the oil business but didn't understand the risk. I was on a canal barge trip in France with my girlfriend when it all came together. We talked about all the things I could do other than just retire and came up with this. She thinks my background and experience will help me sort out crooked deals from good ones, I can keep up my contacts in the business, and I can be involved."

"Well, I'm glad you decided to follow through. You've come at the right time for us."

We sipped the wine and talked for twenty minutes. From Mary, I learned raising and showing the right horses could be a good business, took a lot of work, and a lot of start-up money. Mary had prospered at it and traveled all over the world with her horses. Julie and Randy had run the old home place and acquired land in western Kansas. Most of it was irrigated so they ended up raising corn rather than wheat. Corn prices had gone through the roof with the advent of ethanol so they'd done very well with it. She said Evan was a great help and was going to school at Colorado State University part time. He'd rather be at the ranch.

When I finished my glass, I stood and said I should go. They walked me to the front door. "Goodbye, Cort, and thanks again. Send us your bill and don't be a stranger. You're welcome anytime." Mary shook my hand.

Julie stepped out on the porch, closed the door and said, "Watch out for Jeff. He can be very mean and he carries a grudge. He once told Randy he hated him and all the rest of us. Randy carried that with him until the day he died."

"I'll keep that in mind. Hopefully, our paths won't have to cross again. I'll be watching just in case."

She kissed me on the cheek. "Please come out and see us again soon."

***

I got in the 'Vette and started up the canyon toward the ranch entrance. As I topped the hill three hundred yards from the gate, I saw Jeff's Escalade parked crossways on the road outside the gate. *Damn*! I didn't want to deal with Jeff Linfield anymore today.

I geared down, coasted over the cattle guard, and pulled over on the wide shoulder outside the gate. Jeff climbed out of his SUV and walked toward my car. His face was blotchy red so I knew he was still pissed off. I got out of the car before he got there. If we were going to do this, I wanted to confront him at eye level.

"I told you back at the house and I'm telling you again now, *stay the fuck out of my business and out of my way.*" He hadn't come over to reason with me.

"Like I said back there, Jeff, I haven't been in your business or in your way. I was doing a job for your sister-in-law and nephew and I simply answered a question from Mary."

"Look, you son-of-a-bitch, you don't know everything that's going on. Randy and the others have been holding back on me for years and now that I've found something I really want to do, something that would be good for them too, you come along and fuck it up"

"Don't call me a son-of-a-bitch. I'm only going to say that once—- and I'm only going to say one other thing one more time. I haven't intentionally done anything to you. You've gotten yourself into something way over your head. I happen to know a little about what you want to invest in and I assure you, it's a goddamn scam. The people who're trying to sell it to you are scumbags and worse.

They hurt people who don't deserve to be hurt and I don't want to see your family involved. I don't know why you're so desperate to get mixed up with this bunch, just don't drag your family in behind you. Now, move your rig and let's go our separate ways."

His eyes and face telegraphed the roundhouse right he threw toward my head. I blocked it easily, stepped in close and hit him hard with an uppercut to his solar plexus. I knew the punch hurt but it didn't take all the fight out of him. He dropped his arms and tried to bull rush me toward my car. This time, I sidestepped a little, buried my left fist in his stomach, and rabbit punched him behind the ear. He went down on his hands and knees in the gravel.

"*Stay there, Jeff!*" I yelled. "You're no good at this and I don't want to hurt you."

He got to his knees and turned toward me. He was breathing hard and not catching much wind. He shuffled forward on his knees, put his hands up on my car, and pulled himself to his feet. He finally managed to strain out a few words. "This isn't over, not by a long shot. I've got friends and they're not going to like you sticking your nose in this."

"Well, it's over for now, Jeff. Get your hands off my car. As far as I'm concerned, we can forget about this. I'm telling you though, if Julie or Evan or Mary call me again, I won't hesitate to come back out and help them any way I can. Now back away and get the hell out of here."

Jeff did as he was told, crossed over, and got in the Escalade. He did a three-point turn and floored it toward the county road. He slowed just enough to make the turn and hit the gas again. Maybe an Arapahoe County Sheriff would be on the road into Byers. I returned to my car and followed the same route as Jeff. I hoped he wouldn't want to go another round. I didn't think he would. For a three punch fight, he had taken a good beating.

***

I drove the speed limit all the way back to Parker which added fifteen minutes to the hour I'd spent getting to the ranch. It was 5:15

when I turned south onto C-470 and the sun was setting behind the mountains in spectacular fashion. I kept thinking over the events of the day and was bummed about ending up in a fight with Jeff Linfield. With Bob and Julie's votes, Mary could control the family corporation, however they couldn't stop Jeff from raising hell with them. Because of the way they'd changed the rules, now he could get his hands on a lot more of the investment account and spend it any way he wanted. I doubted he'd be making wise choices, however he wasn't interested in my opinion and I didn't think I'd heard the last of Jeff Linfield or Black Blizzard.

chapter

SIX

I was at my conference table studying Ohio oil field maps when the phone rang. I checked caller ID and was surprised to see Black Blizzard Petroleum on the screen. I answered, "Cortlandt Scott." I tried to use a TV detective voice.

"Cort? Jerry Biggs here. We've met before and I think we have several mutual acquaintances." I smiled to myself wondering why he hadn't said *friends*. "I was wondering if you have time to come over to my office and talk about our deal with Jeff Linfield? He's about to invest some money with us and we understand you represent his family corporation. We'd like them to join us and thought if we could explain our deal, you might be willing to recommend it."

"I can't see how that would happen," I said. I was thinking this guy's got the balls of a cliff diver. Obviously, Jeff had told him about what happened so why in the hell would he think he could get me to come around? "If you're still pitching the Mosquito Basin area, there's no way I'm going to be interested and I'm definitely not going to recommend it to the Linfield family."

"Cort, I don't think you understand. There's a lot of money to be made here. This company has some pretty substantial backing and we have plans for doing a whole bunch of different kinds of deals. If a guy like you wanted to join us, I think there could be millions in it for everyone."

"You're wrong, Biggs, I understand exactly what's going on. I told Jeff and I'm telling you, this isn't a deal for the Linfield family. What Jeff does is his own business as long as he doesn't try to drag his family in. You need to listen to what I'm saying, and for the last time, I'm not interested."

Biggs' friendly tone changed. "No, you listen, Scott. You've been sniffing around where you don't belong. If you don't want to be involved, it's up to you, just keep the fuck out of our deal. Some of my friends don't take kindly to being interfered with, and if you keep mixing in our business, you're liable to regret it."

I kept my voice steady. "Are you making a threat? If you are, you called the wrong guy. I've already got the Denver cops involved in this and they've talked to New Orleans PD and the feds too. If something happens to me, you're the first guy they're coming to see." That was only partially true, but I wanted to make a point.

I heard him suck in his breath and exhale slowly. "You're a wise-ass prick, Scott. I don't give a damn who you've talked to or what you've said. Stay the hell out of our way."

"I wouldn't have it any other way, pardner."

He slammed the phone down. My heart was pounding and I felt prickly heat climbing my neck. Although I'd tried to sound tough, Denver was a small town when it came to the oil and gas business. Even if I wanted to stay out of Black Blizzard's path, I didn't know if I could. I'd had one case as a private investigator and now I had a threat to go with it. I started thinking that working up drilling prospects wasn't such a bad idea. With winter coming on, maybe I should dust off some old prospect files and see if I could spark some enthusiasm for generating deals…deals that wouldn't involve being threatened or end up in fist fights in the middle of the road.

chapter

SEVEN

Gerri and I took a couple of short winter breaks to thaw out and re-connect. She was frustrated because the weather systems had covered the entire Rocky Mountain region. Rigs couldn't move and drilling had come to a standstill. Her company's Green River Basin well had been delayed and would be at the mercy of the runoff and mud. They might not drill until mid-summer.

Although our relationship had waxed and waned over the years, we never drifted too far apart. We'd both seen other people periodically, sometimes for long periods. Somehow though, we always ended up together. Although we didn't use the "L-word," love, it probably applied and, early on, we'd even talked about marriage. The timing never seemed to work out, and now we were too comfortable with the relationship to risk sullying it with a wedding.

Gerri was a bright, innovative geologist with a head for business. She'd made a good living generating and selling prospects. After I'd cashed out from The Crude Company and bought my house, I used most of the rest of the money to buy into her new company, Mountain West Gas Exploration, so I had a vested interest in seeing her prospect drilled.

***

It was now spring, not much had happened over the winter, so I assumed everything was normal. I'd gone for a mid-morning run. My wind was good but after a couple miles, my legs were burning and felt like lead. Luckily, I'd taken a route that left the last half mile downhill. I let myself in the patio door and headed straight to the hot tub. As I walked in, the telephone rang. I answered without looking at the caller ID and was surprised when I heard Evan Linfield's voice.

"This is Evan Linfield." His voice was strained and I knew something bad had happened. "Mom and I would appreciate it if you could come out to the ranch as soon as possible. Aunt Mary's been killed and we need some help."

I had to sit down on the little corner bench. "Jesus, Evan, I'm terribly sorry to hear that. What's happened? How did she die?" Talk about a stunner. My knees and legs were weak and I felt sick to my stomach. My first thought was Jeff Linfield. Could he have been this desperate? Next, I thought about Biggs and Black Blizzard. Was their threat aimed at the Linfields and not me? The timing was too close for this to be a coincidence.

"We think she was killed yesterday afternoon or evening—-we're not sure yet. She fell off the rim rock on the West Bijou Creek trail. Her horse was outside the stable this morning when I went over to muck out the stalls. He was saddled and everything, but Aunt Mary wasn't around. I looked all over for her, and then called Mom." I heard Evan sniff and try to clear his throat. "When Mom got here, we saddled our horses and started searching for her. We know the trail by the creek is one of her favorites so we went there first. We didn't see anything until we got clear up on the very top and could see back down the canyon. We saw something blue down below the overlook—- when she left yesterday, she was wearing a blue wind-breaker. We went back down and saw her in the rocks. There's a place farther down where I could get over the edge and hike back. She was really banged up, Mr. Scott, and—- she was dead." Evan had made it through that far without too much trouble. When he said "dead," I heard him suck in a big breath and let it out again with several catches.

"Of course I'll come, Evan. I can be there in an hour. Have you called the sheriff's office?"

"Yes, sir, it's the first thing we did. We found her about 8:30, used Mom's cell phone to call the sheriff, and a deputy was at the house by 9:00. I rode back, saddled another horse, and brought him back here. Mom and I are still here and there're a whole bunch of people down there by Aunt Mary. The deputy called for a helicopter as soon as he saw her and they flew four people out here. They've been taking pictures and measurements ever since. I think they're getting ready to bring her out."

"Okay, Evan, I'll be there as soon as I can. Is there any place handy I can drive close to where you are now? I'm not much for horses or riding." That was an understatement. I'd grown up out in the country west of Eugene, Oregon. We'd never had a horse, I wasn't comfortable being around them. I preferred not to ride if I could avoid it.

"We're about a half mile from the house by horseback. The closest road is probably two miles away and it's a rough walk. The road is just a four-wheel-drive track."

"I guess it's a horse ride for me then, like it or not. Do you have a gentle one? They seem to sense I'm not comfortable as soon as I get on their back."

"Yeah, we've got a twenty year old mare we use when kids or old people are here to ride. I'll have her ready when you get here. I'm thinking the sheriff's people will've brought the body out by then. Does that make any difference?"

I appreciated Evan's concern for my feelings and thought the elderly mare designated for kids and old people sounded just right. "The horse sounds fine. Although I don't know exactly what I'll figure out, I'd like to see where she fell. I don't want to interfere with the sheriff's people. Some of them, like the crime scene investigator types, will still be there. Regardless, I want to see the place."

"Thanks, Mr. Scott. I'll meet you at the stables in an hour." Evan sounded better than when he'd first called.

I disconnected and called Tom Montgomery. Tom listened as I repeated what Evan Linfield had said. I told Tom I didn't know exactly what I'd be doing for the family, although I doubted if Mary's death was an accident or a suicide—- too many things had been going on. I asked if he knew anyone in the Arapahoe County Sheriff's office who might help me.

"My advice is stay out of the way and don't mess up anything that might be evidence. I'll call Jim Weaver. He's the sheriff and a friend of mine...used to be a Denver PD lieutenant. I'll tell him who you are and find out who's assigned to the case. You need to tell whoever that is everything you know. Then, like I said, stay out of the way while they do their job. I'm sure Jim will keep you informed if I ask him. One last thing, buddy, watch out yourself, okay? If Biggs or Jeff Linfield was really threatening you, it sounds like they've started playing for keeps."

"Thanks, Tom. There isn't a doubt in my mind this is related to those assholes. I'll talk to you as soon as I know anything."

I put the phone down and stood there a moment thinking. Mary Linfield had probably ridden that trail thousands of times. She'd stopped at every overlook hundreds of times. She wasn't going to fall off and, from what I knew of her, she sure as hell wasn't going to jump. Somehow, Black Blizzard was mixed up in this. I hoped Jeff Linfield wasn't, although I couldn't see any way it didn't touch him.

I raced upstairs, threw on some jeans, a wool shirt, and some hiking boots. I grabbed a baseball hat and a rain jacket, and threw everything in the Bronco. I drove as fast as I usually pushed the 'Vette and it still seemed like hours before I got to the ranch.

When I turned off the county road into the ranch, I saw the helicopter on the ground on the flat plateau to the east. I couldn't see the canyon separating us. An Arapahoe County Sheriff's car was parked inside the gate with an officer inside. As I pulled up, he got out, came to the window, and asked, "Are you Cort Scott?"

"Yes." I pulled out my driver's license and my PI card. It was the first time I'd used it. From the look on the deputy's face, it may have been the first time he'd seen one.

"Thanks. The sheriff called and said to expect you. Evan Linfield is waiting at the house and he'll take you to the crime scene."

"You just called it a *crime scene*. Have you already figured that out?" I hadn't been surprised at his choice of words.

"I don't think there's going to be much doubt. I've known Mary Linfield my whole life and she ain't the kind to fall or jump off a cliff. This either has something to do with her horse or somebody pushed her. Everybody out this way likes...uh, 'liked' her and they'll want us to figure out what happened as quickly as possible. Evan and Julie are in pretty bad shape. I hope you can help them."

"I'll try. It was Evan who called me. I better get down there." The deputy raised his hand like he was going to salute, thought better of it, and stepped back.

As I started down the ranch road into the canyon, I wondered what else could possibly happen to the Linfields...and to me.

chapter

EIGHT

Evan was standing in front of the stable holding the reins of a big brown horse. I grabbed my jacket and hat and hurried to meet him. His eyes were red, his face was flushed, and he didn't look well. As we shook hands, I noticed the grip wasn't as firm as usual. "Thanks for coming out. Mom and I really appreciate it." His voice was still unsteady.

I tried to make my voice as calm as I could. "I don't know exactly how I can help. At least I can keep you informed about what the cops are doing. I have a friend in the DPD who'll help. He's good friends with your sheriff."

"We're friends with Sheriff Weaver too. Mostly, though, you'll help by giving us someone to talk to. Are you ready to go? This old girl's name is Nellie and she's a gentle soul. You'll be fine on her."

"I hope you're right. I have a deal with horses. I don't get on their back and they don't buck me, bite me, or stomp me."

Evan smiled as he handed me the reins. I put them around Nellie's neck and stepped back alongside her. I turned the stirrup out, put my foot in, grabbed the pommel, and pulled myself into the saddle. Nellie turned her head toward me as I mounted and, thankfully, stood still.

"She's neck-reined—- you don't have to pull her head around. Just touch her with your heels, click your tongue, and she'll go. Take her around the stable and I'll meet you in back. When we start up the trail, she'll fall in behind my horse and you can let her go at her own speed, which won't be too fast. You'll be fine."

I did as Evan said and joined him behind the stable. His horse was a huge black gelding I would've been scared to get close to, let alone ride. We started at a gentle trot which was about all I could handle in terms of staying balanced. The trail was wide and sandy with hundreds of hoof prints. We didn't talk and made good time. We were at the rim in twenty minutes.

Twenty people, mostly uniforms, were bunched up around sheriffs' ATVs. They must have come cross country from the road Evan had mentioned. Several cops were at the edge of the cliff, so I assumed still more people were down there. The helicopter was sitting about fifty yards away. Julie was standing by herself a few yards from the others. She looked up when she heard our horses. I got off Nellie rather awkwardly, handed the reins to Evan, and hurried over to Julie. She walked slowly to me and I folded her into my arms. She was trembling and stood for what seemed like an hour. It was probably only a minute.

Finally, she tilted her head back and said, "Thanks for coming, Cort. We didn't know who else to call. We called Bob and he's on his way and we've tried to reach Jeff. So far we've only managed to leave messages. Oh God, this is so awful! Randy dying last year and now Mary being murdered! What's happening to this family? Are we all going to die?" Julie was on the edge of hysteria. She was shaking her head violently from side to side, wringing her hands, and crying.

"It's too soon to be speculating about murder, Julie. We don't even know if there's a crime yet, do we?"

Julie jerked back and looked at me like I was crazy. "Of course there's a crime! Somebody killed Mary. She's too good a horse woman to get bucked off. She rides out here almost every day and knew better than to get too close to the edge. Somebody murdered her! We've had nothing but trouble since Randy died and all that stuff started with Jeff and that stupid oil company deal of his." Julie's hands went to her face, her eyes widened, and a look of shock appeared. "*Oh my God, you don't think Jeff's involved in this, do you? Oh no, Oh no, Oh...*" She put her hands over her eyes and began rocking.

"Julie, listen—- like I said, it's too early to start speculating about things like that. I'm sure the cops will get to the bottom of everything. I'll help any way I can—- I want to know what happened too. You know, of course, I'll need to tell the sheriff about that meeting we had with Jeff last fall." I also knew I'd have to tell the cops about my fight with Jeff and my conversation with Jerome Biggs. I hadn't told any of the other Linfields about those. I moved to her side and slid my arm around her waist. She leaned into me and seemed grateful for the support. We walked farther away from the group gathered around the vehicles.

"I'll start nosing around here and try to talk to the sheriff's people. I might see or hear something that'll help me figure this out. The one thing I can do is move quickly. If Jeff *is* involved, I might be able to check it out faster than the cops. I'm going to want to talk to him and sooner rather than later. You said you've been leaving messages—- do you know where he is? Is he in Tahoe?"

"The last we heard he was—- Mary said she talked to him about a couple weeks ago. He'd just returned from LA."

"Okay, I'll try to talk to him when he shows up. I'm sure he'll come as soon as he hears about Mary. If the cops have finished with you, go on back to the house. I'll talk with them, snoop around a little, and ride back with Evan. We'll need to go over this more later."

Julie scuffed the ground with her boot. "Please look out for Evan, will you? He's very strong——- he's also very young. All of this is going to come down on him pretty hard and I'm scared for him."

"Sure, Julie, I'll do whatever I can. I'll see you in a little while."

She slowly walked to where Evan was holding the horses. They shared a long embrace before she mounted and started down the trail. I watched her until the trail took her below the hill. She never looked back.

***

The sheriff's deputies had strung yellow crime scene tape outlining an area about fifty yards long and stretching from the cliff to the other side of the trail. I was standing outside the tape on the downhill side. A couple of people in gray windbreakers with 'Sheriff' on the back walked carefully around inside the tape and along the trail putting down small yellow cones in several places. I motioned them to me and was a little surprised to see a woman walk over. Her hair was tucked up under an Arapahoe County sheriff baseball hat.

When she reached the tape, I put out my hand. "I'm Cort Scott. I'm a private investigator working for the Linfields. They've asked me to come out. May I come inside the tape and walk around with you?"

The lady sheriff smiled. "We were notified you're working for the Linfields. You must have some stroke with somebody——- Sheriff Weaver said to give you full cooperation. I'm Lindsey Collins with the Scene of Crime Division. The guy over there is my partner, Bill Mackey. Come under the tape and we'll walk you through this. Try not to step on any tracks or anything that could turn out to be evidence. When we're done in here, we'll need impressions of your shoes so there won't be any confusion about who's been walking around."

"Thanks, Ms. Collins. I'm new at this. Point me to wherever you want and I'll try to stay out of your way."

"Call me Lindsey."

Lindsey was an attractive blonde in her thirties. She was five-eight or so, athletically built, and had a wide smile with pretty teeth. I noticed she was not wearing a wedding ring——- maybe crime scene investigators couldn't wear them. She lifted the tape and I ducked under. I felt like I had crossed more than just a yellow line. I felt like I was taking on something entirely new and unknown. I liked the feeling. I didn't like the reasons for being here.

We walked toward Mackey who was putting down more cones. He glanced up and scowled as we approached, "You must be Scott. Don't step on anything and stay the hell out of our way." Mackey was a medium-sized guy who looked like he'd never had a good day in his life. He was quite a contrast to Lindsey, who rolled her eyes and flashed a rueful smile. Mackey was already staring back at the ground so he didn't see her expression.

"I won't move till you tell me," I said. I didn't see any reason to piss him off more than he already was. "What are you marking?"

Lindsey replied, "We're trying to mark every track regardless of whether they're horses, shoe prints, or even other animal tracks. You can see the trail itself is soft because they've spread gravel and sand along it. The rock on both sides is pretty hard so we don't see many tracks on it."

I thought I would throw around a few geologic terms and maybe establish some credibility. "The rock on the sides is silica cemented sandstone so it's harder than hell, about the same as pure quartz. The only thing you might find are metal scrapings from horseshoes because the rock is harder than steel."

Lindsey studied me and smiled again. "Maybe you *can* be of some help after all." Mackey just looked pissed off.

We systematically covered all the ground within the tape. They put down about twenty cones mostly marking hoof prints. One cone marked a black scrape on the rock near the cliff edge they said they thought might be from a shoe sole. They photographed it with a high magnification lens and collected as much as they could with a scalpel and tweezers. Another cone even closer to the edge marked a shred of gray material they also photographed and collected. Mackey grunted something about how he thought it might be from an athletic shoe. Eventually, they shot pictures of every hoof print within the tape. Mackey said they'd have to get imprints from every saddle horse at the stables to match the tracks. That sounded like a big job; they'd have to be lucky to get any results.

We crossed outside the taped area and walked uphill about twenty-five yards. From here we could see down to where the others were working around Mary's body. I asked, "What do you guys think? Is there anything you can rule in or rule out yet?"

"What the hell? You think we're going to solve this deal with two rock scrapings?" Mackey was definitely a prick. "I hate it when you amateurs get involved in our business. You watch a couple of CSI shows on TV and figure every crime in town can be solved by somebody taking a goddamn picture and running a spectrometer analysis. Just stay out of our way. We'll tell you what we find because Weaver told us to. Don't think we're going to like it."

This had gone far enough. My Mr. Nice Guy routine wasn't going to work with Mackey. I didn't know who'd put the pinecone up his ass, but we needed to get some ground rules laid down. "Look, Mackey, I get it that you don't want me hanging around with you. I told you I won't get in your way and I'll make sure of it. The Linfields want me involved in the investigation and I intend to be. I don't give a shit one way or another about how you feel toward me. I'm telling you one thing though, if you don't work with me, I'm going directly to Weaver. And if you keep up the comments, I'm going to go out of my way to kick your ass, and don't think I can't. From now on, I'll get my information from Lindsey. You don't have to say a goddamn word to me and I'll return the favor. Are we squared away here?" It probably wasn't too smart threatening a cop, still—- enough was enough.

Mackey didn't say anything. He started to turn away until Lindsey grabbed him by the arm. "Goddamn it, Mackey! You heard what Weaver said and Scott hasn't caused us any grief here. I'll be the go-between and keep him informed. You won't have to say another word to him. Don't you dare try to cut me out of anything or he won't be the only one going to Weaver. Is that a deal?"

Mackey stared at both of us for a couple of seconds, dropped his gaze, and muttered, "Yeah, whatever."

We started back toward the ATVs with Mackey a few feet ahead of Lindsey and me. She said in a low voice, "He can be a pain-in-the-ass and he's really good at this kind of work. I've seen him pull this crap before and usually it works, even on cops. You're the first guy who's ever called him on it. He won't forget, though he'll go along. I'll make sure I keep you informed. Since you said you're new at this, let me give you a big piece of advice—- threatening police officers is good way to get arrested."

"I don't want trouble with him and I'd rather talk to you anyway." I gave her my impression of a good guy PI smile. "I think I'll go back to the ranch and talk to Julie Linfield. Do you know who will be the lead investigator yet? I have some information that needs to be checked out."

She smiled back. "George Albins. He's down with the body. When he gets back, I'll tell him you're at the ranch. Don't go too far with Mrs. Linfield because George will be asking her a bunch of questions too. He's kind of old-timey—- a good guy and a damn fine investigator, the best we've got. He'll appreciate anything you can tell him."

"That's good. I'll talk to you soon, and thanks for all your help." We traded business cards and she promised to call as soon as they knew anything. As we walked past the ATVs, she had me stand on an impression pad and labeled the prints with my name and the date. I had a fleeting thought about being "in the system" now. I wondered if this was going to come back to haunt me.

chapter

NINE

I said good-bye to Lindsey Collins and walked to where Evan was standing with the horses. "How are you holding up?" I asked. I didn't know what his answer would be because he looked like hell.

"I guess I'm all right. It sure hurt watching Mom ride back. She's taking this pretty hard. I'd just started thinking she was getting over Dad and all the fighting over money. Now this has to happen."

"She said almost the same thing about you. You two are going to have to lean on each other for a while."

"I know you're right about that and Mom's a pretty tough lady. I think she'll make it through, maybe better than me." This kid had grown up fast.

"We'd better get back. There are some things I need to talk to your mom about and I don't think I can learn anything up here."

"Did the sheriff's people find anything that'll help figure out what happened?"

"It's too soon to know. They took lots of pictures and found some marks on the rocks. They've promised to let me know what's going on."

We climbed on the horses and headed down the trail. Like before, Evan rode ahead and Nellie followed with me clinging to the saddle. It wasn't much fun going downhill and I felt like I was going to slide down Nellie's neck and out over her head. I found it ironic—-- I would be getting off her and stepping into a Bronco.

When we got to the corral, I saw a white van parked next to my truck. Evan pointed and said, "Uncle Bob's van. He made good time getting here." We got off the horses and I saw a tall man walk through the stable toward the corral. I hadn't seen Bob Linfield in several years and he hadn't changed much. A little heavier maybe and he favored Randy and Mary more than Jeff. He had a bit of gray at the temples. He embraced Evan and they held on to each other for several seconds. When he turned to me, I saw tears in his eyes and his jaw was clenching and unclenching rapidly.

"Hello, Cort. I want to thank you for everything you've done for us and I sure appreciate your coming out here today."

"Hello, Bob. I'm sorry for your loss. I was shocked when Evan called with the news about Mary. I'm sure you know I was out here a few months back. I talked with her and Julie about the deal Jeff was pushing."

"Yes, Mary told me. I also understand Jeff was a big jerk at your meeting. He's a tough guy to understand sometimes." Bob glanced at Evan who was leading the horses into the stable. He gripped my arm and whispered, "This is hard for me to ask...is Jeff mixed up in Mary's death? I hope to God he's not, but truthfully, I'm afraid. He hasn't been on good terms with any of us for several years and it seems like everything's gotten worse since Randy died."

I had to be careful with my answer. "Julie is worried about the same thing. I told her it's too early to speculate on anything. I *do* know that some of the people Jeff's been talking to are bad actors. To say he'd be involved in his own sister's death is a big stretch——- and it's way too soon. I'll have to give his name to the sheriff, though. I've never told Julie——- or Mary, but he waited for me out by the gate arch after that meeting. We got into a scuffle before it was over. I'm afraid he got the worst of it and he was mad as hell when he roared off."

"Oh, *Christ*. This just gets worse. You and Julie and I need to talk."

"We do."

***

Inside, we heard Julie's voice coming from the living room. "Jeff, don't you understand? Mary's *dead*. She was killed up where the riding trail gets close to the cliff edge...I don't know, Jeff...I don't know that for sure, either...It must have been yesterday evening or this morning...Because Evan saw her ride out yesterday and her horse was back at the corral gate this morning with the saddle still on. Yes, Bob is here, I saw him drive up a few minutes ago...We called Cort Scott and asked him to come out and he's here too. *Jeff, my God!* How can you say that? Cort is here to help. He hasn't been here since last fall...*Please* stop saying things like that. Are you going to come here? Okay, goodbye, Jeff."

Julie disconnected. "Jeff will try for the first flight from Reno to Denver. He'll rent a car at the airport and drive out."

She caught my eyes, "Cort, I don't know if you should be here when Jeff arrives. He said some really ugly things about you being here."

I nodded and said, "I'll do whatever you think is best, Julie. There's something I need to tell you about what happened after the meeting here last fall. Jeff waited for me out by the gate and we ended up in a fight. We'll all have to face the fact Jeff will be what the cops call *a person of interest* in this. The cops will take a look at him, although it's a long way from proving he's involved."

Bob's gaze shifted from me to Julie and back. "Jeff's a jerk. I refuse to believe he'd be involved in something like this, but the fact remains, he's a jerk. He's been feeling sorry for himself for years and doesn't care who gets hurt when he gets it in his head *he's* being treated wrong. Julie, I picked up some vibes from your voice and Jeff is way off base with whatever he was implying. Cort, I want you to keep investigating Mary's death. I'm sure Julie and Evan feel the same way. We appreciate your help. You're welcome to come and go as you please and don't worry about Jeff being mad. We'll handle him."

"Thanks. I'll try to avoid Jeff for now, although I'll have to talk to him eventually."

We all turned as the helicopter's engine wound up then faded away. No one said anything.

We watched a sheriff's car pull up in the front yard. A tall, lanky guy unwound himself from behind the wheel, put on a narrow brimmed western hat, and headed toward the porch. We gathered in the foyer and Julie opened the door as the tall sheriff topped the steps.

"Mrs. Linfield? I'm George Albins. I'm real sorry to have to be here under these circumstances. I'll be in charge of the investigation into what happened out here today and I'd like to have a few words if you're up to it." George Albins was six-four or five although he probably wasn't over two hundred pounds. He wore western style clothes with a dove gray, suede sport coat over straight-legged trousers and polished cowboy boots. As Julie opened the door, he doffed his hat, exposing a full head of salt and pepper hair. He looked the part of sheriff.

"Yes, I'm Julie Linfield. My son Evan and I live in the next house down the valley." Evan stepped onto the porch behind Albins. "This is Evan." They shook hands and Julie turned toward Bob. "This is Bob Linfield, my brother-in-law and Mary's brother. This is Cortlandt Scott. He's a private investigator, a friend of the family, and we've asked him to represent us."

Albins nodded and extended his hand to Bob first, "I believe we've met before, Mr. Linfield. It's been several years, though."

Bob and I each shook hands with the sheriff and headed toward the living room. Julie and Evan started to the couch, I took the love seat, and Albins and Bob each sat in one of the leather club chairs. Julie fidgeted like she had a lot of nervous energy and needed to burn some off. "Can I get anyone something to drink? I've got coffee, sodas, water." Albins and I opted for coffee. Evan and Bob wanted water. Julie went to the kitchen, returned with a tray of drinks, taking a seat next to Evan.

Albins put his hat on the floor beside the chair and cleared his throat, "Mrs. Linfield, I need to ask you and your son some questions. Although I'm sure my officers have already asked, I like to hear everything for myself." He took out a digital recorder. "I'll be making a recording of our conversation so there won't be any question of its authenticity."

He turned on the recorder, stated his name, the date, and who was present. He began questioning Julie and immediately included Evan when it became clear he'd been the last person to see Mary. Evan repeated everything he'd told me and was able to add more precise times. Julie hadn't seen Mary for a couple days only talking to her on the phone the day before. Albins asked about that conversation and how Mary seemed at the time.

Julie's eyes misted and her voice caught as she realized it was the last conversation she would ever have with Mary. "Pretty normal, I'd say. Maybe a little distracted. She didn't say anything was out of the ordinary, though."

Albins nodded and made a note. "Mrs. Linfield, I need to ask where you were yesterday afternoon and early this morning?"

A look of concern passed over Julie's face. "I was at my house all day yesterday. And I was there this morning...until Evan called about Mary's horse."

Albins made more notes, "Can anyone confirm that?"

"Just Evan, he was there all evening, we had dinner together and watched some TV. I fixed breakfast this morning before he came up to the stables."

Albins moved his gaze toward Evan, "Can you confirm what your mom says?"

"Yes, sir. Yesterday, I went back to our house about half an hour after Aunt Mary left on her ride. Mom told me dinner would be ready in an hour, so I showered, got dressed, and helped her set the table. This morning she made bacon and toast. She was putting dishes in the washer when I left."

"Did you come directly to the stables from your house?"

"Yes, sir."

"And that's when you found your aunt's horse still saddled?"

"Yes, sir."

Albins smiled for the first time. "That's all I need from you for now, although I may have some more questions in the next few days." He turned to Bob, "I gather you weren't here at the ranch yesterday, Mr. Linfield. Is that correct?"

Bob nodded. "Haven't been here in several weeks. I arrived about half an hour ago. I'd been out at a feed lot east of Greeley until almost ten last night and back there at 7:30 this morning---several sick cows; Julie called about 9:15 and I left immediately."

"I assume there will be somebody to corroborate those times?"

"Yes, that's one of Iowa Beef's lots and their manager was with me all the time. I've got his card out in my van. I'll give it to you."

"Did you stay in close contact with your sister?" Albins drained the last of his coffee and set the cup on a sandstone coaster.

"You could say that, yes. I spoke to her at least once a week, mostly on Saturday mornings, and we would discuss the family business. Sometimes those were conference calls with our brother, Jeff, in Nevada, and with Julie." Bob seemed worse off than when we'd first met at the corral. I thought the full impact of what had happened was starting to set in.

"Have you spoken to your brother lately?"

Bob stared down at the cup in his hands, thought for a few seconds, then answered, "No, not recently. I think the last time was back in January or February during one of the conference calls. He hasn't been available for them since then. Is that about right, Julie?"

Julie nodded. "I think that's the last time I spoke with him until just now. I know he'd called Mary several times, though. She told me about it."

Bob said, "Mary mentioned that to me also."

Albins turned to Julie with renewed interest. "Do you know what he was discussing with Mary that he didn't want to talk to the two of you about?"

Bob cut in. "Money. The only thing Jeff ever wanted to talk to Mary about, and Randy before he died, was money."

It felt like all the air had gone out of the room. Julie's shoulders slumped. Several seconds passed before Bob said, "I hate saying this, but none of us get on very well with Jeff. He's always felt like an outsider even within the family. He's made no secret of his wishes to go his own way—- even wanting to dissolve our family corporation, get his money out of it, and into his own hands. He's my brother and it hurts me to talk about this. Still, I can't help wondering." Bob's face was splotchy red and his voice was hoarse. Tears filled his eyes and he looked away.

"Mrs. Linfield?" Albins shifted his position.

"I hate it too. We've certainly had some terrible arguments and disagreements recently."

Evan sat up straight, glanced at his mother, and spoke to Albins. "I don't know if anybody's told you about what happened here last fall. It might be important."

Albins raised his eyebrows. "What happened?"

Again, Evan glanced at his mother; she nodded to continue. "Uncle Jeff had been staying here for a few days and I overheard him and Aunt Mary talking in the stable. I didn't mean to listen, but they got pretty mad at each other and were both yelling so loud I couldn't help it." Evan's face flushed and he shifted uncomfortably next to

Julie. He told Albins about Jeff arguing with Mary over the family's investments. He said Mary had gotten mad when Jeff told her he'd "promised" a Denver oil company the family would buy shares in the company and invest in one of their drilling deals. Evan seemed embarrassed when he talked about his aunt and uncle screaming at each other.

Julie picked up the story. "Evan was so upset when he told me about the argument that we sat and talked over what we could do. We'd just seen Cort Scott's announcement in the paper about doing oil field investigations. So Evan went into Denver and told him what we were facing. Cort reviewed the drilling deal and began a background check on the company Jeff was trying to get us to buy into. The next week, we had a meeting here and Jeff got really mad about what Cort told us. He stomped out of here and we haven't seen him since." When she finished, Julie stood and stared out the back window. She took several deep breaths.

Albins checked his notes for a moment. "What's the name of this oil company?"

Evan answered, "Uncle Jeff called it Black Blizzard Petroleum."

Albins made a note and I could see him underlining it.

He asked, "Evan, did you hear your uncle threaten your aunt?"

"No, nothing like that. He just said those guys weren't going to wait around forever and they were pushing him really hard. He said he might get sued for breach-of-contract if he didn't come up with the money pretty quick."

"What did your aunt say to that?"

"She asked him if he'd signed any papers or if they had any legal hold on him."

"What was his answer?"

"He told her he hadn't signed any papers *but* he'd given his word and didn't think he could get out of it."

"And what did Mary say?"

Evan looked at his mom's back and cleared his throat. "She said, 'Tough shit.'"

chapter

TEN

Albins picked up his hat from the floor and stood. "Thanks folks. I'm sure I'll have more questions after I've had a chance to review what we've got. Mr. Scott, could we have a word outside?" The sheriff let himself out.

I shook hands with Bob and Evan and gave Julie a hug. "I'll speak to the sheriff and then go back to Parker. If you'll tell Jeff I need to talk to him, I'd appreciate it—- as soon as possible after he and Sheriff Albins have talked. Tell him he can call me anytime."

Outside, Albins stood by his cruiser gazing over the ranch grounds. I strode up to him and he asked, "Where'd you get your information on this Black Blizzard outfit and what've you got on them? You think they're involved in this?"

"Most of my information came from Tom Montgomery in the DPD who got it from contacts in New Orleans. There's lots of bad sounding stuff about who's involved. The bunch who formed Black

Blizzard are mostly high profile New Orleans hoods who play rough, and, somehow, never get caught. One of the guys on the list is Jerome Biggs who's in charge of Black Blizzard's office in Denver. He's a geologist, like me, and I know a little about his background and people who've had dealings with him.

"I wrote everything up for the Linfields and I'll fax you a copy. The scary thing is Jeff Linfield is the connection——- after you've had a chance to talk to him, I'd like to do the same.

"If Mary Linfield's death turns out to be a murder, and I believe it is, I'm betting, at the least, that Black Blizzard is involved. From what you heard in there, what do you think about Jeff?"

Albins scuffed the ground with the toe of his right boot then shined it on the back of his left calf. "It's too early to say. Although I wouldn't repeat this to anybody doing TV news, he's definitely a person of interest. As far as what you should do, don't go charging into something that might end up backfiring on you. If you've got questions, call me first. Deal?"

"Deal," I said. We shook hands.

***

I didn't get home until almost four. I'd had my cell phone turned off all day and laid it beside my desk phone, which was blinking for messages. I decided to make a sandwich and have a beer before delving into both phones.

From the kitchen, I glanced into the back yard. A big doe, obviously pregnant, was munching on choke cherry leaves sticking through the scrub oak. I got a bottle of Anchor Steam out of the refrigerator and stepped out to the deck. The doe glanced up but didn't stop browsing. I took a long swallow, saluted the doe, and went back in the kitchen. I made a multi-tiered sandwich from left-over pork tenderloin, grabbed some jalapeno chips, another beer, and returned to the phones.

The desk phone screen indicated seven messages and my cell showed five. Most were oil field guys; and Gerri had left one on each phone. She said the same thing on both phones, "Big news, call me."

The last message, from Julie Linfield, had come five minutes before I got home. She said Jeff had called and was catching a flight out of Reno arriving in Denver at about 8:30 p.m. local time. He'd be at the ranch by 9:30 p.m., however he planned to get a hotel in Denver. Julie said she'd pass the information on to George Albins.

I called Gerri, got her voice mail and left a message. Next, I called Tom Montgomery and had a brief conversation about the Arapahoe County Sheriff's office. Tom said he didn't know George Albins personally, although he'd heard a lot about him over the years. Sheriff Weaver had told Tom that Albins was a good investigator, tough but fair. I told Tom I wouldn't want to cross swords or anything else with Albins. He looked harder than anvil steel.

Gerri called back. "Where the hell've you been? I've been trying you all day."

I told her about my day and what had happened at the Linfield ranch.

"Oh man, Cort. That's rough. I guess my news won't seem very big by comparison. I just wanted to tell you Ensign Drilling said they're moving a rig onto our location by the end of the week. The funny thing is, my office called about noon and said there was huge volume in the stock today. It was up almost twenty-five percent on the close. You made one hell of a lot of money. Wanna go celebrate?"

"Paper money, sweetheart, it could go down just as much tomorrow. That doesn't mean we shouldn't celebrate, though. How about driving out here? I'll fix spaghetti and we'll drink some Chianti."

"I can't come to Parker tonight. I'm meeting with our partners and Ensign first thing tomorrow morning for a pre-drilling conference. I was hoping you'd come downtown."

"Nope, can't. I've got a bunch of calls to make and I need to put an outline together to work this case. Sorry, babe, maybe we can get together in the next couple days."

"You just don't want to celebrate." I could tell she was disappointed although she had laughter in her voice. "I'll call you as soon as my schedule settles down."

"Sounds good. Hey, good luck on the well."

"We don't need luck...remember, *I* did the geology. This is going to be a major discovery."

"If that's true, the stock oughta go through the roof and we won't regret not celebrating a few hundred grand in paper profits, right?"

"Must be nice to be a rich private 'dick' like you and not need a pot full of money...whatever. Goodnight, I'll see you soon."

"Night, babe."

Damn, it would have been nice to see her tonight. I'd have to take solace with more money...too bad it was still a few months before I could sell any stock. Being a founder of a company had some drawbacks, still—- what the hell, maybe the Green River prospect would really work. Maybe the company would be into a big development drilling program by the time I could sell.

I finished my sandwich and downed the second beer. I got out a legal pad and began making notes. Most were questions I needed to ask Jeff Linfield. Each time I thought of something, I had to wonder how I'd get any answers out of a guy I'd beaten up.

chapter

ELEVEN

The next day, time moved so slowly I was kicking myself for not going to see Gerri the night before. I sat around waiting for the phone to ring. Finally, in mid-afternoon, it did. It was George Albins.

"Hello, Cort. I just got out of a meeting with Jeff Linfield. He came to the Sheriff's office...said he didn't want to meet at the ranch."

"How'd that go? Did you learn anything?"

"Not a lot. I came away with the impression Mary's death has shaken him to the core. This guy may have been playing tough before, but he's scared as hell now. He might be mixed up in her death some way, but I'd bet my last dollar he didn't have anything to do with planning it."

"I'm glad to hear it. If he's cooperating, sounds like a big change in attitude since the last time I saw him. Did you mention I wanted to talk to him?"

"He said he'd call you tonight. I'm hoping he'll tell you something he wouldn't...or couldn't tell me. After you talk, I'll need you to tell me everything he has to say."

"Okay, I can do that. Did he give you anything that'll help him out?"

"He gave me the name of a restaurant in Tahoe where he said he had dinner the night before last and the names of five people he was with. Before he got to my office, I'd checked with the airline to make sure he was on the flight he claimed to be on. Since cell phones went international, somebody can say they're nearly anywhere and you wouldn't know the difference. In this case, the airline had his flight record so at least we know he wasn't physically involved in Mary's death. He was definitely in Nevada at the time."

"That's some relief...can I tell the Linfields? Even if they think he might be mixed up in it, they'll feel better knowing he didn't push her over the cliff."

"Go ahead. Incidentally, Lindsey Collins dropped by to say one set of the scrapings they got at the crime scene came from an athletic shoe. The other was from a hard leather-soled shoe. They're running a bunch more tests to see if they can narrow anything down."

"I hope something pops up. I didn't see any other human shoe prints around, even in the sandy areas, and it didn't seem like a place where a lot of walkers would be. After all, it's a private ranch and a long way from a road."

Albins exhaled loudly, "The crime scene is already screwed up as far as finding other foot prints. I'm sending them back out there tomorrow and have 'em check up and down that ATV trail to see what they might find."

"Thanks for calling, George. I'll let you know what I find out from Jeff."

"Sounds good."

After I hung up, I sat for a minute thinking about what George had told me. I was glad Jeff hadn't been in Colorado although I felt he had to know something. George's observation about Jeff being scared was also interesting. He hadn't seemed like the sort to scare easily. I hoped he would tell me something that maybe he was afraid to tell the sheriff.

George's call broke the ice and the phone rang again. "Cort Scott? This is Jeff Linfield." He didn't sound like the same guy I'd gut-hooked in the middle of a road last fall. "I'm in trouble and I need to try to get out of it before someone else gets hurt. When can we talk?"

"Hello, Jeff. Thanks for calling...right now is fine with me. Where are you and where do you want to meet?"

"I'm sitting in the parking lot of the sheriff's office in Littleton. I've been here for over an hour, I don't know where else to go. I don't think it's safe to go back to my hotel and I don't want to stay at the ranch. That could put Julie and Evan in danger. Where are you? Could I come to your place?"

"Sure, I'm not far from you." I gave him directions. "It should take you about forty minutes."

"Okay, I'm leaving now...uh, listen, I'm sorry for what happened between us out at the ranch last time. Thanks for seeing me."

"We'll talk about it when you get here." I hung up the phone thinking Jeff Linfield *did* sound scared. The phone rang again.

"It's Julie. Do you have a minute?"

"Sure, I just got off the phone with Jeff and he's headed to my house now."

Julie heaved a great sigh, "Oh, God, what a relief! Jeff was here last night and we talked for hours. He feels responsible for Mary. He's completely different than he was last fall and when I told him you wanted to talk to him, he seemed happy about it. He told me some really awful things...it's best if he tells you directly. Maybe later we can compare what he says to each of us to make sure it matches."

"That sounds like a plan. Julie, George Albins said Jeff has a rock solid alibi for the time when Mary was killed."

Julie's breath caught. "That's good—- no, *great* news! I never believed for a minute he would have killed Mary, although he seems to feel guilty. You'll see when you talk to him."

"If he can explain what led up to that point, it'll go a long ways in helping us understand what happened."

"I hope you're right. Thanks, Cort."

"I'll be in touch, Julie. Take care of yourself."

I was looking forward to talking to Jeff. If he could shed some light on Black Blizzard, I could get George headed down the right track. If anybody in Black Blizzard murdered Mary Linfield and George could prove it, we'd slam the prison doors on them for a very long time. What I really needed from Jeff was a timeline for his involvement with Black Blizzard and how everything was tied back to New Orleans.

chapter

TWELVE

A gray Ford Taurus pulled into my driveway. I watched from my office window as Jeff Linfield got out and started up the sidewalk. Jeff appeared to have aged ten years since I'd seen him last. I opened the door as he reached for the bell and mentally increased the aging by another five years.

"Come on in." I motioned him inside and extended my hand. This time, we shook hands. His grip was firm but damp. He was wearing a flannel shirt that hung loose on him like he'd lost weight. His eyes were red rimmed and glistening.

"Thanks for seeing me. I'm sorry about everything that happened out at the ranch. I don't know what else to say." From his demeanor and the shaky sound of his voice, I wasn't sure he was going to make it inside.

"Take it easy. Let's sit down. Can I get you a drink? You look like you need one." I managed a smile, closed the door, and led Jeff into the living room.

"I could use a drink, scotch, if you have it. And, I'm serious about setting things straight. I was a complete fool and a real asshole and I—- "

I cut him off. "Sit down, Jeff. Let me get your scotch and then we'll talk. Ice?" I asked.

"Please, a couple of cubes."

I put two cubes in a large tumbler and poured him a generous double of Johnny Walker Blue Label. It would be a twenty-five dollar drink in the cigar room at the Brown Palace Hotel. I decided to stick with beer. I carried the drinks back to the living room and set Jeff's on a sand-painting coaster on the end table next to the over-stuffed leather chair and ottoman. I sat on the couch.

"Start at the beginning, Jeff, and we'll see what we can figure out. I'm not an attorney and I can't guarantee what you tell me can be kept confidential. If it comes to a court case, I'd have to give it up. You know I'm working for Julie and Bob and I've already given George Albins my report on Black Blizzard. I told him about our dust-up, too. You need to tell me everything and trust me to use it as best I can to help unravel Mary's death. If you're straight with me, I'll put you in the best light I can."

Jeff gulped his drink, a man easing his pain. "I didn't kill Mary. It's driving me crazy when I think about what I told those guys, these fucking killers, about my own family. You gotta believe me, I didn't want to hurt Mary or anybody else. Her death is my fault, but I didn't know it would happen." He had another sip. "You were right about me being in over my head and not knowing how to get out. When we had that meeting last fall, I already knew Black Blizzard was mixed up with drugs and all kinds of shit. The problem was, I'd already given them most of my own money. I'd promised them I could deliver a lot more...the family's money. When I couldn't get Mary to even bring it up with Bob and Julie, I thought

I could just bullshit my way through, you know...talk 'em into it." The scotch was working, his color was better. "I thought if I made it sound good enough, they'd eventually agree to buy in, if for no other reason, just to shut me up. I didn't figure on them getting an outside opinion—- especially from you. When you showed up and started explaining everything to them, I panicked. I was so scared about everything, I completely lost it. I don't know what the hell I was thinking when I tried to threaten you." He shifted his gaze and drummed his fingers on the table.

Finally, he looked back and continued. "After you shut me down, I went straight back to Tahoe. I called Metropolit, told him I couldn't get any more money and I wanted my own money back. I told him I wanted out. At first he laughed, then he went ballistic and started screaming about how things didn't work that way. He said I knew too much to get out and I was part of the deal. He said if I didn't come through with the rest of the money, he could paint me as a major drug player. He said they'd 'sacrifice' a piece of their business and make it look like I was at the top. I'd be facing fifty years in prison."

Jeff leaned forward in the chair. "That was when I made the biggest mistake of all. I thought if I convinced him more people knew what was going on, he'd back off. I lied and told him Mary knew everything. That's what's eating me alive—- I think it's what got Mary killed."

I had the answer to one of the things bothering me. What was the motive behind Mary's killing? If the Black Blizzard assholes thought Mary or Jeff would blow the whistle, they'd try to shut them up any way they could. They probably believed threatening Jeff with a frame job wasn't enough. Killing Mary would sure as hell get the message across. I wasn't going to let him off the hook easily. "It definitely could've led to it, Jeff. I know they scared you but that was a stupid thing to tell Metropolit. It put Mary on their radar."

He nodded and swallowed several times.

I wanted to know more about how he had gotten in so deep he couldn't walk away. "Jeff, go back to how you made contact with them. They didn't just walk in the door one day with a scheme to drag you into the drug business and follow it up with a crooked oil deal. You must've done something to get it all kicked off."

Jeff talked for almost two hours. I tried not to ask many questions because I didn't want to break the flow. His story seemed innocent enough at first. The closer we got to the present, the scarier it became.

chapter

THIRTEEN

Jeff sat back in the chair, sighed deeply, and began talking. "I moved to Tahoe ten years ago after I started receiving royalty income. I didn't want another house at the ranch like Randy and Julie and I sure as hell didn't want to live in the big house with Mary. Mostly, I wanted to get as far as I could from Byers and Colorado. I ended up checking out Tahoe and decided to take a stab at commercial real estate. I made a deal on an improved campground site in South Lake Tahoe plus some adjacent undeveloped land. I put up a commercial building and got a convenience store and a mailbox store to take long-term leases. Everything took off and in a couple years, the place was cash flowing. By then, the oil royalties were really pouring in so I paid off my mortgages. The next year, I acquired more land in west Reno and built a small office building, which filled up with dentists, some lawyers, and a coin dealer. Real estate deals were cropping up all over the area and I was becoming a player.

"I started spending some time in casinos in Reno and Lake Tahoe—- not gambling, I liked the shows. I met this gal, Maria Suarez, who was ticket manager for all of Harrah's entertainment when I signed up for advanced tickets in the main show room. Man, she was beautiful and incredibly professional in her job. I asked her out, she accepted, and we began dating regularly.

"Maria was bright, talented, and wanting to move into real estate so it wasn't much of a stretch to offer her a job managing some of mine. It wasn't long before she moved in with me in Tahoe. A year later, we decided to get married in Reno.

"By that time, I was pushing for access to more of the family corporation money. Mary refused to change the rules and I was really pissed off. I purposely didn't invite them to the wedding—- Hell, I didn't even tell them I was getting married!

"Maria invited her entire family and there were a bunch of them. They filled the courthouse lobby where we had the ceremony. She introduced me to her mother, three brothers, and a sister. I hadn't met any of them before that day.

"Everybody seemed prosperous. Two of the brothers owned a realty company in the San Fernando Valley; her sister's husband, her brother-in-law, was a lawyer in private practice in Van Nuys. He specialized in insurance litigation and, from Maria's description, was extremely successful."

Jeff shifted positions in the chair, took a drink, and sat up straight before he continued. "The youngest brother, Ron, had just been divorced and brought his new girlfriend to the wedding. When I inquired about what he did for a living, he just kinda muttered, 'Oh, this'n'that, a little bit of everything' and changed the subject. While Maria and I were waiting for our flight to New York for our honeymoon, I asked her what Ron did. She said she didn't know... thought it had to do with leasing warehouses and storage units in LA.

"Maria is several years older than Ron and she'd left for college when he was still a kid. After college, she worked in San Jose for a year and then moved to Reno. She said Ron didn't go to college and moved out of the family home shortly after their father died. She knew he'd started working as a delivery and warehouse man, however for the last year or so, he'd started wearing suits and working out of an office. Maria said she hadn't seen Ron for a while and was a little surprised when he showed up at the wedding.

"After we got back to Tahoe, we got busy on the real estate deals and I was scouting for more opportunities and ways to diversify. I kept pushing the family for money and complained to Maria about their conservative outlook and wishing I could figure out ways to leverage their cash. Maria offered to talk to her brothers about opportunities in the San Fernando Valley, however I didn't want to be in residential real estate. I asked her to call Ron about the warehouse leasing business. Two weeks later, Ron called and said he had some things that might interest me. I'd have to come to LA to talk about them. Maria begged off because of a flu bug so I flew to LA alone.

"Ron picked me up at LAX in a brand new, green Jaguar. We drove south to Long Beach and he quizzed me about what kind of investments I was looking for and about how much money I had to invest."

Jeff pause and rolled his eyes. "That's when I really put my foot in it and made a huge mistake. I told him I could invest a couple hundred thousand immediately and had access to a lot more if the first deals panned out.

"He kept asking me where the money was coming from, what other investments we had, and about the total amount available. I started feeling uncomfortable answering some of the questions. But, stupid me, I continued to say if the family got interested, we'd be talking millions.

"After half an hour or so, I asked him to explain his business and how he'd made so much money. He made it sound like he'd just been a hard working delivery guy who'd met the right people. I thought it had to be a lot more complicated than that. Finally, he said he'd been approached by a friend about making some deliveries that weren't on his route sheets. His 'friend' was a Mexican illegal he'd known since junior high. The guy told him he had lots of family in Mexico and they were moving drugs across the border. They needed a better delivery system once it got to LA and Ron's routes might be just the ticket. Ron asked what kind of money they were talking and about the danger of getting caught. His friend told him all deals were prepaid and he wouldn't be handling any money, just delivering product a couple days a week. He could make a thousand a week and since the packaging was similar to his regular deliveries, the chances of being caught were low.

"He jumped on it. Everything went great, no problems, and by the end of a year, he'd accumulated forty thousand in cash. He said he was stashing the money in an athletic bag in his work locker. It was getting bulky, and he wanted a safer place...like in a bank. He knew he couldn't deposit that much cash because anything over ten thousand had to be reported to the IRS, so he asked his buddy what he did with his money. His friend told him about another guy who'd take the cash and invest it in a company that owned things like warehouses and apartments and laundromats—- any kind of business receiving a steady stream of cash. The company would make it look like the money was a loan and they were paying back by check. The checks could be deposited in any bank. Because it was a loan repayment, no tax was due and everybody went away happy. Ron said he needed to talk to the money man, so he met Myron Metropolit.

"Metropolit was older than he'd expected, looked and talked like a New York Jew. He kinda pissed Ron off when he laughed at the forty thousand...said most of the other guys he worked with were turning hundreds of thousands. He said he was happy to see a young guy like Ron trying to do the right thing and clean the cash before using it. Guys who started buying lots of stuff for cash attracted attention and represented a risk to their organization they didn't need. He said his bosses, the guys in New Orleans, had organized the whole deal, recruiting the Mexicans, setting up the networks, and were even involved in production. Their biggest need was for more American citizens who could buy and sell property, make investments, and work in the laundering side of the business. Ron said Metropolit told him, 'We leave the actual handling of the product to the fucking wetbacks. We keep our hands clean and make a hell of a lot of money off our legit businesses. If you're interested, you can move up immediately by leasing warehouses and apartments. You can start making legit money with a company salary and get out of handling drugs.'

"Ron told me he was more than interested because delivering dope two or three days a week was making him crazy. He asked Metropolit how much salary he'd be paid and said he nearly passed out when Metropolit told him a hundred thousand a year to start.

"He cut his deal with Metropolit, got all kinds of paper showing a loan and repayment schedule, and even got an employment contract from 'LA Warehouse Leasing and Storage' showing he was being hired as a 'district leasing coordinator' for ninety-six thousand a year. He said his first job, though, was to recruit a couple of drivers from the delivery company to take over his old routes—- particularly the 'special' deliveries."

I got up, took Jeff's glass to the bar, and refilled it. I wanted to hear the whole story. I couldn't wait to ask how come he hadn't walked out right then. "Why the hell did you keep sitting there talking to Ron Suarez? Couldn't you see he was just a goddamn drug dealer? Why didn't you grab your bag and head back to Tahoe?"

Jeff sipped the scotch, stood, and walked to the window. He didn't say anything for a moment, then sighed, and returned to the chair. "I've asked myself the same thing a thousand times. I don't have an answer. I was so pissed at my family, I wanted to show them I could make lots of money without their help. Mostly, I'm just fucking stupid." Jeff's eyes glistened. I pretended I didn't see although it convinced me he was telling the truth. I asked him to go on with Ron's story.

"Ron knew a couple of drivers he could recruit. One guy had a record and had done a short stint in the California Youth Offenders system. The other one was a mutual friend of Ron's and the guy who recruited him. Both of 'em were Mexican, but he didn't know their immigration status.

"He said everything went as planned for the better part of a year. He got the other drivers, started wearing a suit to work, and discovered he was pretty good at the warehouse leasing business. He started giving Metropolit a suitcase full of cash every week and was getting 'loan repayment checks' in return that he deposited in legit bank accounts. By the time I talked to him, he was taking in over twenty thousand dollars a month.

"He said the only reason he'd given me a call was Metropolit complained they were maxed out on laundering in the LA Warehouse Leasing and Storage scam. They needed another way to wash money so Metropolit made a couple trips to New Orleans and one to Denver. Ron said when he got back, he was excited and told him they'd found a perfect solution.

"He said Metropolit laid out their scheme for forming an oil company with some geologist in Denver, putting in a bunch of cash, and buying some legitimate oil and gas properties. Next, they planned on buying and promoting drilling deals. Ron told me that Metropolit was laughing all the time, because they didn't give a crap about finding oil and gas. They could sell partnerships in the prospects for more money than it cost to put them together. If they drilled dry holes, they'd still make a profit—- and it was clean.

"Ron explained that if lightning struck and they found oil, they'd make even bigger profits and their cash still got washed in the process. In a year or so, they'd do a public float and sell stock in the company. The leveraging effect would be huge because there's so much interest in the oil and gas business. If they sold stock on the open market, they'd increase the value of the founders' shares by several times. They'd have to hold on to the shares for a couple years before selling them back into the market. Since they'd be making twenty or thirty bucks for every dollar they put in, who cared?

"I was seeing dollar signs when Ron said they planned to buy five million dollars of properties, do some deals, and go public for fifty to seventy-five million. Black Blizzard Oil & Gas would be totally legitimate as far as anyone knew. It would conduct real oil and gas exploration and operate its properties. The New Orleans guys would stay in only long enough to wash and multiply their cash. Everybody else could do as they pleased. I figured it was a chance to show up my family and make a bundle of money."

Jeff asked me to point out the bathroom. I was having trouble understanding why his new brother-in-law, whom he barely knew, would talk openly about drug money and fraud.

When he returned, I said, "I don't get two things. First, why would Ron tell you all his dirty secrets? And, second, I *still* don't understand why you didn't walk out."

Jeff was pacing around. "Because of Maria—- he believed I wouldn't say anything that would get him in trouble because it would hurt her. Plus, I made it way too clear how frustrated I was with my own family." He stopped, cracked his knuckles, and looked directly at me. "I stayed because I was a fool. I wanted to get back at my family for treating me like a baby. I thought any money I put in Black Blizzard was so far removed from New Orleans or LA or drugs, it could never be connected. I thought I was going to be an insider, prove to everyone I was a big deal."

He continued. "I knew the whole damn thing was bogus, but I kept thinking, 'What the hell? I'm not in the goddamn drug business.' I'll just be in the oil company and I could get rich. I'll show Mary and Bob I'm not the baby brother any more. If anything ever came up, I would swear I didn't know anything about the drugs."

I got up to stretch my legs. "Did you put money in right then?"

"It was more like I 'pledged' some money. I said I'd put half a million dollars in the private placement. I didn't want to be tied directly to New Orleans—- that would've been too close to the drugs. I fucked up again when I promised Ron I'd get my family to invest. I thought for sure they'd buy into the drilling deal and the IPO. If they bought stock, I'd be making money off them and they wouldn't even know about it. I'd be getting even with them."

I thought about that for a few seconds. "When you were after money last fall, was your first bill due?"

"Yeah. They wanted the family to take a twenty-five percent interest in the Mosquito Basin deal. It was going to cost about a million bucks with my share at two-hundred and fifty thousand. They were planning the private placement no later than June this year so I needed to come up with three-quarters of a million. I don't have that kind of money. Just before Ron called in September, I'd gone out on a limb, bought five-hundred acres south of the lake, and was planning to put in a resort-style golf course, tennis facility, and a fancy restaurant catering to RV owners. I'd had to pay cash up front to close the deal, so I couldn't cover Black Blizzard's call."

It was beating a dead horse, still, I wanted to hear him say it. "You went to the family to get more money out of the corporation, plus get them to invest, right?"

"Yes, that was the idea, but Mary said no—- and I found out you were involved. I panicked and lost it. I'd already tried to stall Ron. He said if I didn't come up with the money as planned, they had ways to 'convince' me. He said they'd get an anonymous tip to the Tahoe and Reno DAs about me being involved with drug money in LA. Even though there wasn't anything on paper in LA to back it up, that kind of investigation could screw me up for years."

Jeff was talking faster now, the scotch was taking hold. "Everything snapped at the ranch that day. I felt like my whole life would go down the shitter if I didn't get the money. You were the guy standing in front of me, so I blamed you. That's why I went after you out by the gate."

I couldn't help myself. "That didn't work out too well either. What happened after that?"

"I kept calling Ron and telling him I couldn't come up with the money, my family wasn't going to back me up."

"What'd he say?"

"Mostly he just swore at me. He said it would cause trouble all the way up and down the line and he'd already told Metropolit I had cold feet. Metropolit told him the guys in New Orleans wouldn't like that. He said they were into 'sending messages' to people who didn't do things their way. It scared the shit out of me. I still didn't have the balls to call Mary and Bob and let them know what was going on. I wish I had."

"That would have been a good thing." I drained my beer and tilted the glass toward Jeff. He shook his head no. "What happened next?"

"I didn't hear anything until Christmas when Ron called and said I needed to call Metropolit. I told him I wasn't going to do it. He said if I didn't, something real bad would happen. That scared me enough to make the call. I thought I might be able to stall because I'd kept in touch with Biggs, knew the Mosquito Basin deal hadn't sold, and they weren't ready to drill. If I just wait for three months, I'd get a chunk of cash out of the family corporation. I might be able to scrape up enough to at least pay for my part of the well. I called the number Ron gave me and got Metropolit's cell—- he was in New Orleans. I tried to explain what was happening. He wouldn't listen and put some guy named Mike Landry on. Landry said if I didn't come up with two hundred and fifty grand in the next week, they'd have to 'send me a message.' Even after that, I thought they were talking about going to the Tahoe DA. I swear it never occurred to me they were threatening something physical."

I couldn't believe Jeff was that stupid or naïve. What the hell did he think they meant? "Did you tell them you couldn't come up with that much cash right then?"

"Absolutely. I said it fifty times. They just acted like they didn't believe me. They just kept telling me to get it."

"What'd you do?"

"I kept thinking there had to be a way out. I made one more call to Mary about getting half a million out of the trust. I told her a cock-and-bull story about another land deal in Tahoe. I don't know if she believed me or not. It didn't make any difference because she said no again."

Jeff stepped behind the chair and put his hands on the back. "I was at the end of my rope. I finally sat down with Maria and told her some of it...mostly, I lied to cover my ass. I told her Ron was mixed up with some guys who weren't doing everything by the book and he owed them a bunch of money. I said I'd agreed to help him out and then found out it was going to cost a lot more than I'd thought. I sugarcoated my part in everything as much as I could. I kept blaming my family because they wouldn't let me get at my own money. I couldn't bring myself to tell her the truth. The whole thing was making me crazy."

"I can't argue that point with you." Again, I couldn't help myself even though I knew I should keep my big mouth shut.

"Next thing I knew, Maria called Ron. He told her I was a liar who shouldn't make promises I couldn't deliver on. He said his partners were legitimate businessmen who had made investment decisions based on my pledges of funding. They were at risk of having their business plan fall apart because I was backing out at a critical stage. He said his partners were very concerned and they were trying to apply whatever pressure they could to get me to keep my end of the bargain."

"What did Maria say to that?"

"At first, I think she believed Ron. She tried to shame me into coming up with the money. By that time, I knew I had to come clean so I told her the whole story."

"How'd she take it?"

"She didn't say anything for a long time and then started to cry. She told me she'd suspected Ron was into something bad and hadn't wanted to believe it. She said I should call Mary. But you know what? I *still* couldn't make myself do that. Finally, we decided to call Ron, let him know Maria knew everything, and see if they would back off."

"No luck, I suspect."

"No. Even worse, Ron told us it was too late to back out. Either I came up with the money or something real bad would happen."

"Why didn't you call the cops? He was threatening you for real."

"What proof did I have? There wasn't anything on paper. Besides, as weird as this may sound, Ron is Maria's brother and I didn't want to be the one who'd cause him to go to jail. He was into so much shit, he'd of gone down for a long time and I didn't want Maria or her family blaming me. Now, I know he would've screwed me over without a second thought. He didn't give a crap about me or Maria And what's more, he's not the worst of them. Still, back then, I didn't think they'd actually hurt anybody."

I threw my hands in the air. "You should've told *somebody*— at least your family. Whether you believed it or not, they were in danger."

"Christ! Don't you think I've thought about that? Now look what it's come to."

I didn't know where to go with all of this. "How much of this did you tell Albins?"

"Not very much. I just told him where I was when Mary was killed. I wanted a chance to talk to you and get your advice before I said something to the wrong people. I guess I'm still covering my ass. I'd like to get as much cleared up as I can."

"Well, I think you need to tell all of it to George. First, though, you need to tell the story to a lawyer. Do you have one?"

"I've got one in Reno...he isn't a criminal lawyer. He does my real estate and development work."

"Okay, I'll call my guy, Jason Masters, and set you up with him. I think it's time you came clean with Bob and Julie too. They have a right to know what led to this, plus they might be in danger."

Jeff's shoulders slumped and he hung his head. I could barely hear him. "I know you're right. It's going to be the hardest thing I've ever done. No, that's not right—- the hardest thing was hearing about Mary." He raised his head and gazed at me. "Will you come with me when I talk to them?"

"No. You need to man up and do it by yourself. I'll come with you when we find an attorney for you. If I'm present, I can argue whatever you tell him, even in my presence, is attorney/client privilege. I won't have to answer any questions. I don't know if it carries any legal weight, but it sounds good. Let's get some things worked out. Where are you staying?"

"I'm at the Courtyard downtown. I paid cash and registered under the name Jeffrey Lyons."

"That's good. How'd you rent the car?"

"Oh, shit...I used my real name and credit card. You have to show a driver's license and credit card to rent one."

"That's all right, we'll return the car tomorrow and I'll loan you my Bronco. Returning the car might even be a good thing if the Black Blizzard shitheads check the car rentals. They might think you've gone back to Reno. Where's your wife? She's in danger too, you know."

"We've handled that. As soon as I heard about Mary, Maria and I agreed she needed to be someplace other than Tahoe. Since Ron never talks with his family, the safest place is with one of her other brothers. She told him she and Ron were on the outs and not to tell Ron."

"That sounds like a plan. Have you talked with her since you've been in Colorado?"

"We talk every night and I called her before I came here."

"Good. Why don't you call Bob right now and see if he can meet you at the ranch tomorrow afternoon?" Jeff's body seemed to shrink as I continued, "First thing in the morning, I'll make some calls about an attorney. I'll meet you at the rental car agency at 10:30 and you can return the car. I'll bring you back here, you can take the Bronco to Byers, then back downtown after you've talked to Bob and Julie. When you get back, give me a call, and we'll see where you stand." I was anxious to get things moving. "I see my job in this as keeping you and your family safe while the cops sort everything out. I don't want you to go anyplace or talk to anybody without clearing it with me. Don't tell anyone, Bob and Julie included, where you're staying. If they need to get in touch, have them call your cell or call me. If you need anything, you call me. For now, go back to the hotel and try to get some rest. Are you all right to drive? You've had three double scotches."

Jeff stood and put out his hand. "I'm fine. It's probably adrenaline. I don't even feel a buzz." I shook his hand. His grip was drier than when he'd arrived. His eyes were clear and I didn't catch any smell of booze.

"Use my office phone to call Bob. I'll give you some privacy."

We went in my office, he picked up the phone and began punching in the number. I went to the kitchen and emptied and cleaned the coffee maker.

Jeff came out fifteen minutes later and gave me a half smile. "That went better than I expected. Bob actually sounded relieved. I told him the basics and asked if we could all meet at the ranch and I'll tell the whole story. He agreed, so I called Julie. We're meeting at noon tomorrow. It's tough admitting to being a fool. It's worse when I think about what happened to Mary."

"Bob and Julie will want to get all of this behind them."

"I hope you're right. I'm going to fly Maria in, so she can go with me."

I shook my head. "Hold off on that until things get a little more sorted out. I'm having second thoughts about you going to the ranch. It wouldn't surprise me if Landry or somebody else is hunting for you, maybe watching the ranch. If they're involved in Mary's death, and I think they are, they obviously know where it is."

"Oh, God! You're right. I didn't think about that."

"It's my mistake. Call them both back right now and ask them to come here instead."

Bob and Julie agreed, we decided on 1:00 p.m. rather than noon, and I gave them directions. I planned to go to another part of the house while Jeff told them the story. I'd join them afterward to discuss where to go from there. I saw Jeff out and thought to myself I wished I knew where to go. As it turned out, I could never have anticipated the direction things would take.

chapter

FOURTEEN

I checked the clock. It was only 8:30 p.m. Listening to Jeff had worn me out. Hearing what people will do to take advantage of others or steal their money was exhausting. I ran through my mental check list of things to do: call Gerri, get back to Albins, and get my thoughts in order. I needed to check in with Tom Montgomery too. If Black Blizzard was involved, DPD would have a piece of the action. That could wait for tomorrow. I decided on another beer and was headed to the fridge when the phone rang.

It was Lindsey Collins, the CSI from the sheriff's office. "Hi Cort. Is it too late to talk for a minute? I've got some news for you."

"Hey, Lindsey. No, it's not too late. I was just sitting down with a beer."

"Mmm, a beer sounds good—- it's been a long couple of days. I just got out of George's office going over the results from those shoe scrapings. One turns out to be from a Nike athletic shoe. The only way it'll help is if we find someone wearing a Nike shoe and match it exactly. That's probably not going to happen. The other one, however, is very interesting. It came from a hard rubber sole material for a hiking boot manufactured in Mexico and sold in Mexico, Texas, Arizona, and California. Although I can't prove it, I'm sure whoever wore that boot came from one of those places and was involved in Mary Linfield going over that cliff."

"That seems like a pretty big assumption. The Linfields have ranch help every year who come from Mexico on H2 visas. What makes you think whoever was wearing the boot killed Mary?"

"Those scrapings were fresh. There isn't any sign of weathering or deterioration so whoever left them was standing on that rock within the last day or so."

"That'd sure as hell make a difference all right. It would be a big deal if we find two guys together wearing shoes to match."

"Stranger things have happened. Uh, Cort, do you mind if I ask you something personal?"

"No problem, ask away."

"This is probably *way* out of line—- I was wondering if you might like to have a drink sometime."

That came out of the clear blue. "I would love to. Is now too soon?" I said it with a laugh.

"Now is exactly what I had in mind. Can you meet me at Cool River? Do you know where it is?"

"I know it. I've been there a couple of times. I can be there in half an hour. Will that work for you?"

"See you in a few."

I hung up and replayed the conversation in my mind. She'd said "personal." That didn't sound like something to do with the case. Was she hitting on me? The idea triggered some immediate second thoughts about agreeing to meet. I wondered what I'd say to Gerri—- if anything.

***

It was quarter after nine when I walked into Cool River. Like usual, the place was crowded and the noise level was damned near painful. I gave the room a once over, couldn't pick out Lindsey, so crowded my way over to the bar next to the service station. I'd found it to be the best place to get the bartender's attention because they had to come there to pick up the servers' drink orders. I was right.

"Can I help you?" The bartender was a put-together blonde with very short hair, dangly earrings, and a hassled expression on her face.

"I'll have a Bud Select in the bottle, thanks."

"You can't stand there. You're in the servers' way."

"No problem. I'll move over by the door."

"Here's your beer. It's five bucks." She didn't smile, frown, or express anything. I gave her a twenty and she made change from the register. I left a single and turned back toward the crowd. I spotted motion to my right, a hand waving above the crowd. I headed in that direction and saw Lindsey sitting in an alcove cubicle at a counter height table. I waved back and wove my way through the revelers.

"Hi, Lindsey, I didn't spot you when I came in." She looked a lot different in a beige, low cut, chemise top and some slinky brown pants. The ensemble fit her better than the sheriff's uniform she'd been wearing at the Linfield ranch.

"Thanks for coming out this time of night. Sorry about sitting up high like this. It was the last open table."

"It's a little conspicuous for sure. I'm late, I picked up a phone message from my girlfriend." Even though Gerri hadn't called, I said it to establish a few things. One, I had a girlfriend. Two, I thought enough of her to take a call before leaving. And, three, I was here anyway. I watched Lindsey carefully. Her eyes sparked, I think she got my "message."

"I'm glad you came. I really wanted to see you again and knew I'd have to make the first move." She'd got it all right.

"Then I'm glad you called."

"And, I heard what you said about a girlfriend. In fact, I'd already checked you out. George Albins told us to share information on this case with Tom Montgomery at DPD and while I was filling him in, he mentioned he's a friend of yours so I asked a lot of questions. Like, if you're married, he said 'no' although you have a girlfriend. I figured, what the hell, I've had boyfriends and still went out with other guys. God, I sound like some kind of stalker."

"It's okay, I *do* have a girlfriend. She has the occasional drink with male friends and I have drinks with female friends. I'm not looking for something else, but that doesn't mean I live a cloistered life either. My old friend Hedges used to say, 'Just because you're on a diet doesn't mean you can't look at the menu.'" It made a good story, although I wasn't so sure how much of it I believed.

Lindsey laughed out loud and it was a great laugh, kind of husky and deep in her throat. "Fair enough," she said.

I had a couple pulls on my beer, set it down, and said, "What are you drinking? Have you had anything to eat? We could get a couple of appetizer plates, a bottle of wine, and call it dinner."

She drained her wine glass. "You certainly push the right buttons—- I'm drinking red wine and I haven't eaten since 11:30 this morning, I'm hungry as hell and I'd love to share a bottle of wine."

I signaled a server prowling the area, asked for a wine list and the appetizer menu. I asked Lindsey if she had a favorite wine and what kind of food she wanted. She said she liked red wine and definitely wanted some kind of meat. She couldn't decide between chicken kebobs and some steak-on-a-stick things.

When the server returned, I ordered both appetizers and asked for a bottle of 2005 Erath Pinot Noir from Oregon. A pinot would go with most foods and I knew this particular one was an award winner.

"That was impressive. Are you a big wine guy or what?"

"I don't know what a 'big' wine guy is. I like wine, buy a lot of it and I happen to be familiar with this one. It's pretty common in a lot of better restaurants."

"Maybe there's more to you than meets the eye."

This girl was definitely hitting on me. It was decision time. "Look, Lindsey, even with what we just said about boyfriends and girlfriends, this seems to be advancing pretty quickly. Where are we headed with this?"

"I don't know where you're headed, Cort...I'm interested in sport fucking, no emotions involved, if you know what I mean." She used the f-word without the slightest hint of embarrassment and with no perceptible change in inflection. My first problem was I "did" know what she meant. My second problem was I didn't have any experience with it. I didn't know how my conscience would react. My third and biggest problem was I knew I was going to find out.

The server brought the wine, uncorked it, and poured a generous tasting amount. I pinched the cork and smelled it, which always looks good although it rarely yields any valuable information. I swirled the wine, checked the legs, and sniffed the nose—- ripe black berries followed by spice and leather. I sipped, rolled it over my tongue, held it in the back of my mouth for a second, and swallowed. I nodded at the server and said, "This will be fine. Would you mind decanting for us? It could stand to be open a little—- decanting will probably do the trick."

She set the bottle in the center of the table and went back through a service door next to the bar. She returned with a decanter and a filtered pourer. "Do you want me to filter the wine, sir?"

"I don't think so. If I remember correctly, the Erath is filtered before bottling."

She decanted and set it in the center of the table. "Should I pour now or do you want to wait until your appetizers come out? They should be about five minutes."

"You'd better pour now. We wouldn't want a good wine to turn to vinegar." She poured the two glasses, filling them to the exact mid-point of the belly curvature. She knew what she was doing.

Lindsey watched this with a bemused look. I picked up my glass and gestured toward hers. "Let's check and make sure this stuff isn't poison."

She carefully picked hers up and asked, "Would you show me how to taste it? What should I be doing?"

"Swirl your glass, take a whiff, then drink some." I reached across, touched glasses with her, swirled mine, checked the nose, and had a sip. It smelled and tasted better than the official tasting I'd just done.

Lindsey carefully swirled her glass, set it down, and took a drink of water. She swirled it again and checked the nose. She tried a small sip and rolled it around in her mouth before she swallowed. She set her glass down and smiled at me across the table. "That's the best wine I've ever had."

"Great. It'll be even better with the food."

The waitress arrived with our appetizers. Lindsey took one of the beef skewers and I grabbed the chicken. We had a couple bites and smiled at each other. It was as good as it looked. We polished off half of each plate quickly, switched plates, and finished the food. The server returned, cleared the plates, and divided the rest of the wine equally between us. "Would you like another bottle?"

"We would love another bottle, but we're not going to have one," I said. "We'll sip the last of this and be off."

We didn't exactly sip the wine, we didn't talk much either. We both knew what came next. I finally stared at Lindsey until I caught her eyes and held them, "To make a classic comment, 'My place or yours?'"

"Mine's probably closer. I live in a townhouse about five minutes from here. You can follow me. I'm parked right by the entrance. It's a copper colored Ford Edge. What are you driving?"

"I've got a yellow Corvette with a black top."

"I could have guessed that. I'll see you at my place."

I followed her out of Cool River. She was parked a couple of rows outside of me so I walked her to her car intending to double back to mine. She keyed the locks and the interior light came on as we reached her door. She turned to me, put her arms around my neck, and pulled my face close to hers. The kiss was long, hard, and mostly open mouthed. I could taste the remnants of the pinot noir on her tongue. Finally, she said, "Follow me."

chapter

FIFTEEN

Sex with Lindsey was new, different, exciting, and exhausting. She had a wonderfully athletic body, knew what every part was for and how to use it. She wore a light fragrance behind her ears, between her breasts, and in some other regions I found to explore. Getting used to her height and the length of her legs took some adjustments on my part. When I first slipped under the covers, I had a brief thought about the amount of alcohol I'd consumed over the day. I didn't want to be plagued with what Hedges referred to as "Brewer's Droop." As it turned out, there was no reason to worry although subjects like stamina and staying power crossed my mind. Lindsey apparently didn't have such thoughts mucking up her brain. Her love making was enthusiastic and vocal. She liked being a leader and wasn't shy about telling me what she liked and what felt good. I liked it all. We didn't cover any new ground as far as techniques or positions. The ones we did use were made to seem new.

When we finished, we assumed the classic post-coital spoon position. Lindsey reached for a remote and turned off the lights and music. Looking over her right ear, I saw the digital display on her alarm: 2:30 a.m. So much for being rested and ready for tomorrow.

I awakened when Lindsey stirred and couldn't believe we were still spooning. I checked the clock: 6:30. Four hours of totally dreamless sleep. Now would come an awkward moment, however, as it turned out, it wasn't.

She rolled over, faced me, and said, "Good Morning. Race you to the bathroom. I've gotta pee like a racehorse!" She leapt out of bed without waiting for an answer. I had to go although I figured I could hold out a few minutes. As she exited the bathroom, Lindsey, being keen on the social mores, sensed my need. "Next," she said with a smile. "Take your time if you want, I can wait a few minutes to brush my teeth and fix my hair."

When I came out, Lindsey had made the bed and was pulling on a golf shirt over a pair of jeans. No bra, I noticed. "Hurry up and get dressed. I'll start some coffee and toast."

I did as instructed and when I got to the kitchen counter said, "I feel kind of overdressed."

"That's because you are." She was smiling and her voice was happy. "I'm going to duck back in the bathroom and brush my teeth. I've got the coffee going and the bread is in the toaster. Start it in about five minutes— I'll be right back." She came around the counter, put her left hand on my shoulder, and looked me in the eyes. She gave a slight squeeze and headed down the hall.

I opened the front door and picked up the newspaper. The coffee maker chimed so I went in the kitchen, pushed down the toast, and opened the paper to the sports section. The Nuggets had lost in OT to the Trailblazers in Portland. The Avs had won big, five to one, over the Wings at home. Both teams were already in the playoffs, which would start in another week.

Lindsey sat on a bar stool on the living room side of the counter. "Is there any service in this beanery?"

"Coming right up, Miss. What'll it be? Say, I have an idea. How about coffee and toast?"

"Sounds good to me. Let's eat!"

I poured us each a cup and watched as she ate her toast. She ate like a man with big bites followed by sips of coffee. She finished hers before I had started on my second slice.

"Looks like getting a good, uh..."night's sleep" makes you hungry, young lady."

"I guess you could say that, sir. Sleeping does that to me."

This wasn't awkward at all.

"What's up for you today?" I asked. "I assume you have to go to work."

"That would be correct. We're trying to pull the trace evidence together from the crime scene. I'll probably spend most of the day in the lab."

"Do you like doing that kind of work?"

"I really do. You never know when one little clue is the key to a whole case. We don't get many murders in the county so we devote nearly full time to each one."

"I'm glad you're on it. I hope we can put it together quickly."

"Me too. There isn't much to go on yet, though." She swallowed her coffee and glanced at the kitchen wall clock.

I got the hint. "I've got to go. I need to get home, change clothes, and meet Jeff Linfield at the airport rental car return. I'm bringing him back to my place to meet with his brother and Julie. As soon as I get home, I'll call Albins and fill him in too. Are you done with your coffee?"

She shook her head and stared intently. "I know I came on pretty strong last night...I'm not sorry. I described it as 'sport fucking.' That's way too crass...I wanted to say the words for shock effect. Even with all that's going on, I'd like to see you again. If you want to tell me to back off, that's fine—- I'll understand. I guess what I'm saying is if you'd want to try this out for a while, I'd like that. I won't put any pressure on you. We can just have a good time and see where it takes us...if anyplace."

She was a very unusual girl and said the things nearly every man had dreamt about hearing. The little conscience man standing on my shoulder was silent. "Let's just take it slow and easy to see what happens. I've been with one woman for a long time and I'll probably continue spending most of my time with her, but I'm going to make room for you. too. I don't know how this will turn out...I'll be honest with you if it isn't working."

"Don't be so serious. We'll just play it by ear and have some fun. If it gets too heavy for you, tell me and we'll go away friends."

Lindsey came into the kitchen and put her arms around my neck. We stood for a few seconds in a loose embrace, then she leaned back, pulled my head down, and we kissed. It was one of those soul-wrenching kisses that take you back to your first date—- or the first time you got laid.

When we pulled back, I said, "I've got to run. I'll call you this afternoon after the Linfields leave."

I kissed her cheek and went down the short hall to the garage. I hit the garage door opener, got in the 'Vette, and backed out. The tachometer in my mind was red-lining as I watched her reach to close the door. What the hell was I doing?

chapter

SIXTEEN

My mind continued to over-rev as I drove. Last night was a lot to process and I needed to get my brain cleared and ready for today. I was running against the commuter traffic so it was a quick trip home.

Inside, I went straight to my office. The message light was blinking and I had three messages: Tom Montgomery and Gerri had called after I left last night. The most recent was from George Albins fifteen minutes ago. I sat down, ran my conversation with Jeff through my head, and pushed the recall button. George picked up on the first ring.

"Hi, George, it's Cort Scott. I was out for an early run and just walked in. I missed you by about ten minutes."

George hesitated before replying. "I'm anxious to find out what Jeff Linfield had to say yesterday."

"A bunch. There's no question he has some involvement, but I agree with you that he didn't do anything leading directly to Mary's death. He told me a long story about getting sucked into a business deal with one of his wife's brothers who happens to be running drugs in LA." I gave him the short version. "Jeff's beating himself up pretty bad. He's taking the blame for what happened. We've arranged a meeting for him with Bob and Julie at my place today. He's going to tell them everything."

I heard George take in a long breath and slowly let it out. "From what he told me, I don't think he's implicated in her death. Plus, his alibi checked out. He didn't say anything about being involved in drugs and money laundering. I definitely sensed something was bothering the hell out of him though, and he told you a lot more than me. You say his brother-in-law is involved?"

I said, "He's the contact between Jeff and Black Blizzard."

"Does that put Jeff's wife in the frame too?"

"I don't think so. Jeff said he's told her everything. She's estranged from her brother, Ron Suarez, the one who's involved."

George didn't say anything for a few seconds. "Do you think Jeff and his wife are in danger?"

I sighed. "I think there's a damn good chance of it. Suarez and Metropolit have both threatened him. He believes they were sending him a message by killing Mary. Now, he thinks they're hunting for him. He checked out of one hotel and registered at another under a different name. Hopefully, it'll be enough to keep them off him for now."

"I hope you're right. It sounds like you've got that part under control. Didn't you tell me the Black Blizzard guy in Denver knows you advised the family against investing in their deal? Do you think they might put two and two together and come after you too?"

"I doubt it, but I'll keep my eyes open." I wasn't too sure about anything right now.

George said, "Good idea. Thanks for the info. Let me know if anything new comes up. I've asked Lindsey Collins to keep you up to speed on the lab stuff."

"Thanks for that. She gave me a call last evening and told me about the shoe scrapings. What do make of them?"

"Not much at this point. It would be a real long shot to put them together with a person at the crime scene."

"That's what Lindsey said. Still, it's all you've got. Maybe you'll get lucky."

George laughed softly. "'Maybe' is right. I'll let you go for now. Keep in touch and I'll do the same."

I hung up and wondered if George had bought my story about the run. What the hell? He didn't have anything over me and shouldn't be worried about Lindsey either, unless something compromised his investigation. I checked the clock. It was 9:00. I headed for the bathroom to shave and shower. It was forty-five minutes to the airport so I needed to get going.

***

I threw on a pair of jeans and grabbed a light windbreaker as I headed out. A blue Chevy Malibu was parked in my neighbor Ed's driveway across the street. That wasn't unusual because Ed's a pilot for FedEx and I never know when he's coming or going, plus he uses a lot of short-term rental cars. I powered onto E-470 from Parker Road and headed east at a little over the speed limit. It was another breezy spring day with some high cirrus. I made it to the rental car plaza in forty minutes and watched Jeff pull in a couple minutes later. I beeped at him as he entered the service road, then followed him to Thrifty. He must have a preferred customer card because he tossed the envelope and keys in a collection box inside the door and came right back.

"How are you doing by now?" I asked as he climbed in.

"All right, I guess. I didn't get much sleep. God, I'm nervous about talking to Bob and Julie today."

"Just tell them everything. They'll be all right with it. Let them make their own decisions about Mary's death. If I were you, I wouldn't tell them you're blaming yourself for it regardless of what you believe."

"I don't know what I believe. It changes every hour. When I left your place last night, I was feeling pretty bad—- like I caused everything. By the time I got back to the hotel, I'd changed my mind. I know I made some bad mistakes, but her death wasn't my fault. God knows I didn't want it to happen."

I made the turn off Pena Boulevard onto E-470 and ran it up to seventy-five. I glanced at Jeff, he didn't look good and his skin had a sickly pallor. I said, "The talking part of it will be over quickly. After that, you need to go back to George Albins' office and repeat everything again. It'll go a long ways toward helping you out of this mess if you tell him in person. I called an attorney friend and he's going to meet you at the sheriff's office at 3:00 p.m. His name is Jason Masters and he's an ex prosecutor, so he knows the ropes."

"Thanks. That's a lot more than I could have expected after, you know, what happened between us. Talking to Albins and a lawyer probably won't be as tough as talking to Bob and Julie. Are you still willing to lend me your car?"

"That's the plan. And it's a beefed-up Bronco, not a car."

We rode in silence the rest of the way to my house. Jeff seemed to be getting his thoughts together. When we pulled in, two deer bounced across the street and up the grassy slope behind Ed's place. As we watched them, I noticed the Chevy was still parked in his driveway.

Inside, I told Jeff I'd put on a pot of coffee. He went to the back deck and stared south toward the big park. I decided to leave him alone with his thoughts and went into my office.

The message light was on; I'd had another call from Gerri. She wasn't going to come out this evening and was driving to Green River, Wyoming. Their well was taking a hard gas kick and threatening to blow out. They had over five hundred feet to drill before the main objective and she wanted to be on site if they needed to make a decision about shutting down and running casing to protect the wellbore. She expected to be gone until sometime next week. The last thing she said was, "This looks like the real thing. The way things are acting, we might have tapped the goddamned mother lode. *If* this thing's as big as I think, we're going to be rich. I mean rolling in it rich! I'm so glad you believed in me enough to buy all that stock. Keep this under your hat, okay? I don't want to set off a big lease play because we still have some leasing to do if we want to control the whole damn thing. Talk to you soon, lover."

If she's right, this was going to be a major gas discovery and Mountain West was going to score big time. Gerri and I would make a lot of money with our stock positions. It also meant Gerri would be out of town for a while. After spending the night with Lindsey, taking Gerri's message made the balancing act in my brain rock like a teeter-totter. I couldn't possibly have developed an emotional attachment to Lindsey already, could I? How could I want to be with her while my lover and companion of the last twenty years was working her ass off trying to make me rich? Jesus, what kind of person was I? I didn't want to wrestle with that right now.

Even though I hated to call Lindsey at work, I found her card and dialed the office number.

"Arapahoe Sheriff's Forensics, this is Mackey."

Crap. "Hello, Bill, it's Cort Scott. Lindsey Collins called me last night about some of the stuff you found at the crime scene. I was wondering if anything new had come up."

"Since last night?" Mackey was in his usual benevolent state.

"I'm just anxious to find out anything that's happening. I don't mean to bug you."

"Do you want to talk to Collins?"

"Please."

"You're outta luck for the moment. She's gone over to Albins' office. I'll leave her a note to give you a call."

"Thanks. I didn't mean to interrupt."

"You did, though." The line went dead.

I hung up. What a prick. I bet Lindsey loves working with him.

I glanced out the front window and saw Bob Linfield's van pull in with Julie in the passenger seat. At the door, I found Evan with them on the porch. We all shook hands and I welcomed them to my house. Jeff stood in the entry, hanging back, until Bob stepped forward and pulled him into a hug. Evan shook his uncle's hand. Julie remained still for a moment, finally striding to Jeff and put her arms around him. She was less enthusiastic than Bob.

I led the way into the living room, brought water and coffee for everyone, and excused myself to the downstairs rec room.

I grabbed the newspaper and a cup of coffee, opened the patio door a little, and turned on an easy listening channel. I could hear the murmur of voices from upstairs, although I couldn't make out any words.

I had another computer downstairs which I booted up to CNBC. I entered Mountain West's stock symbol and was amazed to see the stock had doubled since yesterday. Obviously, the well information wasn't being kept confidential. That was no surprise. With twenty rig hands plus service company people, something always leaked out. Somebody was going to talk and when that happened, a thinly traded stock like Mountain West was going to react.

At a dollar-thirteen a share, I was up over six million dollars from my initial investment. I would've loved to sell some and take profits, however, I was dealing with inside information. That kind of trade would land my ass in prison. I'd seen it happen. For now, all the profits would have to remain on paper.

I read some of the paper, finished the coffee, and walked out onto the patio. The day had warmed up nicely, almost seventy degrees, and I could see bees working on new flowers that'd sprung up in the last couple weeks. I faintly heard my name and went back inside to find Julie standing on the bottom stair.

She stepped down and said, "Jeff finished telling us the story."

"How'd that go? Will you guys be able to work past this?"

"It's going to take some time...I hope we can. Jeff feels terrible about what happened, although so do we. Assuming he's telling us the truth, he didn't do anything except be incredibly stupid. What do you think?"

"Just that. He didn't do anything leading directly to Mary's murder. He just acted incredibly dumb. I think the only thing to do is prove what actually happened. We've got leads on people who know something and Jeff's going to tell George Albins everything he can remember about every single guy he met through Ron Suarez. George will be the one who puts it all together."

"Do you think the rest of us are in danger?"

"That's hard to say. I can't see what these guys would get out of hurting anyone else in your family, although they might be mad enough to want to hurt Jeff. They aren't going to get any money out of you, so my best guess is you and Evan and Bob can probably return to normal life. Jeff, on the other hand, needs to be careful until we can get this wrapped up."

Upstairs, the others were standing in the kitchen talking. The mood seemed good for the first time since the meeting at the ranch. I repeated what I'd told Julie and ushered them to the van. Everyone made the obligatory promises to keep in touch.

After they left, I turned to Jeff. "You need to get to Albins' office a few minutes early to talk to the attorney. Try to remember every guy you met with Ron Suarez. There has to be a lead to the hitters somewhere in that bunch." I handed Jeff my truck keys and led him to the garage. As the garage doors opened, I said, "I'll start working from this end on what Jerome Biggs knows. I'll make some calls and probably then pay him a little visit on Monday."

"After you get done with Albins, give your wife a call to let her know what's going on. Give me a call sometime tomorrow." I shut the truck door and gave it the two-handed thump that EMTs use dispatching an ambulance.

Jeff started the truck and backed out. As he pulled away, the blue Chevy pulled out of Ed's driveway and headed the opposite direction directly in front of my house. I didn't get a look at the driver and didn't recognize the guy on the passenger side. I don't think they saw me standing in the shadows near the front of the garage. I began thinking back to when I'd first seen their car this morning and wondered who they were and what they'd been doing at Ed's.

chapter

SEVENTEEN

My cell phone rang. It was Lindsey. "Hi. Thanks for calling back, your timing is impeccable. The Linfields just left."

"Hi, yourself. What the hell did you say to Mackey? He's been ranting about being a goddamned answering service."

"He's a dickhead, if you'll pardon the expression. Forget about that, though...would you be interested in coming out to my place? I can fix dinner, give you a tour of the house, and, you know, see what comes up."

"I'm interested in the 'what comes up part.' Dinner would be a bonus. I'd love to come out." She sounded excited.

I gave the directions and said seven o'clock would be good. Mentally, I was answering my own question about what kind of person I was. Gerri hadn't been out of town for even a day and I was already playing her for a fool. Or maybe I was the fool?

Since Mark Mathey had been the first to mention Black Blizzard over drinks at the Mandarin, I decided to start my detective work with him. I punched in his number. "Hey, Mark, what's the haps, pards?"

"Hello, Cort. Long time, no hear, man. What's happening with you? How's the crude detecting going?"

"All right, I guess. I've only worked one case and it turned deadly. I'm afraid I might be in over my head a little. I'm calling to see if you've heard anything new about Biggs or Black Blizzard."

"Not much. I see him and his shadow all the time, though. I heard he was trying to promote a Mosquito Basin drilling deal."

"Who's his shadow?"

"Guy named Mike Landry who Andy Thibodeaux thinks is a fake coon-ass. I never see Biggs without him hanging around."

"Yeah, that's who I thought you meant...Andy pointed him out one time. How much of the Mosquito Basin deal have they sold? Do you know?"

"I don't. If it's like the old days, I'd bet on about 150%." Mark laughed—- not in an amused way. "You know as well as I do the Mosquito Basin is dry hole heaven. If Sid Bonner couldn't find oil there, no one can—- and Jerome Biggs sure as hell isn't Sid!"

"You got that right. You know anybody who's taken a piece of their deal?"

"Nobody locally. I heard he sold some in New Orleans."

I thought that's not exactly a news flash. "Thanks, Mark. I'll keep in touch and you do the same."

"You got it. Come by the Mandarin and I'll buy you a beer."

I called Tom, didn't get him, so I left a message asking if anything new had come up. I checked the clock: almost four p.m. I went to the bedroom and changed the sheets in anticipation. I went downstairs to check the wine cellar, opened the top on the hot tub, and put in some gardenia fragrance. I wanted everything to be just right for tonight. Christ, I was acting like a high school kid on prom night.

The doorbell chimed and I sprinted upstairs into my entry. I couldn't make out the faces of the two guys standing on the porch through the water glass of the front door. I glanced out the dining room window at my driveway and saw the blue Chevy that'd been parked across the street most of the day. That should have made me stop in my tracks, but my mind was on other things. I wasn't thinking straight.

I opened the door to find a silver plated .32 automatic pointed at my stomach.

chapter

EIGHTEEN

Mike Landry, holding the gun in his right hand, and a big
guy who looked Mexican were standing there. Landry was about my
height, pudgy, and probably out of shape although the gun made up
for a lack of muscle definition. The Mexican was really big—- maybe
six-four and well over two hundred pounds. He wasn't fat either.

"Hey, fellas, come on in." My throat was too tight to try anything more amusing.

"You're a pain in the ass, Scott. Some guys I work for say you're
fucking around in their business, causing a bunch of problems. They
told me to have a talk with you about that." He did have a southern
accent, although not a pleasant one like Andy's. I didn't know how
much talking he intended to do. A lot of my Army Rangers' hand-
to-hand combat training flashed through my mind.

Landry jabbed with the gun motioning me to back up. The
Mexican slid behind him as they started in. As soon as Landry start-

ed to step up into the house, I jumped forward and slapped at the gun with my left hand. It was just enough to knock his arm sideways as he pulled the trigger. The shot sounded like a bomb going off in the entry. Before he could swing the gun back, I punched him in the temple with a hard right. Off balance, he bounced against the door jamb, and crashed to the floor on his hands and knees.

The Mexican tried to push around him, couldn't get any leverage, and was too slow. I threw a sharp left hook into his stomach. It wasn't my best punch, although he grunted and dropped his hands a little. I had time to throw a roundhouse right. He tried to duck and the punch hit him high on the forehead. Pain shot through my wrist and up my forearm. I followed with a chest-kick and drove him back across the porch. He lost his footing on the steps and flailed backward, crashing into a low bush.

I heard Landry struggle to get up. I turned my attention to him. He was still on all fours with the gun in his hand. I stomped his hand while his fingers were under the trigger guard. He screamed, got to his knees, tried to switch gun hands, and didn't make it. I kicked him under the jaw. He went ass over teakettle onto the porch. I picked up the .32 and stepped into the doorway.

The Mexican was scrambling back, stopped when he saw me with the gun, and let all his air go out. Landry rolled over and got to his knees. He was holding his right hand in his left, blood dripped between his fingers, and his jaw was out of line.

I yelled, *"Get the fuck off my porch! Or I'll cancel your fucking ticket!* You said just enough to let me know who I need to go after. I'll be sure to tell them where I got the information." I was pumped up with adrenaline and my voice was tight. I was holding the gun in my left hand because my right one hurt like hell and I had to concentrate on holding it steady. Landry groaned and tried to stand. "Stay on your knees, you prick. I want you to crawl to the car." I looked at the Mexican on the bottom step. "How about you, shithead? You speak English?"

He nodded. "Yeah, I speak English." He didn't have much of an accent.

"Where the hell are you from?" He was wearing Nikes athletic shoes.

"California."

"I hope the hell you can drive because your buddy here isn't going to feel like it. When he gets to the car, you can help him get in, then I want you to get the fuck out of here. I know the whole damn story and all the players. The whole bunch of you assholes are going away. You got all that straight?"

The Mexican nodded. "Yeah, I've got it."

I watched as Landry tried to crawl on hands and knees down the sidewalk. His hand hurt too much, so he knee-walked to the car. The Mexican opened the door, helped him get in, and went around to the driver's side. Landry continued to hold one hand with the other. He was keeping them both in the air, probably trying to slow the bleeding. They both shot glances at me as they backed out. Landry was trying to hold a stare and look tough. He couldn't do it.

***

My whole body started shaking as the juice ran out of my synapses. It hit me like a kick in the balls that I'd just screwed up big time. Why the hell hadn't I kept those two bastards here and called the cops? What a dummy! At the very least, I could have had them arrested on any number of charges like assault with a deadly weapon or home invasion or menacing, plus Landry *had* to be involved in Mary Linfield's murder. If I'd have hung on to him, the cops could've had time to pin something big on him. *GODDAMN IT!* How fucking stupid could I be? Now, Albins or Tom or I would have to run him down again. *GODDAMN IT!*

I walked back in the house, put Landry's .32 on the hall table, and called Albins tell him what had gone down. He didn't make me feel much better. "That *was* stupid. You should've kept the gun on them and called me."

I knew he was right. "I know, George. You don't have to keep telling me what I already know. I just wanted them the hell out of here. What I *really* wanted to do was shoot the sons-a-bitches."

"I hear you. Problem is…I doubt you've seen the last of those guys. You need to be damn careful. If they're the ones killed Mary Linfield, they were able to do it out in open country. I've been through your neighborhood and it would be real easy for someone to find a hiding place and pick you off as you're coming or going."

"You're right of course——- I'll keep an eye out for a while. Damn it, I wish to hell I'd called you."

George exhaled loudly. "I do too. Chalk it up to a 'rookie' mistake. I know you live in Douglas County, so I'll call Sheriff Weaver and make sure he's on board with having my Arapahoe County forensics people work this. At least we've got some evidence now. We can try to trace Landry's gun and run his blood through the system. Who knows what that might turn up? With your statement, we can get search and arrest warrants for him. We don't have anything solid to tie him to Mary's murder, so being able to search his place might give us something."

He was silent for a moment and then said, "You know what? Actually, I think we should hold off on an arrest warrant. I'll give Tom Montgomery a call and see if he can get a couple Denver guys to stake out Landry's apartment and Black Blizzard's office. You rattled his cage pretty good, I'd like to know what he's up to, and, more importantly, who he's seeing. That is, unless you want to get him off the street for a while?"

I thought for a moment. Since I'd already screwed up, allowing the professionals to do their job was probably a good idea. "Go ahead and see if Tom can watch him. I'm betting Landry will be in contact with Biggs and maybe even New Orleans. If we're lucky, we can get enough to pull the whole damned bunch in and get this settled."

"That'd be nice, although you're right about getting lucky. I'll call Tom and get the wheels turning. I'm also gonna call the California Bureau of Investigation and ask them to take a look at Ron Suarez."

"I'm sorry I screwed up, George. Everything happened pretty fast. This thing's growing all sorts of arms and legs, isn't it?"

"Yeah. I'm not sure what we've got a hold of. I hope it quits expanding soon."

"George, can I ask a favor?"

"You can always ask, and I can always say 'no.' What do you need?"

"Could you send Lindsey to work my 'crime scene?' I don't get on too well with Mackey."

I heard George laughing as he hung up.

chapter

NINETEEN

I inspected my entry and found a scrape on the stone tiles where Landry's bullet had ricocheted. I followed the scrape and found a hole in the baseboard. I'd let Lindsey dig the slug out. I'd made enough mistakes for one day. Maybe someday, the "evidence" would make a nice conversation piece for visitors. Next, I looked around the area inside the door and spotted the ejected shell casing from the automatic. I left it in place for Lindsey to photograph.

I glanced at the hand gun on the table. I was pretty sure Landry's prints, as well as mine, would be all over it. Mine were on file with the attorney general's office from when I got my PI license. I had to believe Landry's were on file someplace.

Landry had left several drops of blood on the tiles and a small puddle on the porch. I wanted, more than anything, to hose off the porch and scrub the tiles with Lysol—- another job for after Lindsey finished.

The phone rang and Gerri's name was on caller ID. I answered as calmly as I could. "Hi. Where are you and what's going on?"

She paused and laughed. "Where the hell do you think I am? I'm about sixty miles northeast of Green River in God's country. You know why they call it that? Because nobody else wants it. What's going on with you? You sound out of breath."

I didn't want to talk about my visitors. "I just came up from the exercise room. Nothing much going on around here."

"Weird time of day to be exercising. What's the matter? You feeling guilty about your out-of-shape body?"

"I wasn't exercising. I was just rearranging some wines. Besides, I haven't heard you complaining about my body."

"I'm complaining about missing it—- and it doesn't look like that'll change anytime soon. The well is, for sure, trying to blow out and we're barely keeping control. Some of the partners want to quit drilling, but I think the real goodies are deeper. I wanta run casing, use a smaller bit, and drill another five hundred feet." Gerri's voice rose and her words came faster. I'd never heard her so excited about a well.

I got excited too. "Everything so far says you've been right about the prospect. I'd hate to see the main objective go untested. Stick with your plan. Congratulations! This is a great piece of geology."

"Thanks. Getting any prospect drilled is hard, a success validates the effort."

"You're right about that. How big can this thing be, anyway?"

"I don't want to talk about that on a cell phone. Why don't you go down to my condo and pull the prospect file? I believe every acre inside the prospect outline is going to work. We need to think about leasing more acreage outside the lines."

"I'll do that. It'll be Monday before I get down there, though. Things are starting to happen pretty quickly on the Linfield case and I'm going to be busy as hell the next few days."

"Why? What's going on?"

"Too much to talk about now. How long do you expect to be gone?"

"Could be two weeks. We'll take a couple days to run casing, so I'm going to the county courthouse and check lease records. If there's anything open, I'll play landman for a few days to see what I can pick up."

"I'll miss you. We'll have some serious catching up to do when you get back."

"I'll miss you too. Hold that thought."

She disconnected and I stared at the phone for several seconds. Gerri and I had kidded around about the nonbinding and comfortable nature of our relationship. We'd had those discussions several times. They sounded good at the time—- not so good now. The second thoughts or, as Hedges called them, "the remorses" made another trip through my brain.

Three p.m. Too late to make Black Blizzard calls. On Friday afternoons everyone was already hitting the bars. I'd make the calls Monday, then go downtown to check out Gerri's maps. I'd already made up my mind to make a personal visit to Biggs, also.

chapter

TWENTY

When I saw Lindsey's Edge turn in the driveway, I went to the garage, opened the overhead door, and motioned for her to park inside. As soon as she was in, I lowered the door. She was wearing a uniform, so I felt a little odd when she took me in a long embrace.

When she pulled back, I noticed tears in the corners of her eyes. Her voice was low and soft. "George sent me out. He just said your place was a crime scene and I needed to work it. He told me to make sure I brought a blood kit. What happened? Are you hurt?"

I said, "No, I'm all right...just a sore wrist. I had a visit from some guys who are probably involved in the Linfield murder and we had a pretty good go-round in the front entryway and porch. There's some blood out there from one of them and George wants to get samples into the system quickly. Hey, did you bring your overnight bag? The 'work' gives you a good excuse for you getting here early."

Lindsey reacted like I'd slapped her. "What the *hell's* the matter with you? George said shots were fired, you say there's blood evidence, and you're asking if I plan to spend the night? C'mon, show me the blood and anything else you've got. I'll do the forensics, get the samples to the lab, and *then* we'll sort out what we're doing!" There was nothing soft in her voice now. She sounded mad.

Properly chastised, I waited as she got her kit and then led the way to the entry. "There's a little blood just inside the door and more out on the porch. It's all from the same guy. There were two of 'em here, but the other guy wasn't cut that I know of...me neither. The bleeder was a guy by the name of Mike Landry. He's part of Black Blizzard. The other guy's a big Mexican dude, I don't know his name.

"If you look here," I pointed at the scrape on the tile, "You can see where a bullet clipped the floor. It bounced into the molding over there." I showed her the bullet hole. "The slug should be in the wall and the casing is over by the door. I put Landry's gun on the table."

She put a scaled ruler next to the bullet hole and began snapping pictures, moved the scale next to the shell casing and took more. She opened her kit, pulled on surgical gloves, and began using Q-tips to swab blood from the tile putting each one in a small sealed tube. She used a pair of rubber tipped tweezers to pick up the casing and put it in a plastic bag. Finally she said, "What have you touched?" Her voice was all business.

"Nothing except the gun."

She took blood samples from the tile and the porch before asking, "Are those more blood drops going down the sidewalk and out to the driveway?"

I hadn't noticed. "Probably. Landry did a knee walk from the porch to the car."

She gave me a sideways glance. "Why'd he do that?"

"Because I told him to."

Finally, a smile, "I shoulda figured." Each drop got a swab, each swab went in a separate, numbered tube and each tube was placed beside its blood drop. She took more pictures of the driveway, side-walk, porch and entry.

When she finished with the blood evidence, she got a slender, flexible probe from her kit, began playing around in the bullet hole, and popped out the slug. "It's pretty beat up, but it looks like a .32."

She returned to the table and, using the probe in the barrel, picked up the gun. "Well, everything seems to match up...it's a .32 all right." The little automatic went in another evidence bag and into her kit. She gathered up the rest of the evidence bags and said, "Okay, I'm going to drive this stuff over to our lab. George told Mackey to hang around and start processing everything as soon as I can get there."

We walked to the garage, she put the kit in her car, and re-moved a small carry-on bag. "Here, hotshot, put this in the bedroom. I'll be back as quickly as I can and we'll talk. And, please, *don't do anything else stupid while I'm gone!* George told me you let two perps walk away."

I didn't say anything because I wanted her to return, I wanted her to spend the night, and I wanted to hear the soft, low voice again.

chapter

TWENTY-ONE

My wrist and hand hurt like hell. I was soaking it in an ice bucket and gazing out the front window when I saw Lindsey turn in. I repeated the garage door exercise and opened her door. As she stepped out, I saw she'd changed out of the uniform and into a pair of beige slacks, daffodil yellow top, and tan strap sandals. It was a good look for her. This time, she offered her face and a kiss.

I led the way through the kitchen to the deck which overlooks the open space behind the house. Lindsey said "This is absolutely *gorgeous*. Oh, there's a deer." One of my "wants" was answered...her voice was soft again.

The small doe walked across the back lawn and disappeared into the scrub oak. "They're pretty common back here. The buggers keep my flowers trimmed. How about a glass of wine? You can sip it while I give you a tour. I've got a sauvignon blanc open and chilled."

"I'd love one. I'm 'off duty' now...no thanks to you! Wow, this deck is great."

"Thanks. I think you'll like the rest of the place too. If you'll indulge me for just a minute, I'll open a red wine and light the grill."

As I was opening a bottle of 2006 Acacia pinot noir, Lindsey stepped inside just in time to watch me grimace as I worked the wine opener. She looked at my wrist which was swollen and red. "What's the matter with your hand?"

I finished pulling the cork and rubbed my wrist. "I hurt it when I punched out the Mexican...hit him too high on the head, I guess."

"You *dumb* shit! That looks bad. Why don't you go to the urgent care clinic in Parker and get an x-ray?"

"Because it's not *that* bad, you're finally here, and we're both *off duty!*"

***

The house tour took fifteen minutes and she was suitably impressed. She really liked the hot tub room windows with their laser-etched Colorado mountain scenes. I told her about the house rule of no hot tub attire. She smiled and said, "I didn't bring any."

After the tour, I refilled her glass and she sat outside while I prepared dinner. I fixed a salad, Lorraine potatoes, and grilled lamb chops followed by a store-bought cheesecake topped with strawberries marinated in Grand Marnier. When we finished, I said, "Help me pick up the dishes and we'll go in the tub. I've got plastic glasses downstairs, we can finish the wine there."

Later, as I reached to turn off the bedside lamps, Lindsey murmured, "Why not leave the lights on low? I'd like that."

***

I awoke to the sound of birds and realized Lindsey wasn't in bed. I sat up and saw her in the glider on the bedroom deck. The smell of fresh coffee wafted through the bedroom. What a way to wake up. I rolled out of bed and walked to the door. "You'd make a great cat burglar, Linds. I didn't hear you get up." She was wrapped in a long robe and was sitting with her legs folded under her.

"You seemed to be sleeping pretty soundly, so I slipped out, washed up, and went out to the kitchen. I found the coffee stuff, made a pot, and brought mine out here. Would you like me to get you some?"

"That'd be great. I'll brush my teeth and join you right here."

She stepped inside and put her face up to be kissed, which I did without exhaling. I didn't want to wilt her with morning breath. "More of that later," I said and headed into the bathroom.

I did all the morning things, dressed, and came back to the deck. Lindsey was in the glider with two cups of steaming coffee on the little table. I joined her, picked up a cup, and took a sip. It was good. Strong with a hint of cinnamon and French vanilla. "That's good. Where'd you get all the flavors?"

"You had dark roast coffee so I added a dash of cinnamon, some vanilla extract, and a touch of brown sugar."

"It really hits the spot." I gulped and managed to scald my tongue.

"Slow down, dummy. There's lots of coffee." She laughed. "How much wine did you feed me last night? I'm kinda foggy this morning. Which reminds me, how's your wrist?"

I extended my arm and flexed my fingers. "Better...the swelling is down although it's still pretty sore. I musta sprained it on that asshole's head."

Lindsey took my hand, rotated the wrist, and said, "Looks better, all right. You wanta tell me about yesterday?"

I picked up the cup without wincing just to show her I could. "There's not a whole lot to the story. Those two lowlifes showed up on my porch and we ended up in a fist fight. I slapped Landry's hand and his gun went off. After that, we did the hurt dance for a couple rounds till I stomped on his hand. I got in a big haymaker on the other guy...that's when I hurt my hand...and all the fight went out of him. I picked up the gun, made Landry do the knee walk I told you about, and ran them the hell out of here.

"That was my screw-up. I shoulda kept 'em here and called the cops. I realized what I'd done as soon as they drove away. I guess that's why George was so mad."

Lindsey snorted and her expression hardened. "What about me? Why do you think I was pissed? George calls and tells me to grab my kit and come to your place to work a crime scene. Jesus, Cort! I didn't know if you were shot or cut or, even, dead! And, then you have the gall to ask if I'm spending the night! I was mad the whole time I was here. I didn't make the decision to stay until we were back in the garage. Frankly, I'm not too sure why I did."

I gave her my best hang-dog expression and said, "I don't know why either. I'm glad you did."

Her face softened. "Thanks. Look, I'm 'involved' in this, in more ways than one. I care about what happens to you, just don't take me for granted...for anything."

chapter

TWENTY-TWO

At 2:00 p.m. on Sunday, Lindsey took my face in both hands, kissed me, and whispered, "I've got to go. My folks call at four o'clock on Sundays. I don't want to miss them." I walked her to the car and watched as she backed out and drove away. I missed her before she rounded the corner.

My phone rang as I reentered the house. Caller ID indicated my friend at Denver PD, Tom Montgomery. Thinking about Lindsey, I was smiling when I answered, "What the hell do you want on a nice Sunday afternoon?"

"Listen, dipshit, cut the joking around." Tom's grating voice was more serious than usual. "After I talked to Albins on Friday, we put some guys on Landry's place. He finally showed up this morning with his hand all bandaged up. He went in for half an hour, came back out with a suitcase, and took a cab to the airport. He just got on a flight to New Orleans scheduled to arrive about 6:30, our time, tonight. I called down there and NOPD will trail him after he lands. Now, get this—- the California cops are watching Ron Suarez and *he* caught a plane to New Orleans too. It arrives a few minutes ahead of Landry's."

"Have you been watching Black Blizzard too?"

"No. I don't have enough guys to go around. Why?"

"I'm wondering how deeply Biggs is involved. Even though he's an asshole, it's hard to believe he'd get mixed up in murder and dope peddling."

Montgomery didn't say anything for a moment, "I'll put the guys who were watching Landry on Biggs. What are you planning to do now?"

"I haven't thought it through yet. I might go see Biggs tomorrow and maybe shake him up a little."

"Don't do that, you dumb ass! Everybody needs to back off a little and see what's coming down. The cops in New Orleans and California are going to check in on a regular basis and keep us in the loop. I'll do the same for you and Albins. As much as I hate it, I'm going to give the FBI a call. The drug and money angles make this a federal rap and they've got more resources than we do. If we keep an eye on everybody for a while, we might figure things out and prevent anymore really bad shit from happening." It was the longest speech I'd ever heard from Tom. He sounded involved and excited at the same time.

"Okay, I'll leave Biggs alone...for now. I don't think he's the violent type, although he's definitely dirty in some of this. I guarantee he knew about Landry coming to see me and just for that, I'd like to kick his ass up between his shoulders." I thought I sounded plenty tough with that kind of talk.

Tom laughed. "I hear you, but you'd best pick your spots. Of course, you could have short circuited a lot of this if you'd held on to those two mutts yesterday. Having guys come see you with guns isn't much of a ticket for a long future. Here's a deal for you—- if we find out Biggs knew about your visit ahead of time and we've got the rest of 'em under wraps, I'll let you have a few minutes alone with him before we put the cuffs on. Work for you?"

"That would do. Thanks."

"Don't mention it, pal, and I mean that *literally*."

"I got it, Tom. Let me know as soon as you hear anything."

"I said I would. See ya."

***

I tidied up around the house, packed a shave kit, my Beretta .38, and a shoulder holster. I decided to go to Gerri's condo to look at her Green River Basin prospect map and lease outline. I'd stay overnight and have lunch at Andy Thibodeaux's tomorrow. I might even run into Biggs which I wouldn't mind, although Tom would have a shit fit.

As I got in the car, I thought about what I'd told George so I turned the key and opened the garage at the same time. There weren't any cars in my driveway to block me so I hit the gas and backed out as quickly as possible.

It was another nice day and I was enjoying the drive. The biker bar, three miles south in Franktown, must've shut down the Sunday afternoon twofers because about fifty Harleys were also traveling north on Parker Road. Bikers seem to have an affinity for Corvettes and I got lots of low fives as I passed the chopper jockeys. I took the turn for E-470. The bikes continued north probably headed for the Emerald Isle or maybe Caledonia's.

An Earl Thomas Connelly CD made the trip downtown go quickly.

I parked in Gerri's spot in the underground parking area of her building. She'd given me a pass card to access the elevator, which I rode nonstop to her floor. The twelfth floor of One Larimer Place had four penthouse condos. They'd been constructed so each had a private hallway and entrance. When I got to Gerri's door, it was open about two inches. I dug the Beretta out of my bag and set the rest of the stuff in the hall.

I listened at the door for several seconds. Didn't hear anything, so moved to the side where I knew the hall closet was located. I rapped hard and called out, "Ms. German? Are you in there? It's James Ruiz, the lobby guard. Are you there?" I didn't expect anyone to answer and no one did. I knocked again and said, "I'm coming in now." I pushed the door open until it banged against the door stop. I listened as hard as I could. Still couldn't hear anything. I stepped inside and silently made my way down the entry hall. I could see most of the living room and patio deck. I carefully slipped in and looked around. Everything seemed okay. The furniture was all in the normal places, even the throw pillows. The kitchen was clean with nothing on the counters or the table. Her bedroom was undisturbed. Gerri's office was a different story.

Files were scattered around the floor, the desk, and on top of filing cabinets. Maps had been pulled from the racks and thrown about like jackstraws. Some were unrolled on her drafting table with map weights on the corners. The file drawers were mostly open and had gaps where files were supposed to be hanging. I picked my way through the debris to the drafting table and spotted the map lying on the top of the stack. It was the Green River Basin prospect I'd come to see.

I quickly scanned it and spotted the areas Gerri had indicated she wanted to pick up more leases. Anyone with an idea of the play and the well location could do the same, so whoever had broken in knew what they were looking for. I didn't know whether they'd scattered all the other stuff around to confuse the issue or if this map had been the last thing they'd found. Either way, Gerri needed to know as soon as possible.

I used her office phone, dialed her cell phone, and waited for the interminable delay before hearing it ring. Gerri's voice sounded good when she finally answered. "Hi, lover! How come you're calling from my phone? What's happening?"

"Gerri, I'm in your office and you've had a break-in. It——"

"*Shit!*" She didn't sound happy now. "What's gone?"

"I don't know if anything's gone. I think whoever broke in was looking for the maps and files on your prospect. The maps are on your drafting table and the files are scattered all over."

"*Shit!* How'd they get in, can you tell?"

"I haven't had a chance to look around yet. The door was open a couple inches. I didn't notice any damage like it had been kicked in or anything. The rest of the place seems okay, like they knew exactly what they were looking for, and went directly to your office."

Gerri said, "It ought to be easy enough to figure out who broke in. They'll be filing on the federal and state lands and trying to buy up the fee leases in my outline."

"I agree, but unless whoever broke in was really careless and left their prints or something, it's going to be awfully hard to pinch anyone...even if they go after the exact leases you want."

Gerri sighed. "I guess I'd better get as much done as I can right now. I've already identified the lease owners so I'll start calling them tonight and try to make some deals. I can't do anything about the state and federal until their offices open tomorrow. Do me a favor, would you? Call Tom Montgomery and ask him to handle this as quietly as possible. Every geologist and independent company in Denver knows we're drilling. Most of 'em don't know the play and I don't want them snooping around. I sure as hell don't need more competition up here. Can you do that for me?"

"Sure, I'll call Tom soon as we hang up. You have any idea who would know enough to break into your place, especially right now with what's going on at the well?"

"No. It's almost like someone has my phone tapped. From now on when you want to talk, call me on this cell, and I'll go to a secure landline. When I call you, I'll use a landline."

"All right. I'll call Tom and see what we can track down on this end. Be careful and watch your back."

I went back to the door and looked carefully at the lock. I couldn't see any obvious damage so whoever had been inside either picked the lock or had a key. I didn't like that idea very much. I went back to the office and called Tom. He said he'd be right over. He gave me the usual cautions about not touching anything and I assured him I'd only touched the office phone, nothing else. He growled, "Keep it that way, dipshit."

I checked the patio door, without touching anything, and decided it hadn't been opened. The half-inch dowel Gerri had laid in the track was undisturbed. I'd given her a bad time about having a dowel in a door twelve stories up. It still seemed silly and I made a mental note not to bring it up with her anymore. I wished the building had gotten around to installing the security cameras they'd been promising.

"Where are you?" Tom's voice rang down the hallway. He'd made good time.

"I'm in the office, last door on the right."

Tom appeared at the door and glanced around at the mess. "What have you fucked up while you've been here?"

"Nothing but your day as far as I know."

"That's for sure. Where's Gerri?"

"Up in Wyoming. I just talked to her and we think whoever was in here was trying to find out where her play is headed. They'll try to beat her to some of the leases. She's already working so she'll probably be able to hold them off for a while. She asked if you can keep the wraps on this as much as possible. She doesn't need more competition."

"I can handle that. I gather she's on to something up there?"

"Yeah, I think so. Did you buy any of her stock when I told you to?"

"A shit load, buddy. Her well going to drive it up some more?"

"Damn right it will. I'll be surprised if it doesn't double again."

"That sounds good to me. I might be able to retire someday after all."

"Good luck with that. It'd help if you figure out who broke in here and head 'em off before they screw up her lease play."

Tom nodded, took out his camera cell phone, and began taking pictures of everything. He fixed me with a stare. "You're sure this is just the way you found it and you haven't touched anything other than the telephone?"

"That's right. I even opened the front door with the toe of my shoe. It was open about two inches when I got here. I didn't see any damage so they either had a key or picked the lock."

"Good observation, Sherlock. They picked it. I saw scratches on the inside of the lock. I looked at it with a penlight when I came in."

"In a way, that's good. I'd hate to think somebody has a key to her place."

"I assume you have one."

"I do. And I also have a key card for the elevators. Gerri registered my license plate with the building so I can park in her space."

"Security in this place is a joke. I parked around the corner, walked into the parking garage, and got in an elevator with some old couple who were nice enough to hold the door for me. I didn't have to bother going to the lobby and checking in with the concierge or anything. The old couple got off on the seventh floor and wished me a nice day. The way the penthouse hallways are arranged, someone would have all the time they needed to stand out there and pick the lock. Nobody would see them unless they were specifically coming to this condo. This must be the last condo in Denver without hall security cameras."

Tom looked around and took more pictures. "I'll get a crime scene tech over here to dust the place for prints. My guess is he won't find shit." He shook his head and muttered, "This isn't going to be easy especially if nothing was taken. They probably wrote down information or took pictures of the maps. Unless someone suddenly gets religion and walks in and confesses, we'll probably never have an arrest."

"I was afraid of that. About the only thing I can think of that will give us a lead will be watching who goes in the BLM offices and checks leases around the play. Even at that, probably fifty landmen a day look at records; it might be a waste of time."

"I don't have any jurisdiction in Wyoming and wouldn't know where to start anyway. Give me Gerri's number, I'll call her and tell her to keep her eyes open. At least she knows exactly what records they'll need."

"I was going to study Gerri's maps and spend the night here. Is that all right?"

"No. I'll have the crime scene tech here in a couple of hours. I don't think you should be around when he's here. And pick up your crap out in the hall when you leave."

"All right, you don't need to be a hard ass about it. Call me tomorrow if you find out anything."

"Don't hold your breath."

We closed the door without locking it so the crime tech could get in and went down the elevator together. At the lobby stop , Tom stepped off and headed toward the concierge's desk. I continued to parking and drove out. I'd wanted to have a much better idea of Gerri's prospect area before making my "office visit" to Biggs tomorrow. Now, I'd probably end up spending the evening worrying about Gerri. I planned to spend some time contemplating how to bust Biggs' balls. Actually, that wasn't a bad plan—- literally. The more I thought about it, the more I couldn't wait for tomorrow.

chapter

TWENTY-
THREE

When the phone rings at 5:55 a.m., it's rarely good news. I hit the snooze button a few times before figuring out it wasn't my alarm, fumbled around with the phone, and finally said hello without looking at caller ID.

Tom's voice was strained. "Cort, it's Tom. You need to get up, make some coffee, and get yourself together as soon as you can. I'm turning onto South Pinery Parkway and I'll be at your door in five minutes. I don't know any other way to say this other than just say it—- Gerri's dead. The Green River, Wyoming police just called me. They found her in her motel room this morning. Get up and open your garage door. I'll be there in a minute."

I couldn't move. I sat on the edge of the bed and stared at the telephone. My gut began to churn and my stomach rolled. I dropped the phone, ran for the toilet, and started puking out my guts. As I raised my head, my bowel clenched and I barely had time to turn to take care of that. Everything in my system flushed in less than a minute. It took all my strength to push myself up and get to the sink. I splashed cold water on my face, looked in the mirror, and watched the tears coursing down my cheeks.

My mind began to fill with memories and questions. Why hadn't I treated her better? Why hadn't I made a commitment? Why have I been an asshole? Why Gerri?

Numbly, I walked to garage and pushed the opener. Tom's unmarked Crown Victoria pulled up as the door rose. I didn't wait to let him in, just turned around and went back to the bedroom to pull on some clothes. When I returned to the kitchen, Tom was measuring coffee into the coffee maker. He didn't say anything, just put me in an embrace that must have lasted thirty seconds. I heard the coffee start to brew and Tom's breathing. It seemed unreal.

"I hated being the one to tell you. I didn't want you to hear it from anyone else. I got a call from the Green River PD a half hour ago. I talked to them yesterday after I spoke to Gerri about the break-in and asked them to keep an eye on her. I gave my number as a contact." Tom pulled out the counter stools and sat down. He motioned to me and I managed to get on the other.

"She left a wake-up call for 5:00 and told 'em she'd set her alarm. She said she was afraid of sleeping through and needed to be up. They have an automated system, however if there's no answer, it alerts the desk clerk who follows up. He couldn't raise her so he sent a maid to her room. She found the door wasn't closed all the way, so she pushed it open. Gerri's feet were sticking out between the beds. The maid ran back to the desk and the clerk dialed 9-1-1.

"The police were there in two minutes and phoned it in. Their computer system automatically brings up any history associated with a name that's been entered and when they typed in Gerri's name, my number came up. They called me and I took off for here. Cort, I can't tell you how sorry I am. I don't know what to say to you."

I didn't say anything. I couldn't. I got out two cups, poured coffee, and sat down again. My hands were shaking so badly I had to use them both to bring the cup to my mouth. The coffee was too hot and burned my lips and mouth. I didn't care. Tom was watching me and I saw tears form in his eyes. "What the hell?" I whispered. "How could this happen? Jesus, Tom, Gerri never hurt anybody in her life. Why would someone want to kill her? How'd she die?"

Tom blew across his coffee. "I don't have any answers. All the cops said was it looked like she'd been hit on the head. I've got a lot of questions, though, and I'm going to ask you some things that are probably going to hurt. I hate to have to ask, though it might help me figure out what's going on. First, do you—-"

I held up my hand. "Hold it, Tom. I need to go to Wyoming. You'll have to wait until I get a chance to see for myself."

"There's nothing in Green River for you to do. You'll just be in the way."

"This isn't a debate. I'm going. If you want to come along you can. You can ask questions on the flight."

"How are you getting there?"

"Didn't you just hear me say 'flight'? I'm calling my friend, Kirk, right now. He's got two jets and a helicopter in his charter service and can be ready to go with an hour's notice. We can be in Green River before noon."

"You'll still need to answer my questions."

"I promise I'll answer anything you ask. And, Tom, someone had to tell me so I'm glad it was you."

***

It was 6:42 a.m. I dialed Kirk Chase's cell number and waited through four rings until he answered. "What's up, Cort? I know you're an early riser but it's pretty early even for you."

"Kirk, listen—- something really bad has happened. As soon as you can get wheels up, I need you to fly me and Tom Montgomery to Green River, Wyoming."

"No problem. What's going on?"

"Gerri's dead."

"*NO!* Not Gerri! Oh, *God!* I don't believe it. How soon can you be here? I'll be ready to fly in half an hour." Kirk had flown Gerri and me several times for both business and pleasure. His wife was one of Gerri's few non-business female friends.

"I'm leaving the house in ten minutes so we'll be there by the time you're ready. Thanks, Kirk."

I hung up and looked at Tom. He was wearing the same clothes as yesterday. They'd obviously spent the night on the floor. "You can borrow some of my stuff if you need clothes," I said.

"I've got a travel bag in the car with everything I need. Go pack your stuff while I make some calls and we can take off. I'll follow you to Centennial so we'll both have cars when we get back."

I didn't plan to stay overnight in Green River but threw a change of clothes in a sports bag just in case. I got the Beretta out of the gun safe, checked the clip, and threw a box of ammo in the bag. I pulled on running shoes, grabbed a jacket, and headed toward the garage as Tom came out of my office. We poured coffee into go cups, dumped the rest, and hurried to the cars.

It took twenty minutes to reach Centennial Airport and Kirk's hangar/office. We grabbed our bags, went in, and spotted Kirk near the exit to the tarmac. He stuck out his hand to Tom and then to me. "I'm so sorry, Cort. C'mon, I'm ready to take off. Clark's already onboard so we can leave as soon as the door's closed."

"Thanks for this, Kirk. We'll settle up after we're back, okay?"

"There won't be anything to settle. I'm doing this on my own—- for Gerri."

"Thanks, man," I said. Tears filled my eyes as we climbed the stairs into the Falcon. Probably for the first time ever, I didn't think about being a nervous flyer. I could only think about getting my hands on whoever had murdered Gerri. I needed to be in Green River and make someone pay.

chapter

TWENTY-
FOUR

We were airborne in two minutes and hadn't cleared down-town Denver before Tom got out a small notebook. "Let's get to those questions."

"Just a minute." I picked up the thermos Clark Larson, Kirk's co-pilot, had loaded, and got out two cups. I poured coffee and gave Tom one. "Go ahead. What do you need to ask?"

He pulled up the seat table so he could set his cup down while he was writing. "Do you know of anybody who'd want to kill Gerri, had a grudge of some kind, or had lost money in a business deal with her?"

"I don't know anyone who'd feel that way about her. She was a friend to everyone. I imagine there are people envious of her business or who she got the better of in a lease sale. But surely not enough to want to kill her."

"This one isn't fun to ask—- do you think someone would kill her to get back at you for anything you've done?"

"Jesus, Tom. What the hell are you driving at? You're not trying to say somebody would kill Gerri to get to me are you? You think I'm responsible for this? *Fuck you!* That's bullshit and I won't listen to it."

"Don't take it personally, Cort. I've gotta ask. She didn't go around beating up people, or getting shot at, or 'investigating' things. She hadn't made her money yet. You have. You're rich and well known and she was your girlfriend. You can see where I'm going with this. Someone could definitely want to hurt her to get to you."

"Ah, man, don't lay that on me." Despite my words, I'd already had the same thoughts from the moment I was retching in the toilet. Gerri had never given anyone a reason to murder her. On the other hand, I rubbed lots of people wrong and had made plenty of enemies along the way. "Look, Tom, I'm not mad—- I know you might be on to something. It's just too hard to hear it out loud and know it could be true. Let's start making a list and see if it goes anywhere. I'll give you everybody I can think of."

"That'll be a start. I hoped you'd see it that way."

We brainstormed back and forth for several minutes. The ride was smooth and the view of the northern Front Range, the Flat Tops, and the Laramie Mountains was spectacular although we weren't looking. Most of our ideas kept coming back to Mary Linfield's murder and Black Blizzard. It was hard to connect those things to the break-in at Gerri's condo, her company's new well—- or her. We kept returning to me being the connection. Clark told us to buckle up and prepare for landing.

Green River airport was entirely devoted to general aviation and most of it catered to oil companies. The private jet facilities matched anything in the world. We taxied to Red Carpet Jet Services, Clark lowered the stairs, and we strode inside. Two uniform cops and a guy in a suit waited by the counter. As we approached, the suit stuck out his hand to Tom. "I'm Jack Carstairs. These officers are Jim McDonald and Bo Randolph. I'm Green River PD's only homicide detective, so I've caught the case. Jim and Bo were the responding officers."

His tone changed when he turned to me. "You must be Cortlandt Scott. Lieutenant Montgomery called me from your house to tell me you were flying in." He took my hand and gave a firm shake. "He didn't tell me much about your relationship to Ms. German... I'm truly sorry for your loss. I hope we can find whoever did this quickly and bring you some closure. The crime scene people are wrapping up at the motel and her body's being taken to the morgue at City Hospital. There'll be an autopsy done tomorrow. We can go to the motel if you'd like, although I don't know how you feel about that. Otherwise, we can go to the station to talk."

Carstairs was an ordinary looking guy I judged to be in his early forties. Some slight scarring around his eyes and on the point of his chin indicated he knew his way around a boxing ring. He filled up his suit jacket and didn't have a belly. Hearing the reference to "her body" hit me hard and I struggled to keep my voice steady, "I'd like to help anyway I can to solve this—- I need to help. I want to see Gerri's killers strung up."

Carstairs studied me quizzically and said, "I notice you say 'killers'. Do you have reason to believe more than one person is involved?"

I had to think about that. "There's nothing I can say for sure. It just 'feels' like there would have to be more than one. I'd like to go to the motel, take a look around, and then talk it over." The three cops nodded as if they knew what I meant about a "feeling."

***

A black-and-white prowl car and a gray Crown Victoria were parked in front of the jet service building. Tom and I got in the Vic with Carstairs, the uniforms got in the prowl car and led the way. It was ten minutes to the motel on the east end of town just off I-80. Carstairs asked if I knew why Gerri had been in Green River and I told him a little bit about what she was doing. I mentioned the break-in at her condo and Tom said that's what had prompted his call about keeping an eye on her.

At the motel, Carstairs parked under the overhang in the check-in area and we went inside. Two more uniforms were talking with McDonald and Randolph. Carstairs didn't introduce us. "The room's down this way. Are you sure you want to see it?"

"I *need* to see it. You said she's, uh, I mean…her body is out, right?"

One of the other cops spoke up. "Yes, Sir. She's been taken to the morgue."

It didn't feel right referring to Gerri as a "body." I was having trouble accepting she was dead.

I said, "Let's go then."

The hallway was taped off and the doors to the rooms were all open. Gerri had been in one-twenty-six. I was shocked at what the forensics team had left behind. Every surface in the room was covered with fingerprint dust; the floor and drapes appeared to have been freshly vacuumed. The beds were stripped; the towels and wash cloths were gone. Gerri's toiletry kit had been bagged and was sitting on the bathroom counter. Her clothes were hanging in the closet.

The dresser drawers were pulled and her underclothes were in disarray. She would've hated knowing people had been pawing through her underwear regardless of whether it had been her killers or the cops.

Carstairs saw my look and shrugged. "Sorry, we have to go through everything." I nodded and tried to swallow. My throat was too dry.

Randolph pointed. "We found her over here, between the beds. She was on her left side." I walked past the first double bed and stopped when I saw the blood stain. Gerri's blood. It was pooled in front of the night stand between the beds. The tape outline on the floor was just like TV, with the blood stain coming from the outline of the head. My stomach rolled and I shuddered.

Tom grabbed the back of my arm. "You all right? You see enough?"

I shook off his hand. "No, goddamn it! I haven't seen enough! I need to see everything there is to see and hear everything there is to say! I want to find the sons-a-bitches who did this and I want to put out their fucking light!" The anger felt good. I needed to say it out loud. It would probably screw me up with the cops. I didn't care.

Carstairs leveled his gaze at me. "I can understand how you feel. It won't help us find the killers if you go vigilante." There were things he had to say too, although I could see in his eyes he understood and was just going through the protocol. I appreciated that.

I tried to calm down. "You're right, I hear you. I *have* seen enough, except for one thing. Were her purse and briefcase here? And, she never went anywhere without her cellphone."

Carstairs shot a glance at McDonald and Randolph. McDonald answered. "Yeah, they were both here. The forensics people bagged and tagged them and took 'em to the lab with the towels and sheets. We didn't look inside for a cellphone."

I nodded and said, "Let's go out to the coffee shop and talk." Everyone took a breath and seemed to relax.

We trooped out of the room and back to the lobby. Carstairs told the other two uniforms to return to duty and asked Tom and me if we needed any more from Randolph and McDonald. I said I had a couple of questions. Carstairs motioned them over. "Ask your questions."

I asked, "Do you have any theories of how they got in her room and what happened?" The two cops looked at each other and at Carstairs, who nodded.

Randolph said, "We think whoever did it was already in the room before she got there. The first thing we checked was the sliding door to the interior courtyard and it was open. Her purse was sitting on the second bed like she'd walked through the room, set it down, and turned around. Someone could've been inside the closet, inside the bathroom, or even behind the wall where the room opens out. She'd been hit high on the left side of the forehead—- like she'd turned around and faced someone. It probably indicates the guy who hit her was right handed. The ME will be able to tell us more after the autopsy. Forensics got prints from almost everything in the room so it's going to take forever to sort 'em out. We didn't find an obvious murder weapon in the room so we think the killer took it with him."

McDonald spoke up. "Those sliding glass doors don't have much of a lock so it's easy for anybody to slip the catch and get in. There are four different entrances to the interior courtyard and two are open to the parking lot. The motel has a surveillance camera on those two and we'll look at the tapes later today. Unfortunately, the entrances from the hallways don't have cameras and there's no system for the courtyard itself. For that matter, someone could've gotten to the courtyard from a room too. We're going through all the room records, although we don't know who we're looking for."

I couldn't help thinking about Gerri's deck doors in Denver. They were twelve stories up and she still put dowels in the tracks.

I looked at Tom who shook his head. "Thanks, fellas. If we think of anything else, we'll get back to you." We shook hands all around and Carstairs told them to go back to the station and fill out their reports immediately.

The three of us strode through the lobby to the coffee shop. It was pushing lunch hour and the place was starting to fill. Carstairs motioned to the hostess and pointed toward a six seat booth in the back corner. She frowned about using the six-top for the three of us, but nodded and took us back. We sat down and a teenage waitress stepped up, ready for our orders. Carstairs wanted coffee. Tom and I were coffeed out, so Tom ordered a vanilla malt and I asked about an Arnold Palmer. The waitress threw a blank stare my way. "What's that?"

I told her to mix iced tea and lemonade in a large glass over ice cubes. She looked at me like I was crazy, wrote it down, and walked away. I said, "She isn't old enough to know who Arnold Palmer is. I guess Tiger Woods needs to invent a soft drink of some kind." They smiled, although neither thought it was funny. I didn't either.

Tom asked about any recent murders in southwestern Wyoming matching Gerri's. Carstairs didn't know of any and said most crime in the area was oilfield theft or simple assaults from bar fights. The drinks arrived and everyone took long swallows before sitting back. Carstairs said, "This is going to be tough unless we catch a break on the prints. If something's going to pop big, it might have to come from you guys in Denver."

Tom agreed. "We're starting with people who were pissed off at Cort and might have gone after Gerri as a way of getting to him. Cort's working a murder case out east of Denver that may involve some wise-guys from New Orleans and LA. We're checking it for a connection."

Carstairs' head jerked up. "You on the job?"

I shook my head and said, "No, I'm private. I'm doing some oil business investigations. Which raises a question---Have you seen any signs of organized crime associated with the drilling activity?"

Carstairs thought for a moment. "Nothing I can put my finger on. I've been hearing stories about geologic consultants and independent lease brokers selling their lease positions at less than the going acreage price. That seems real strange considering the rumors flying around about the well Ms. German's drilling."

That got my attention. Even the cops had heard something about the well. "What have you heard about the well?"

"Oh, just the usual scuttlebutt---you know, stuff about how it might be a big discovery."

"When did you start hearing about brokers selling their lease positions?"

"Just the last couple of weeks," he said.

I glanced at Tom, then asked Carstairs, "Do you know who they've been selling to?"

"No, I didn't have any reason to follow up. I'll ask around now."

Tom sipped his malt, leaned forward, and asked, "Do you know any of the sellers personally?"

Again, Carstairs paused before answering. "I might. A guy by the name of Kevin Wright up by Pinedale. I go fishing with him two or three times a year and the last time we went, he said he had a pretty good lease position in the general area of Mountain West's drilling location. I called him two days ago—- his wife said he was in Denver making a deal on his leases. It's probably worth a call."

"When you talk to him, ask if he was contacted by Black Blizzard Petroleum," I said. "They're the outfit connected to New Orleans and LA. We think they're involved in the Colorado murder."

Tom put down his malt with a bang. "Hold it, Cort. You're talking out of school. You don't have any proof tying them to the Linfield murder."

"*Goddamn it*, Tom! I don't care if we have any 'proof' or not! Those bastards are involved and Jeff Linfield's story ties it all together. I don't know if Biggs is giving orders, I doubt it, however, he's supposedly running Black Blizzard and we know the money is from New Orleans. What the hell else do you need?"

Carstairs drained his coffee to indicate our conference was over. "I need you to list every name you can think of in case we come up with anything here we can cross reference. Proof or not, Tom, a list will help us process prints and forensics from here. If we get lucky, maybe we can get something for you to run with."

Tom nodded. "We started a list on the flight up. We'll finish it on the way back and I'll fax it to you as soon as I'm in the office."

Carstairs glanced at his watch and signaled waitress for a check. "If that's it for now, I've got a lot on my plate the rest of today. I'd like to take you guys to the airport and start pulling this together."

I said, "I'm sure something will occur to me later, I'll give you a call if it does."

"Mr. Scott, remember what I said about going vigilante—we'll do a lot better if we work together."

I looked directly at him. "I hear you."

We walked to the cash register and Carstairs paid the tab. Tom said, "Thanks. It'll be our turn when you're in Denver."

"No problem. I expect we'll be seeing a lot of each other for a while."

I called Kirk at the airport and told him we were ready. He said they'd be ready to fly by the time we got there.

***

As soon as we were airborne, I got out a bottle of scotch, put two ice cubes in each glass, and poured a double for each of us. I handed a glass to Tom and leaned back in my seat. "Carstairs seemed like a good guy."

"Yeah. I've never worked with him, it looks like he's on top of it."

"Let's finish the list."

"Okay. I'll fax him a copy when we get back."

We started with all the members of the Linfield family. Jeff's name was underlined although he couldn't have physically committed either murder. He was, however, the link to Black Blizzard. Ron Suarez and Jeff's wife, Maria, were added.

Next came everyone we knew of connected to Black Blizzard: Maurice "Mo" DiPaulo, John Marcello, James Davidoff, Myron Metropolit, and my old "friend" Jerome Biggs. Mike Landry's name got a double underline along with the Big Mexican. Now, I *really* wished I'd have grabbed them. If I had, we'd have a name for the Mexican. Tom added the Renoir and Mondragon law firm for good measure.

Tom scanned our list and asked, "Can you think of anyone else, maybe not connected to these slugs, who has a hard-on for you?"

I shook my head.

"What about Gerri? She ever tell you about anybody out to get her?"

"We've been over this. Both of us probably made people mad at some time or another. I don't think anybody would ever have been mad enough to think about murder, though.

"What are we going to do, Tom? I feel totally lost. I don't know which way to turn or what to do. I'm starting to understand how Jeff Linfield must feel...knowing you probably caused someone's death even though you didn't mean to. This is hell."

My best friend, Tom Montgomery, homicide detective in the Denver Police Department, closed his notebook, put it in his inside pocket, leaned over and put his hand on my shoulder. "We wait on the ME's findings, work the case from both ends, and hope for a break. There's not much else we can do. Sometimes these things take a while, Cort. You've got to hold yourself together and not go crashing around trying to solve it on your own. If you do, you're going to get in the way and screw something up. When we do get a lead, we've got to make sure we can tie up every detail and get a conviction."

"I know. I just don't like having to go slow. I'm not sure what Gerri and I had, I don't know if it was 'love.' I know I cared about her and she cared about me. We had lots of good times together and were planning more. She didn't deserve this. If someone did it to get to me, they did a fucking good job of it. I'm telling you ahead of time, I'm going to start rattling cages and hope to shake something out."

Tom took his hand off my shoulder and gave me a hard stare. "You can cut corners I can't. You've *got* to keep me in the loop. You need to share everything you turn up."

We started the descent into Centennial Airport and Kirk told us to fasten up. We were on the ground ten minutes later, the pilots buttoned up the plane, came in, and we said our goodbyes. Kirk rarely cursed so it startled me when he said, "I want you and Tom to catch the bastards who did this and fuck them up every way you can." Neither of us spoke as we hurried to the parking lot.

I told Tom, "I'll go home and make notes on everything I can think of about Gerri's business deals, clients, stockholders, and anything else that comes to mind. I'll go over my history too, especially with the Linfields, Mary's murder, and all the crap associated with Black Blizzard. The clues are in there someplace. I hope I'm smart enough to figure them out."

Tom dropped his bag in the trunk. "I'll be in touch when I hear from Green River. Do you know who'll handle Gerri's arrangements? Does she have any family here?"

"It'll end up being me. Her folks are both dead. She has one brother. He's a modern day Robinson Crusoe and lives on some island off Thailand. I'll have to go through Gerri's files to find an address to let him know. You could do me a big favor if you'll ask Carstairs when they'll release her. I'll contact one of the funeral homes here to coordinate getting her back to Denver. I already know she wanted to be cremated and have her ashes spread on the Arkansas River near Salida. We used to go rafting and fishing there, she loved the area."

For the second time in an hour, Tom put his hand on my shoulder as he said, "I can't tell you how sorry I am for you. If there's anything…anything at all, I can do for you, let me know."

I felt the tears well up and replied, "If it had to be anyone, I'm glad it was you who told me. The first thing, now, is to catch the bastards."

I meant what I said, although what I really wanted to do was get home and figure out a way to put a .38 slug in whoever had clubbed Gerri.

chapter

TWENTY-FIVE

I drove home as slowly as I'd ever driven anywhere. I felt like I'd taken a solid beating from someone a lot bigger and tougher than me. My eyes would tear up as I thought of something Gerri and I had shared. The worst part was thinking about what I had been doing the day Gerri had been murdered, who I'd been with, and what to do next. I was assaulted with waves of guilt and thoughts of revenge. Revenge for whom? Was I trying to avenge Gerri or find solace for myself?

Deep in my gut, I knew Biggs and the slime balls from New Orleans were involved in Mary Linfield's death. Although I couldn't make a direct connection between me working for the Linfields and Gerri's death, the warning signs were brighter than the Las Vegas strip. Tom's thought about somebody killing Gerri to warn me off didn't seem logical, but it was out there none the less. My problem was I didn't know how to go about proving anything. I did come to one solid conclusion, I wasn't going to let the niceties of the law and due process get in the way of figuring out who was to blame for the murders.

Inside, Gerri's spirit was no longer in residence. The house seemed quieter than I remembered. The robe Lindsey had used was hanging behind the closet door. It was another, too soon, reminder of what a bastard I was. I'd cheated on Gerri while she was trying to make us both rich. If I'd cared more, I would've gone to Wyoming with her. I could've been running lease records while she watched the well. Instead, I was here with a girl who was little more than a casual acquaintance. What kind of person had I become? And now, what could I tell Lindsey and how would she handle whatever I said? How the hell was I going to survive this?

***

I didn't feel like eating so settled for another scotch which I drank while watching the sun go down. When I finished the scotch, I went downstairs, got a bottle of wine, and went in the hot tub room. I triggered the remote, put light classical on the sound system, stripped and stepped in. The water was a perfect ninety-nine degrees and crystal clear. I sat in the lounger seat with the jets on low and started on the wine. It was good. I wished I could have said the same about me. After the second glass, I welcomed the numbness as it worked its way out from my gut to my legs and back. Whoever said alcohol is not the answer obviously didn't appreciate the fact it is "an" answer. One that was working for me.

***

I needed a schedule for the next few days. I thought I'd work it out mentally and write down everything when I got out. The first item was taking care of Gerri's arrangements although Tom had said to plan on at least four or five days before Green River PD released her body. I'd call a funeral home first thing tomorrow and check out arranging transport. I would have to call Martin Gear, her partner and co-founder of Mountain West, to arrange a memorial. I knew Gerri wouldn't have wanted a church service, she wanted something simple like a celebration of life party and having her ashes scattered on the river. I could take care of that anytime. I wanted her murderer first.

Regardless of Tom's cautioning, I was going to Black Blizzard's office tomorrow. I needed to look directly at Jerome Biggs. I figured he would be the weak link in the chain.

I was pouring another glass of wine when my cell rang. I killed the tub jets, picked it up, looked at the screen, and felt a hot blush. It was Lindsey.

I pushed the talk button. "Hello."

"Thank God, you're home. I just got off the phone with George Albins—- Tom Montgomery called him about Gerri. Cort, I'm so very sorry. I want you to know I'm not going to push anything on you, try to console you, or even talk to you until you say the first word. Anything we find out on the Linfield case, you can get from George. That way, you don't have to see me or talk to me. You need time and space, I shouldn't be a part of it right now."

I felt tears running down my face as I listened to her. It hit me hard hearing her say Gerri's name. I cleared my throat to steady my voice. "Thanks for that, Lindsey. It's hard to know what I need or should do. When I've had time to take care of things, I'll need to talk. I appreciate your calling and putting everything out front. I've got to tell you I'm suffering terrible guilt about...well, about everything. It wasn't wrong. It was just really bad timing."

"Yes, it was." Her voice caught. "I understand, I feel terrible too. Call me if you want to talk or just need someone to listen. I'll be here."

"Thanks. It means a lot."

"Good-bye, Cort."

"Bye, Lindsey."

I disconnected the call and sunk back in the tub. I stared at my half full glass and finished it in one swallow. Making Gerri's arrangements moved down one space on my schedule—- shaking the truth out of Biggs came first and that was going to happen tomorrow.

chapter

TWENTY-SIX

I was up at 5:30, shaved, showered, and dressed by 6:30. The coffee brewed while I was cleaning up. I picked up the paper from the driveway, brought it in, and poured coffee. A small headline in the lower left corner, read: *Denver oil company executive murdered in Wyoming*. The article had two short paragraphs on the front page and continued on page five. I read it quickly, then again slowly. The story reported Gerri German, a principal in a Denver based oil and gas company, had been found dead in a motel room in Green River, Wyoming. No cause of death had been established, pending an autopsy. Homicide was suspected. The police had no leads and were soliciting help from the public who were asked to call Detective Jack Carstairs at the Green River police with any information. It was not much of an epitaph for someone I knew so well, although it was more than the five lines about Mary Linfield last week. I sipped coffee while I stared at the story. Seeing it in print made it all too real. Gerri was dead.

I went to the gun safe, got out the Beretta .38 and shoulder rig, picked up an extra clip, and took a light bomber jacket off the hanger. I dropped the clip in the inside pocket made for carrying cell phones. As I raised the garage door and backed out, I almost wished someone would make a try at me. I hoped they'd miss, of course, although I wouldn't have minded emptying a clip into a real target.

Downtown, I parked in my space and walked the block to my office. I could barely push the door open over the mail shoved through the slot. Most of it was junk except for a thick envelope with a handwritten return address from Green River near the top of the pile. It was postmarked the day before Gerri had been found. I kicked the rest aside, picked up the envelope, and sat down at my desk. I stared at it for a long time. Finally, I grabbed a letter opener and sliced the top. I took out a bunch of plat maps and yellow legal pad sheets with notes. On top was a handwritten note from Gerri.

Dear Wise-ass Investigator,

Here I am in the historic Sweetwater County courthouse. It's lunch time so all the civil servants have taken off, however since I've been such a good customer and regularly bring them coffee and doughnuts in the morning, they agreed to let me stay and work. See? A little bribery never hurts!

I've found something very interesting I thought you should see for yourself and I didn't want to talk over the phone. (I've been hearing lots of weird clicks and stuff on both my cell and on the phone in my motel room.) Anyway, someone has been top leasing virtually every lease in the county due to expire in the next year. Some are on my leases but lots of others are being covered, too. Here's the interesting part. The leases are being taken by LA Warehouse Leasing. Isn't that the name of the outfit you told me the bad-ass Linfield brother was working with? If it is, that could mean everything that's going on is connected: LA Warehouse Leasing is covering for Black Blizzard, Black Blizzard is owned by the guys in New Orleans. Our old buddy, Jerome Biggs works for Black Blizzard, etc.

What I'm saying is—- what you find out down in Denver might be tied into the same guys who are trying to bust my play up here.

I miss you, big boy! It's been a long time up here in the wilds without seeing you. I'm thinking I can wrap this up in the next week and should be back in ten days or so. Let's plan a big reunion celebration with lots of wine and post-dessert desserts, if you catch my drift.

Love, Gerri

I blinked back hot tears. My throat clenched up tight. I could hear Gerri's voice in my mind. This was the link that would tie the people who killed Mary Linfield to Gerri's murder. The bastards must have heard about the well, decided to burglarize her condo, and immediately started taking top leases. They also knew she was my girlfriend and she'd put the names together and make the connection. They'd killed her to shut her up before she could tell me. They had moved quickly, but not quickly enough. The bastards had signed their own death warrants.

I knew I had to let Tom know about Gerri's letter, but decided to make my call on Biggs first.

It was just after 9:30. Black Blizzard ought to be open for business. I pulled the .38, jacked a shell into the chamber, and slid the gun back in the holster. I patted the clip in my jacket pocket and locked the door behind me.

Liz Flint, my office neighbor, was walking down the hall toward me. "Oh, Cort, I just read about Gerri in the paper. God, I'm so sorry. I heard your office door a few minutes ago and I've been trying to figure out what to say. I guess there's not much that..."

I stopped her short. "Thanks, Liz. I've got some stuff to do right now. It can't wait. I've got to go."

"I understand. If there's anything I can do, just let me know."

We walked side-by-side to her office. She went inside and I took the stairs to the lobby and the 17th Street exit. Black Blizzard was in the Anaconda Building, a couple blocks away. My pulse rate had gone up, still I felt calm inside. It was good to be doing something.

I went through the revolving doors and checked the directory. Black Blizzard was on thirty-four, one floor below the Front Range

Room of the Petroleum Club. I took the elevator and stepped out into a lobby with glass doors on each end. To my right, the doors were engraved *Northern Lights Executive Suites*. The ones to the left said, *Black Blizzard Petroleum*.

The reception area was open to the outside wall and had an expansive view of the city to the south. Pikes Peak was visible sixty-five miles away. It was a clear day, no brown cloud. The receptionist's desk was a high counter along the wall left of the entrance. Interior hallways were visible running both ways. The receptionist was a thirty-something brunette with an imposing superstructure, well styled hair, an expensive looking silver-gray pants suit, and an emerald green shirt. She smiled as I approached. "Good morning, sir. How may I help you?"

"You can help me by pointing the way to Jerome Biggs' office."

"Do you have an appointment with Mr. Biggs? He's in conference at the moment."

"I plan to surprise him. Now, why don't you show me the way to his office. Don't touch the phone or the intercom." I opened my jacket. She didn't panic, just opened her eyes wide, stood, and walked to the hallway. She turned back momentarily, and then started to the right. There were no windows, however the doors were open allowing outside light into the hall. I looked in each office as we passed. They were well furnished—- with clean desktops. No maps in the racks or on the drafting tables—- and no one was in any of them. The place felt deserted.

At the end of the hall, a glass door led to a corner office. I saw Biggs sitting behind a large, ornate desk looking to his left. I pulled my gun, reached past the receptionist, opened the door, and pushed her through.

I'd hit the jackpot. Landry was sitting on a leather couch against the wall to Biggs' left. His right hand was in one of those casts that left the thumb sticking straight up. The first two fingers were bandaged and in little wire protective cages. His jacket was open and I spotted a gun on his right side. He must have intended to use a left draw because of his broken right hand.

Landry started to stand. I pointed the Beretta at him and said, "Stay down! Stick your left hand under your ass and sit on it." I stepped across the office, fished out his gun, and stuck it in my jacket pocket.

Biggs' face had turned pasty white and he'd slid down in his chair. "Slide your chair all the way up under your desk, Biggs. Put your elbows on top."

He did as he was told, whining, "What the hell do you think you're doing, Scott? You can't come busting in here waving a gun around."

"Shut up. I *am* doing it and now we're going to continue your 'conference.'" I told the receptionist to move a visitor chair between the two men and take a seat. She did as she was told with no argument.

"Okay, boys and girl, let's see what we can figure out here. Biggs, you get to start. What do you know about Gerri German's murder?"

He got even paler, coughed, and stuttered out, "Whadda you mean, what do I know? I don't know a damned thing about it. Just what I read in the paper. What makes you think I——" I fired a round into the right front of Biggs' desk. The receptionist screamed and started to get up. I motioned her back and turned the gun toward Landry.

"What about you, Landry? You know anything about Gerri getting killed?"

He tried to act tough and cool. I saw beads of sweat break out at his hairline and around his eyes. Before he could say anything, I fired another shot into the couch six inches from his left arm. He stopped looking tough. "Jesus Christ, Scott! Are you crazy?"

The smell of the gunpowder combined with a wisp of smoke from the leather where the bullet had made a sizeable hole. The receptionist was crying and the tears were ruining her mascara. Biggs looked like he was going to have a heart attack.

"I'm completely fucking gonzo, you prick! I'm just crazy enough to shoot out the goddamn window and throw you out of it. How much of a grease spot do you figure a slime ball like you would make from thirty-four stories? I want some answers and I want them right now or you're not going to make it out of here."

The girl screamed and went down on her knees. "Please don't kill me! I don't know anything about what you're talking about. Honestly, mister, I just answer the phones. I've only been her three months. Please don't shoot me."

"Shut up and go stand by the bar. Keep your mouth shut and listen carefully to what these bastards say. You're going to get a chance to repeat it all to the cops." That was bullshit, of course. Nothing these two said at the point of a gun would ever be heard in court.

Biggs found his voice, "You can leave her out of it. She's telling the truth. She doesn't know anything. This was all——"

Landry yelled to cut him off, "*Shut the fuck up, Biggs!* He isn't going to kill anybody. He's bluffing."

I shot Landry in the foot. So much for admissible testimony. This would have to be one of the short cuts Tom warned me about. I didn't care, these guys had killed Gerri.

He pitched forward off the couch, grabbing at his foot. The girl started to scream again then bit her lip to stop. Biggs stared at Landry writhing around on the floor as blood leaked out of his shoe and smeared the carpet as he rolled.

"*Ah, shit! Jesus Christ!* Scott, for God's sake, stop shooting! I'll tell you anything. I'll tell you whatever you want." Biggs stood up to look at Landry.

I was experiencing sensory overload. I'd never shot anybody in plain cold blood before. It was way too easy. All the visions I'd been having about these guys killing Gerri—— bashing her head in a god-damn hotel room in Green River—— went through my mind. Somehow, a disconcerting thought kept taking over——- I wasn't any better than them. I'd just shot a guy who was no threat to me and I did it without any hesitation. I'd done it to keep him from silencing Biggs who was ready to tell me what I wanted to hear. He shouldn't have yelled when he did. Everything I'd been thinking about revenge for Gerri...or really for me...made me pull the trigger. My next thought was I shouldn't have done it. I'd lowered myself to Landry's level. I'd acted emotionally without thinking it through. I almost puked. I choked back the bile and hoped Biggs hadn't seen. Was I really no better than these guys?

"All right, start telling me everything you know. And Biggs, you better tell the truth. If you lie and I figure it out, you'll get some of what Landry got."

I told the girl to help Landry onto the couch. He was groaning and his color had turned chalky. She tried to help him up, getting him to one knee. "Landry, get on the fucking couch. If you do, I'll let the girl help you. If you don't, I'll leave you on the floor and you can bleed to death. It's all the same to me." With the girl's help, he finally managed to crawl onto the couch. I was glad he made it. I didn't know if I had the stomach for too much more of this.

I jerked my head at the girl. "You get to play nurse. Slip off his shoe, pull up his pant leg, and try to get the sock off. We need to look at his foot." Landry gritted his teeth and pressed his left hand on the couch as the girl slid off his shoe. She dropped it when she saw it was full of blood. She pushed the pant leg past his knee and started pulling down the sock. Landry went totally white, took in a quavering breath, and held it as the sock came off. His foot was a bloody mess. The slug had made only a small hole in the top but had blown most of his heel off when it exited. He was bleeding heavily. I looked around at what they had. "Slide the visitor's chair in front of him. I want you to put the pillow from the couch on the chair, then pick-up his foot and leg and let him stretch them out on the pillow. Next, take off your belt and make a tourniquet around his leg just below the knee. Can you do all that?"

The girl realized she wasn't going to die, so she nodded and said, "I think so." She got started. Landry kept groaning and gritting his teeth, however his color got better. When he was situated with his leg up and the belt around his calf, the bleeding slowed nearly to a stop. He wasn't going to bleed to death right in front of us, at least not right now.

I asked the girl if there was anyone else in the office suite and she said no. I asked how many people were in the executive suites on the other side of the floor—— she didn't know for sure.

"There are two girls who work there full time. The people who rent the suites and use the services come and go. Sometimes I don't see anyone for days."

I asked her if she'd seen anyone today and she said only the girls. I knew it was a risk and I was betting the girls on the other side hadn't heard the shots, especially if they were wearing telephone headsets.

I turned back to Biggs. "Let's have it. I need everything you've got, right from the beginning."

chapter

TWENTY-SEVEN

I motioned at Biggs with the gun. "Talk."

He looked at Landry and took a deep breath. "About two years ago, I was in New Orleans doing some consulting work for a guy I know who has some small working interests in a bunch of crappy oil wells out in the swamp. We were having drinks in a Metairie bar one night, and a couple of guys he knew came in and we got to talking about the oil business. These guys were real interested in how money flowed in and out of the business. I was pretty boozed up and told them if you knew what you were doing, you could turn a lot of money and never even drill a well. I told them you could even make money when you drilled a dry hole if you promoted the price and sold more than a hundred percent of a deal. They couldn't seem to grasp that part, so I drew it out for them on a bar napkin. It got their attention and they asked me if I could help them get started in the business. They said they had a money 'problem.' They had a lot of cash that needed to be cleaned up—- and thought an oil company would make a perfect washing machine."

I glared at Biggs. "They were *telling* you they were dirty. And, you didn't object?"

"I'd been having a tough time. I got mixed up in some bad deals here and Shell made sure everybody in Denver knew about it. After I left Shell, I didn't have steady work for years. I even did a little well-site work...nothing was bringing in any money, so I went to New Orleans. I was looking for anything that would give me a big payday. I didn't care if it wasn't on the up and up. I needed the money."

"That sounds like you," I said.

Biggs stiffened but continued. "We agreed to get together the next day in New Orleans. After they left, the guy I was consulting for started talking. He told me these guys were 'connected', you know, with the mob. He figured they were talking about drug money. I told him I didn't give a shit where their money came from as long as I wasn't handling dope. He told me he didn't want any part of the deal and if I was smart, I wouldn't touch it either. I guess I wasn't smart. All I wanted was a big payday."

I checked Landry who sat breathing deeply with his eyes closed. "You proved a long time ago you're not too smart, Biggs...keep talking. Who were your new friends and business partners?"

"The two guys at the bar were named DiPaulo and Marcello. When I went to their office the next day, which turned out to be in the back of a restaurant, another guy named Davidoff was there."

"Jesus Christ, Biggs! Obviously, you didn't listen to your buddy. You *had* to know those guys were mobbed up. How dumb are you anyway?"

"Goddamn it—- I needed the money! I knew who they were. I'd been in New Orleans for a few years. I didn't care."

"What else?"

"We sat there talking until two in the afternoon. I explained how to put together a bogus deal and, if you're positive it's going to be a dry hole, sell more than a hundred percent of the interest. I even got them going on how we could run it straight for a while, particularly if we acquired a bunch of acreage and some legitimate drilling prospects, then do a float and raise a bunch of money in an IPO. We could clean all the money they wanted by buying drilling deals and leases, selling off promoted interests, and taking cash out as finders' fees or even in stock. They were hot and heavy for it. They asked where the best place to locate would be and I told them Denver or Casper, Wyoming. Both places are full of independent oil companies and geologic consultants, so there'd be tons of drilling ideas around that we could get cheap and turn. They decided on Denver because the airline connections are better."

Landry coughed and tried to sit straighter. I asked the girl to get some water bottles from the refrigerator and give Landry a drink. Biggs took one and drained half a bottle before I nodded at him to continue.

"We all went to Pat O'Brien's after that and had some drinks. About six o'clock, this Jewish guy named Metropolit showed up and they brought him up to speed on everything we'd talked about. He got all excited, said it sounded perfect, and he'd get their lawyer started on putting a company together. They planned to start off with four or five million dollars Metropolit was sitting on in LA. He said they could park the money in an offshore bank until we got the paperwork together, print stock certificates for them, and move the money to a Denver bank. We came up with the name Black Blizzard because we were drinking Hurricanes and wanted something connected to oil and storms and shit like that."

"Cute," I said. I hated this son-of-a-bitch. I was tempted to shoot him in the foot too. "Keep talking."

"That got the ball rolling. I came back to Denver the next week. They gave me a cashier's check for a hundred thousand, told me to rent an office, and start looking for deals. It took about three months for their lawyers to get their shit together. They all came to Denver for a big opening party. We had a hell of a blowout at

Morton's——- that's when I first met Landry. They said he would be coming in every so often to keep an eye on the operation——- and on me. The next morning, Landry came up here and told me if anything went wrong, or if they thought I wasn't doing the right stuff for them, he would make it right. He scared the shit out of me."

Landry had one eye open and was looking at Biggs. If pure hate could come out of one eye, it was happening there. He shifted his one-eyed gaze to me, then closed it.

"Fast forward for me, Biggs. How did Jeff Linfield get pulled into this and how did any of it lead to Gerri?"

"Can I have more water?" he asked. I motioned to the girl who'd been listening to all this with her eyes popped and mouth open. Apparently, she'd been telling the truth about not knowing anything. She went back to the refrigerator and got another bottle for Biggs. He opened the lid and drained most of it in one swallow. Confessing to crime must make a guy thirsty.

"About a year ago, Metropolit made a trip to LA and stopped in Denver on the way back. He said they had a line on a guy from Colorado who was living in Tahoe. He and his family had a shit-load of money and a big income from oil production on their ranch. He didn't see eye-to-eye with the rest of the family on investments and was anxious to get his hands on some trust they'd set up. He was ready to invest his own money and said he'd get the family to go along if it looked like a good deal. Because they were familiar with oil and gas, he figured they'd jump on another one. That was Linfield, of course. He said he could put as much as a million into a deal."

The phone on Biggs' desk buzzed. The receptionist said, "It rings through if nobody answers out front. It'll go to message after four rings." They both looked at me.

"Let it ring. Keep talking, Biggs."

"Metropolit got to Linfield through Linfield's brother-in-law, Ron Suarez, in LA. Suarez works for the guys in New Orleans. Metropolit wanted to know what kind of deals Black Blizzard had that he could use to hook Linfield and his family. We didn't want him as a partner, we just wanted to get our hands on his cash. I was fooling around in the Mosquito Basin because it's a great place to put together a cheap lease position, promote the hell out of it, and sell a hundred and twenty-five percent of the working interest. We planned on drilling a dry hole, pocket the cash, and move on to the next deal. You know the odds of hitting a producer there are piss poor, so we wouldn't have to worry about that happening. We started putting leases together and I even tried to get ahold of Sid Bonner's maps to pretty it up. He never even returned my phone calls."

I thought Sid must have forgotten about that because he was so adamant about not doing anything with Biggs.

"About that time, Linfield started crawfishing. He said his family wouldn't agree and he couldn't come up with the million on his own. Marcello sent Landry up here and we talked about what to do. I wanted to back off Linfield, make some really pretty maps, and try selling the deal back East or in California. Landry said Linfield was too big a fish to let off the hook. We'd threaten him with dropping an anonymous tip to the cops, saying him and his wife were mixed up in drugs and money laundering through their real estate business. Even if it wasn't true, it would tie him up for years. They thought they could scare him into coming up with the money and bring his family in too."

"Who did the dirty work? You? Did you threaten Jeff?"

"Not me, Landry went out to Tahoe and told Linfield unless he came up with the money, we'd tell the cops his family was involved in everything. That was bullshit, but we figured it would get his attention."

"How did Jeff react to that?"

"Landry said he acted scared as hell and kept saying we shouldn't contact his wife or family...that he could handle it. I think that was when you had the meeting at their ranch because Linfield came into the office and was crying the blues about how the whole thing was going to hell. Landry went ballistic, shoved him around a little, and said if he didn't get the money, something real bad would happen."

I sat up at that. "What did you think he meant? Was Landry physically threatening him or someone in his family?"

I watched as Landry stirred, opened his eyes, and looked at Biggs who said, "I think so. After Linfield left, Landry said he needed to make some calls and get a couple of guys in here who could 'convince' the Linfield family they needed to go along. He said they'd have a talk with Linfield's sister who headed their family corporation."

"Who showed up after Landry made his calls?"

"Two Mexicans. I think they came from LA. Landry picked them up at the airport and drove out to the Linfield ranch."

"Did you go with them, Biggs?"

"No."

"That's a good thing. If you had, I think I would just throw you out the window right now. I'd get the rest of the story out of Landry before he croaks."

Biggs' hands started to shake. "I'm telling you the fucking truth! I didn't go with 'em. I didn't do nothing other than show 'em where to go on a map. I swear to God."

"God isn't going to help you, Biggs. At the very least, you're an accessory to murder. I haven't made up my mind about you. Keep talking." I stood and walked behind my chair. I needed to move.

Biggs seemed relieved to be telling the story. "I don't know the details about what happened. I know the two muscle guys went out to the Linfields' again the next week. I know Jeff Linfield called and was screaming that what had happened to his sister was no accident. He said he knew we were behind it, and was going to tell you and the cops everything. That scared the shit out of me—- it just made Landry mad. He told me to keep my mouth shut, that he'd take care of Linfield—- and you too. He started looking everywhere for Linfield and couldn't find him. He must have called twenty hotels and car rentals. He even started following you around and staked out your place. He came back one time and said you were screwing some woman cop and it might be a way to shut you up——- he could tell your girlfriend."

When Biggs said that, I turned to Landry who was staring at me. I took two steps and kicked him just above the ankle on his bad leg. He screamed which made the girl scream too. Landry's face went white and his eyes rolled like he would pass out. "Don't fucking faint, Landry," I snarled. "If you do, I'll kick your leg off that chair and let you bleed to death." Landry struggled to stay conscious. I leaned over him. "Is that when you and the big greaser came calling?"

He managed a nod.

"I'm guessing that getting your ass kicked got you pissed off enough to go to Wyoming and go after Gerri, you son-of-a-bitch."

Landry clenched his teeth. "You gotta get me to a hospital. I've lost too much blood. I ain't going to make it unless you get me out of here. If you help me, I'll tell you the rest of it. I ain't going down alone for all this shit. I can hang the New Orleans guys for you. That's who you want. You ain't going to get to 'em unless I help you."

I faked a laugh. "I'd rather just plug you again, Landry. Nothing you or Biggs has said will ever get to court, so killing you might be all I get...I guarantee I'd like it."

By this time, I knew I was bluffing. I didn't have the heart or the guts to murder someone in cold blood. I needed to keep up the front though, so I started to raise my gun. The girl caught her breath. Biggs' eyes bulged. Landry managed to get both eyes open and focused on me.

"Don't shoot me, Scott. I'll tell you and the cops everything I know." I enjoyed hearing Landry beg.

His eyes had changed from before. I couldn't see the hate any more, just fear. He was afraid to die. I wasn't sure he would make it anyway. I knew I wouldn't shoot him again. I needed to hear what he had to say and wanted Tom Montgomery to hear it, too.

"Here's the deal, shithead. I'll have the girl call 9-1-1 and get an ambulance on the way. I'm also calling the cops and we're going with you in the ambulance. You're going to start talking as soon as the cops get here and you'll keep talking until they put you under to work on your foot. If you quit talking for even a minute or try to fake passing out, I'm going to smash your fucking foot. The cops aren't going to 'see' a thing. You clear on that?"

Landry nodded. "I got it."

I took out my cell and punched the speed dial for Tom. I didn't have time to think through what I'd say, so I just told him what had happened.

Tom let out the breath he'd been holding. "You are a fucking idiot. Let me think a minute." The line was dead for several seconds before I heard Tom clear his throat. "Do either of those guys have a gun?"

"Landry had one. I've got it in my pocket."

"Is it an auto or a revolver?"

"An automatic. What difference does it make?"

"Shut up and listen. You're going to create one hell of a case for self-defense. You don't have much time, so here's what you need to do."

chapter

TWENTY-EIGHT

"Drop the clip and make sure there isn't a round in the chamber. Wipe the gun down, including the clip, and don't get your prints on it. Hand it back to Landry, to his good hand, and make him handle it. Make him put the clip in, don't let him jack a round into the chamber. Then have him drop it on the floor. Can you trust the woman and Biggs not to say anything?"

"How the hell do I know?"

"We'll have to take a chance. Okay, this'll be your 'official' notification to the police. I'll call dispatch and we'll have some uniforms there in a couple minutes. I'm less than five minutes away. I'll come rushing in and take charge of the scene. Go ahead and call 9-1-1 to get an ambulance started. That'll add a little more confusion.

"Like you told Landry, we'll ride with him in the ambulance. If he's still alive and conscious, we can listen to what he has to say. You *are* a fucking idiot, Cort. I don't know if we can pull this off. I'll do what I can."

"Thanks, Tom. Get here as fast as you can."

I closed the phone and spoke to the girl. "Call 9-1-1, give them the address and say a man's been shot. If they ask, tell them the police have been notified and are on the way. If they ask anything else, hang up."

She glanced at Biggs, picked up the phone, punched in the numbers, and did exactly as I said.

I turned to Biggs. "You stay right where you are."

Next, I told Landry, "We've got a little housekeeping to do and not much time." He looked confused. "I'm going to drop the clip from your gun and wipe everything down. Then, you're going to handle it with your left hand. Make sure you get your prints on the grip and the trigger guard. Push the clip in with your left hand and get your prints on it, too. Then drop the gun in front of the couch. Don't even think about trying to jack a shell in. My gun will be four inches from your ear, I'll kill you if you make a wrong move."

I focused on Biggs and the girl. "You two aren't going to see him do anything, and you won't say anything different. You got that?"

They both nodded. I took out Landry's piece, pressed the release, and dropped the clip in the chair. I told the girl to get a towel from the bar, wipe the gun down, and hand it to Landry with the towel. She acted like she was being forced to touch a rattlesnake but followed orders. After watching Landry fumble with the gun left handed, it was obvious he wouldn't have had a chance if he'd gone for it when I first came in. He was clumsy. When the girl was ready with the clip, he had to push the gun down between the couch cushions to use his left hand to put the clip in.

I said, "Now pull it out of the couch and drop it on the floor."
He did it.

I nodded at the girl. "Okay, you kick it over toward my chair."
She gave it a push with her foot. It just missed the blood stain under
the chair with Landry's foot.

At that moment, we heard voices in the reception area. Someone shouted, "Denver Police!"

"Back here, end of the hall in the corner office," I yelled. "My
name's Cort Scott, I called this in. I'm holding a gun on three people.
I—-"

The same voice cut me off. "Back up to the door and lay the
gun on the floor!"

I backed to the office doorway, and did as I was told.

"Now, kick it behind you into the hall and put your hands
behind your head."

I kept watching Biggs and Landry as I followed orders, they
weren't moving. I heard footsteps behind me, then felt the cop's hand
on my left shoulder pushing me back into the office. Another officer
stepped past with his service weapon drawn, looked over the scene,
and said, "What's going on here?"

I started to answer when Tom walked in. "I've got it, Officer.
I'm Montgomery from Homicide, I'll take it from here. I know Mr.
Scott. He called this in to me and I forwarded everything to dis-
patch."

"Yes, sir. What do you want us to do?"

"Take the guy at the desk and the woman to the station house.
Put 'em in separate interrogation rooms, get their names, numbers,
and addresses. They're not under arrest at this point, so don't ask
them any questions other than the names and addresses. Unless we
start an interrogation, we don't have to read them Miranda rights."

The cops holstered their guns. One walked around the desk,
took Biggs by the arm, and led him into the hall. The other one did
the same with the girl. As they were leaving, an emergency medical
response team wheeling a gurney showed up.

Two guys in blue scrubs and a woman in green rushed in. The woman said, "9-1-1 dispatch said you have a gunshot victim. That him on the couch?" I wanted to ask if she saw anyone else with a bloody leg and a tourniquet but decided against it.

They immediately began taking Landry's vitals. The woman examined the tourniquet and bloody bandages.

Tom asked, "How's that guy doing? He going to be ready for transport soon?"

"Give us five minutes," one of the guys answered. "He's lost a lot of blood. He's pretty woozy and in quite a bit of pain. We should give him an injection."

"I don't want you to do that," I said.

Tom snapped, "Shut up! I'm in charge here. You need to get your lawyer down to headquarters."

I studied Tom for a moment and realized he wasn't kidding. "Can I make the call now?"

"Go ahead." His tone of voice didn't leave any room for confusion.

I reached in my jacket, found my extra ammo clip in the phone pocket, and remembered my cell was in an outside pocket. I spun through the number list to Jason Masters, my lawyer, who I'd contacted for Jeff Linfield. I punched the speed dial and waited for his receptionist to answer. She said he was in conference. I told her I needed him to call me ASAP and meet me at DPD headquarters. I disconnected the call and looked at Tom. "What's next?"

Tom was looking over the office. "We're riding in the ambulance to Denver Health. *I* will ask him some questions on the way. *You* will ride along, listen, and keep your mouth shut. If you say one fucking word, I'm going to arrest you on suspicion of attempted murder. You got all that straight?"

"Yes."

The woman med-tech shot Tom a glance and said they were ready. Tom said, "Go ahead. Get started. I'll call for a forensics team to go over this place."

The EMTs loaded Landry on the gurney and started down the hall. Landry didn't look too good. His face was splotchy gray and he was grimacing, however he managed to keep his eyes open. Tom and I followed them down the hall, out through the reception area, and into the elevator lobby. The cops had locked off one of the elevators at the floor and it was standing with the doors open. There wasn't enough room for everybody along with the gurney.

Tom said, "You guys on the gurney go ahead. The rest of us will meet you in the lobby." We arrived in the main lobby as they were wheeling Landry out to the street where the ambulance was double parked. More cop cars were blocking traffic. Several uniforms were standing around. Tom surveyed the scene, then shouted, "Shows over. Everybody who isn't involved in transportation, get back on patrol."

The cops climbed in their cars and began to clear the street. As the EMT crew loaded Landry, Tom and I, plus the female tech climbed inside, so it was crowded. The driver and the other tech clambered into the front. They hit the siren and flashers, we flew down 18th, turned on Broadway heading south toward Denver Health.

Tom said, "Okay, asshole, can you hear me?" Landry nodded. "Start spitting it out. Tell me what went down with the Linfields and with Gerri German?"

Landry grimaced, wet his lips, then whispered, "If you keep me alive, I can put you on the guys who set everything up."

"We'll keep you alive all right," Tom hissed, "If you bullshit us, you'll wish we hadn't."

Landry's eyes started to roll, he fought it off. "I didn't do no killings. You gotta understand that. I'm just the guy in the middle. I know people. I put people in touch with other people who need something done. You understand?"

Tom asked, "Who wanted something done and who'd you find to do it?"

"The guys in New Orleans figured they could get to the money if Linfield's sister was out of the picture."

"Who'd you send out there to kill her?" Tom yelled. The woman EMT jerked her head up, gave Tom a hard look, and shook her head.

Landry jumped. "They didn't go out there to kill that woman. They were supposed to tell her that unless she went along, her brother and the whole family would be ruined. If she went to the cops, somebody in the family would get hurt. They were just supposed to scare the shit out of her. When they stepped out onto the trail, she ran her horse right at 'em and damned near knocked *them* over the cliff. They were the ones who got scared. They panicked, pulled guns, and got ahold of the horse. They pulled her off and started pushing her around. The fucking horse got all excited and started jumping around...her own horse knocked her over."

I looked at Tom and shrugged. He'd told me to keep my mouth shut...I felt he'd meant it.

"You don't expect me to believe that crock of shit, do you?" Tom shook his head in disbelief.

Landry fought to keep his eyes open, "I'm just telling you what they told me."

"Who are 'they?'" Tom repeated.

We were already at Denver Health emergency. As the rear door opened, Tom said, "Hold it. I've got a couple more questions for this asshole."

The woman EMT stared at him. "You don't have a minute. We've got to get him inside and stabilized. He's lost a lot of blood—-maybe too much. If you let us do our job now, you can probably talk to him in a couple of hours. He might be a little drugged up, although sometimes that works to your advantage. Now get your ass out of the way."

Tom didn't say anything. He jerked his chin toward the door, and we climbed out. The driver said, "Check with the admitting desk in an hour. They'll have some more information. I assume you want a police hold on this guy, right?"

Tom said, "Cuff his goddamn arm to the bed."

The driver grinned. "Don't worry, he sure as hell won't be walking anywhere for a while."

Tom said, "Tough shit, cuff him anyway. I'm not done with him."

chapter

TWENTY-NINE

Tom and I walked into the chaos of the emergency room admitting area. It smelled like a low level UN meeting. Drunks and homeless were triaged down one wall; people with cuts, bruises and bandages sat in chairs along another wall; people holding vomit trays sat on the floor down a hall.

Tom surveyed the scene. "Let's go around back to the staff break room. They've got coffee and we can probably find a chair."

I was still in the mouth-shut mode, nodded, and followed. He led the way past the pukers, around a corner, and into a door marked "ER Staff." Three tired looking people sat at a corner table. We helped ourselves to coffee and went to a table away from the others. We sat and had a sip or two before Tom finally said, "You could have really fucked this deal up. If Landry spills his guts and doesn't start yelling about being tortured or threatened, you might skate. If he changes his mind, or if Biggs or the girl rats you out, you're in deep shit, bucko. What the fuck were you thinking? You can't go in some office and start shooting people for crissakes!"

I opened my eyes as wide as I could and spread out my hands, palms up.

"Fuck you, Cort. Talk, goddamnit."

I would have smiled but didn't think Tom was quite ready for it yet. "I've had a gut feeling all along that Biggs was mixed up in this. It was just gravy when I walked in and Landry was with him. I'll admit I went there to slap Biggs around—- scare some truth out of him. When Landry tried to shut him up, I wasn't going to get anything. It was spontaneous, though—- shooting him like I did.

"I didn't think it through, Tom. If I would have stopped to think, I probably wouldn't have done it. I damn neared puked when I saw his foot."

"Shooting somebody isn't a good way to start an interrogation, even though you got what you were looking for. Maybe you'll get lucky if we have a story Biggs and the girl can buy into. Something that'll keep your ass out of jail. Did you take care of Landry's piece like I said?"

"I did everything just like you told me."

"Good. Your story is you went to the office to talk to Biggs. You barged in on him and Landry who tried to pull a gun left hand-ed—- the dumb shit, you outdrew him, and ended up shooting him in the foot. How does that sound?"

"Whadda you mean...sound? It's *exactly* what happened. We probably need to 'tell' the girl, though, don't you think? And, maybe Biggs, too."

"Let me take care of that. I'll talk to her first when we go to the station. You going to have a lawyer there?"

"You heard me make the call. I hope he shows."

"Just make damn sure you tell him the story exactly the same way. I'll tell Biggs if he's the first guy to cut a deal, you know, *volunteer*, things will go a lot easier for him."

"That might be a tough sell, Tom. He's seen what happens to people who cross the New Orleans crowd."

"Good point. I'll threaten him with conspiracy to murder, murder for hire, and shit like that—- play him off against Landry. I'll say Landry's ready to talk, but if Biggs goes first, I can probably get his charges down to extortion or maybe even fraud."

"If you start cutting deals, don't forget about Gerri, Tom. I guarantee those bastards are mixed up in her murder, too. I particularly don't want Landry walking on that. I'd rather face some charges myself for 'coercing' his confession than have him get off."

"Another good point although Gerri's murder will get tried in Wyoming. You've got to tell me whether you're willing to let him live. It might be that agreeing *not* to go for the death penalty will be our only bargaining chip. What about that, Cort?"

"That's a tough one. Off the top of my head, I'd say fuck him. Let him try to get out of it. There's probably a better chance of Wyoming injecting him, even if he didn't do the job himself. I'm willing to take my chances to see that bastard fry."

"I'm glad to hear you say that. I'm betting Biggs will go along. I'll try to convince him it's his best chance to beat a murder rap."

I drained the last of the crappy coffee. "Let's go see if Landry is coming around."

***

We threw the cups in the trash and headed to Emergency Admitting. As we approached the desk, the admitting nurse looked up. "Good timing, Detective. They've just moved your guy into a bed in the Police Holding area. He's going to make it, although his foot is screwed up big time. There are lots of bones in a foot and the bullet broke several of them. He'll have a bad limp the rest of his life."

"If we're lucky, that won't be too damned long," I said.

The nurse looked surprised. "He must be a bad dude to generate that kind of hate."

Tom warned me off with a glare. "We need to talk to him, regardless. What kind of shape is he in?"

The nurse eyed me carefully, studied Tom for a moment, and said, "He's conscious and doped up, woozy as hell. He'll probably fade in a few minutes."

"Thanks," we both said.

A uniformed cop sat at a small desk left of the door to the police holding ward. "Hey, Tom, they just wheeled your perp in about ten minutes ago. You wanta see him?"

"We do. This is Cort Scott. He's a friend of mine and a PI working this deal. You got the sign-in sheet handy?"

"Right here. Nice to meet you, Scott. I hear you're the guy who plugged this jerk, that right?"

Before I could say anything, Tom asked, "Where'd you hear that, Bobby?"

"One of the EMTs who brought the guy in. She came by while they were working on him. What's up with that?"

"Nothing special. We're just having trouble getting the whole story. Let's not discuss anything with anybody until we know all the facts, okay, Bobby?"

"You got it. Go on in." The cop hit a switch and we heard the lock click.

The ward held eight beds, four on each side of the room. Each bed was in a cubicle like an office with floor-to-ceiling glass partitions. The privacy curtains were all open and Landry was the only patient. The back of his bed was raised and his foot was elevated with a sling contraption like he was in traction. He had a handcuff around his left wrist attached to a chain and cable bolted to the floor beside his bed. His right hand, the one with the cast and finger cages, lay next to his hip. Landry was awake. His eyes had a morphine stare. We each stood on opposite sides of the bed.

Tom spoke in a cold, hard voice. "Start talking. Same rules as before. No bullshit."

Landry turned his head slightly toward Tom. "I told you most of it. I didn't kill anybody. I just put people in touch with each other."

"Why don't you ask me if I give a shit? Look, scumbag, you're in this up to your ass even if it's just conspiracy or solicitation to murder. Here's the deal——- I'll get the DA to charge you with the minimum possible and in return, you've got to give us the names of every guy you've talked to who's involved."

Landry tried to change position, grimaced, and stayed still. He swallowed a couple times and stared at the ceiling. "Okay."

Tom pulled a digital recorder from his pocket, set it on Landry's tray table, checked his watch, and starting speaking in an official tone. "This is Detective Lieutenant Thomas Montgomery, Denver Police. It is 1225 hours on June 23rd. I'm with uncharged suspect Michael Landry and private investigator Cortlandt Scott in the Police Holding facility at Denver Health. Michael Landry has agreed to be questioned in regard to the deaths of Mary Linfield, an Arapahoe County, Colorado resident, and Gerri German, a Denver County resident. Ms. German's death occurred in Green River, Wyoming. Mr. Landry, please verbally acknowledge you are cooperating with this investigation and you are speaking on your own volition without the benefit of an attorney being present. Please be advised you may request an attorney at any time and, should you not be able to retain your own counsel, an attorney will be provided for you."

Landry studied first me and then Tom. His voice was slurred. "I'll talk to you guys now."

"Mr. Landry, describe any meetings you may have had related to the referenced deaths. Start from the beginning."

Landry cleared his throat and managed to sit up a little. "A year ago, I had a meeting with some guys I work for in New Orleans. They were looking for a way to wash some cash coming out of LA and New Orleans, and——-"

Tom interrupted. "Please name those individuals."

Landry swallowed like he had a rock in his throat. "Maurice DiPaulo, James Davidoff, John Marcello from New Orleans and Myron Metropolit and Ron Suarez from LA."

"What was discussed at that meeting?"

"Another guy, Jerome Biggs, told 'em how to set up an energy company that would look legit. They could pump money into it, drag in some sucker investors, and take out clean money. They set Biggs up in an office in Denver and told me to keep an eye on him. They told me to learn something about the business while I was watching out for their money. So I did. I hung out in the office and sat in on meetings. I even had a title, 'negotiator.'"

"What is the name of the company?" Tom started taking notes.

"Black Blizzard Petroleum."

"Are there any other people working for Black Blizzard?"

"Just some broad who answers the phone."

"How is this related to the murders?"

"Black Blizzard was trying to promote a drilling deal and one of the investors who was supposed to be buying in was trying to get his family to put in a bunch of money. The family wouldn't go along, the guy got cold feet and wanted to back out. The New Orleans guys wanted a way to keep him in and to get the family money too. They told me to handle it. They told me to find somebody who would go 'talk' to him and his family."

"Who is this man and his family? What're their names?" Tom was speeding up his questions.

"Jeff Linfield...and the family's name is Linfield too. They live out in the sticks east of Denver. They've got a family investment corporation that Jeff Linfield's sister runs."

Tom paused and checked his notes. "How did you interpret the word 'talk?'"

"They wanted somebody to scare the guy and his family; threaten them if that's what it took."

"Did you know somebody who would have that kind of 'talk?'"

"Yeah, we had a couple of hitters who'd done some stuff for Metropolit and Suarez. Suarez turned out to be Jeff Linfield's brother-in-law. The button men are both Mexicans—- one of 'em is from California. He speaks normal English, not much accent. He was supposed to do the talking."

"What kind of 'stuff' are you referring to?"

"Strong arm work. One time they grabbed a guy who was short changing Suarez on some drugs and beat the shit out of him. They threatened to kill his whole family if he tried doing it again."

"What are the Mexicans' names?"

"Jorge Benitez and Freddy Aquilar. Benitez is the one from California. He pronounces his name 'George.'" Landry gave up their names easier than the New Orleans mobsters.

"Describe in detail what kind of plan was formulated?"

"We decided to fly the Mexicans into Denver and show 'em where the Linfield family lived. They were supposed to grab the woman who had the purse strings and threaten to ruin the family, even kill her brother if she didn't put up the money. I *didn't* tell them to kill her. That was a fucking accident. She was riding her goddamn horse when they surprised her. When they tried to stop her, she sicced the horse on 'em. After they got her down, the horse started jumping around and knocked her off a fucking cliff."

I caught Tom's attention and raised my eyebrows to let him know I wanted to say something. He nodded. "When you said, 'we would show 'em where the Linfield family lived', who was 'we'?"

Landry blinked and his drug stare sharpened. "Biggs and me."

I said, "Did Biggs know the Mexicans were going to kill Mary Linfield?"

"Hell, no. I didn't either. I told you that."

Tom reached over and shut off the recorder. "That puts Biggs in the frame for conspiracy in case we need a little leverage on him." He turned the machine on again. "When did you find out that Mary Linfield had been killed?"

Landry started to squirm, although it appeared to hurt. "The Mexicans came back and told us what happened."

"You *and* Biggs?" I needed to know how much Biggs was involved. Tom shook his head, signaling me to be quiet.

"Yeah. Biggs got all fucked up. He went in the can and puked after they told us."

I couldn't keep quiet. "You didn't puke did you, shithead?" Tom didn't say anything, he pointed at the recorder, and put his finger across his lips.

"Like I said, they weren't supposed to kill her and I didn't tell them to kill her. I was mad as hell when that happened. We weren't going to get any money out of the deal and cops would be swarming all over it. It was too fucking late to change anything."

Tom flipped a page in his notepad. "What happened to Ms. German in Green River."

This time Landry's expression changed. He glanced at me and turned fully toward Tom, as if he didn't want to see me. He tried to clear his throat and said, "Can I have some water?" Tom got the water bottle from the bedside table and put the straw up to Landry's mouth. He managed to swallow some. Tom set the bottle back on the table.

"After the Linfield woman got killed, Jeff Linfield called Suarez and Metropolit. He said he was going to spill his guts to Scott and the cops. I figured we'd catch up with Linfield before he could go to the cops and put a stop to it one way or another. Scott was going to be a problem if Linfield told him the story so I got Benitez and went out to his place. I didn't know nothing about him except he was supposed to be a geologist like Biggs. He'd had some kinda wild hair and was trying to be a private dick, a real tough guy. I figured if he was like Biggs, I could scare him off or, if that didn't work, I'd take care of him, you know, get him out of the picture."

"Did you plan to kill him?" Tom asked.

Landry shot a glance at me. "I didn't think it would come to that. Benitez was already on the hook for the Linfield woman and needed to cover his ass, so I took him with me. I figured if something happened and he did it, at worst, I'd be an accessory."

"So what happened at Scott's?"

"We walked up to the front door and I had a gun on him when he opened it. We started to go in, he surprised us and got my gun away from me. That's where I got this." Landry lifted his right hand with the cast and the bandaged fingers. "We got the hell out of there and went back to the motel where the Mexicans were staying. My fucking hand was broke up bad and hurt like hell. I was mad as shit. I thought about sending the Mexicans back out there to shoot the son-of-a-bitch, but that was too easy—- I wanted to fuck up his whole life."

We heard the ward door open and a nurse entered the cubicle. She came to my side of Landry's bed, checked his vitals, made the chart entries, and left. She never said a word.

Tom rolled his hands at Landry to continue. "The thing was, a couple weeks ago, Biggs told me there was a big lease play breaking out in Wyoming. He wanted to get some lease guys on it and maybe get in the middle. He said the outfit taking the leases was run by Scott's girlfriend. I hadn't thought much about it when he mentioned it, then I got to thinking—- I could do two things at once. We could screw up his girlfriend's deal and I could get back at him at the same time. Somewhere along the line, when the time was right, I planned to bury his ass."

I could feel my blood rising and I found my fists clenched. I wanted to hammer Landry, however I needed to hear the rest of it.

"We started taking leases in the name of our LA company and had only been at it for a few days when the Linfield woman got killed. I called New Orleans and we talked it over. They were some kind of pissed off. We decided we might salvage something out of the Black Blizzard idea if we could find out *exactly* where Scott's girl-friend was leasing. I told Aquilar to take Biggs and break into her condo. They took pictures of her maps and Biggs figured out what leases to go after. He faxed the outlines to the land guys and they got started."

Landry took another drink. "After Scott busted my hand, I wanted to push it harder so I told the Mexicans to go up to Wyoming, grab his girlfriend, and make it look like a burglary gone wrong. I told them to rough her up pretty good. I didn't care how much. That was just going to be gravy, the first part of my payback.

A couple days later, the Mexicans called and said the job I gave them was finished."

I knew what that meant. The job was killing Gerri. The blood began pounding in my brain. I felt nauseous. I knew there was more, although I was ready to finish Landry.

Landry's voice got weaker. "They'd gone back to LA and wanted the rest of their money. I'd fronted them a few grand each and needed to get the rest from New Orleans. We'd been trying to keep the Black Blizzard books straight, so I couldn't take it out of their accounts. I told the greasers to sit tight, that I'd talk to New Orleans and get them the rest in a few days. They didn't like it and got pissed off. I told them they didn't have a choice if they wanted to get paid."

Landry lay back in the bed. He looked used up and his eyes were starting to roll. I motioned to Tom and he stopped the recorder again. I leaned over close. "I don't know what you're going to get for all this, Landry, life without parole isn't enough. Here's a promise for you, asshole, even if we get the Mexicans, I'm coming after you. I don't care if it's twenty years from now when you get out of prison, or if I have to get some con to shank you inside. One way or another, you're going to get yours for what you did to Gerri."

Landry tried to turn his head away and glanced at Tom. Tom just pushed 'record' and said, "That'll be all the questions for now. I'd advise you to have an attorney present next time. The time is 1317 hours." He stopped the machine and stuck it in his pocket. It was his turn to lean close to Landry. "You change one line of your story, dirtball, and I'll make sure you don't even get to prison. You might not get out of this bed!"

Tom finished his notes, closed the pad, and put it in his inside pocket. We went out, nodding at the officer at the entry desk. Tom didn't say a word until we were all the way outside. "You should have shot that prick in the nuts. I'll make goddamn sure nothing comes back at you. Let's get over to headquarters and we'll go through the paperwork. What're you planning to do now?"

"As soon as you turn me loose, I think I'll fly to New Orleans and have a 'talk' with the founders of Black Blizzard Petroleum. It might be the same kind of 'talk' they had with Mary Linfield."

"I expected you to say that. Don't do it. Unless you give me your word to stay put for a while, I'll slap you in jail while I process the paper."

"Goddamn it, Tom—- I've got to do something. I can't sit still and wait."

"I understand that, however if you go charging off half-cocked, one of two things is going to happen and neither of them is good. You're either going to get yourself killed or you're going to screw up any case we can build against all these assholes."

"All right, all right. How're you going after Benitez and Aquilar?"

"We need to get LAPD involved and see what they can do with Ron Suarez. If they can get him to roll over, they might have a chance of catching those fuckers. At the very least, since he was at the original meeting, we can get him on conspiracy to commit murder. It might get us some leverage. Speaking of which, I'll arrest Biggs on the same charges. He heard 'em talk about Mary Linfield, he showed them where she lived, and he told Landry about Gerri. I'm guessing he's scared enough to cop to most anything we throw his way. He'll go away for a long time."

"He may not be in as deep as Landry, although it hardly seems like enough for him either. If we can get those bastards in New Orleans and the Mexicans, it might make up for some of it. I'm sick about how Gerri came to be mixed up in this. If they'd just been trying to bust her play, it would've been one thing, but because she was my girlfriend and I beat Landry up, she got killed. She didn't have a damn thing to do with anything, just me."

"Regardless of how tough it is, you gotta get past it. Now, give me your word you won't go to New Orleans and I'll get you kicked loose as fast as I can."

I nodded, crossed my fingers behind my back, and wondered how I could get a flight scheduled while I was talking to Tom.

chapter

THIRTY

A patrol unit took us back to DPD headquarters. Jason Masters, Esq., briefcase and all, stood inside the lobby entrance. He didn't look at me. "Tom, are you arresting my client?"

Tom stuck out his hand. "Not this time, although I might arrest you for impersonating an attorney." Tom and Jason knew each other from when Jason had been in the DA's office. "Just for the record, I need to ask him some questions and it'd be good if you're there. It shouldn't take more than half an hour."

Tom took us to an interrogation room and I ran through the story from the time I walked into Black Blizzard's office through Landry's interrogation. Jason took pages of notes and didn't say anything while I talked. He did look at me several times. When I finished, he asked, "How much time elapsed from when you went in the door till you shot Landry?"

"Hardly any. He tried to pull his gun, fumbled it, and I shot him."

Jason wrote it down. "Did you fire just once?"

I thought about the slugs I'd put in Biggs' desk and the couch. "No. I was trying to move when I saw Landry going for his gun and fired a couple of other rounds before I hit him."

"How long before you called Tom?"

"Just a couple of minutes, I guess. The girl and I got Landry situated and I called."

Jason looked at Tom. "You have any more questions for him? If not, I assume we can leave."

Tom pointed at the door. "I don't need anything else. Unless Biggs or the receptionist says something different, the dumb bastard won't face charges."

Jason and I walked out to the parking lot. "What the hell was that load of BS? You and Tom sound like you're reading from a script."

"Hey, man, I just underwent a grueling and exhaustive police interrogation. I don't need another grilling from my lawyer."

"If that's the way you're going to play it, I can't do much about it. I also know you're lying through your teeth about what went down. What are you planning to do now?"

"I'm either going to LA after the Mexicans, or I'm going to New Orleans for the assholes who set the whole thing in motion."

"It's not my business, although the way you're headed, that seems likely to change. You need to think carefully about what you're doing. You're a geologist and oilman, for Christ sake, not a judge, jury, and executioner. You're going to get in way over your head if you're not careful. You could get killed running around in places you don't know anything about."

"I just heard all that from Tom. Hell, I've read all of James Lee Burke's books about south 'Luz-e-anna' and all of Michael Connelly's and Robert Crais' books about LA. What the hell else do I need to know?"

"You need to know you're a wise-ass trying to act like a tough guy and it ain't working."

***

I walked the eight blocks to my office, went in, and locked the door behind me. The message light was blinking—- I had seventeen messages. I scrolled through until one caught my eye. It was from Martin Gear, Gerri's partner and the cofounder of Mountain West Gas Exploration. We'd been friends for years. I hit the call back button and he picked up immediately.

"Cort? Thanks for calling back. I'm so sorry about Gerri. I'm so sorry for you. This is unbelievable. These have been the worst two days of my life. Everything is going to hell in a hand basket. I can't handle everything that's happening and I need some help. Can you take an hour or so and come by?"

I paused before answering. "I'm already underwater, Martin. I'm trying to do several things at the moment."

Martin sounded frantic. "Besides what you and Gerri had going personally, you're one of our major shareholders. I've gotta make a bunch of business decisions and I need to make them right now. You're the only one I can turn to for help."

"I have to look after Gerri's funeral and those kinds of things."

"I understand, but all hell is breaking loose up at the well. Some of this stuff can't wait. You know more about the play than anybody and a lot more about the science and geology than me. I really need to see you right now." Martin's career had been as a landman. He didn't know much about the operations end of the business.

"All right, Martin, I'll come over. I can give you an hour... that's it. Calm down if you can—- we'll get it sorted. I'm on my way."

"Thanks, Cort. I really appreciate it."

I hung up, scanned the rest of the messages, and didn't see anything urgent. Most of them were from friends of mine or Gerri's or both. They were probably condolences or offers of help. I would get to them later.

I opened my locked cabinet and took out the file for the company. It had the board minutes and my notes from technical meetings I'd attended. I checked the wall clock: 3:30. I would give Martin his hour.

***

I walked across to the 17ᵗʰ Street Plaza Building and took the elevator to the twenty-sixth floor. The glass doors, with Mountain West Gas Exploration centered across both doors, were closed as usual. The same glass artist who'd done the engraved aspens and alpine scenery in my hot tub room had done the mountain scene with superimposed drilling rigs on these.

Peggy Sue Crandall was behind the receptionist's desk. Although nearing fifty, under bar lights she looked mid-thirties. Today, she looked her age. She was wearing a green sweater and her dark brown hair was pulled back in a simple ponytail. Her eyes were red and her face was flushed. She'd been crying. When I walked in, I heard her breath catch in her throat. "Go on in. He's expecting you. I'm so sorry about Gerri. I don't know how we're going to make it through this, especially Martin. I think he's at the end of his rope." This was the toughest so far. Peggy Sue had been with Gerri in every job she'd had. She'd known her longer than anyone. "Thanks, Peggy Sue. We'll get through it, I promise." I wished I could believe it.

Her head sank and when she raised up, tears were streaming down her face. Her voice was stronger, though. "You were her rock. I know you'll see everything through just the way she would have."

Martin sat at the side of his desk staring out the window. His office faced east and I saw the circus tent roof of Denver International Airport's terminal on the horizon. I took the guest chair and put the file on his desk. Martin sat still. He seemed to be gathering the strength to talk. "Thanks for coming. I didn't know who else to call." His voice was husky and his eyes were blood-shot and puffy.

"Coming here wouldn't be my first choice. I'll do what I can. I don't have a lot of time so let's get to it. What do you need to do immediately?"

Martin walked behind his desk, picked up a stack of papers, and handed it to me. It was the last few days' drilling reports. I went back four days—- to the last one Gerri had told me about. Since then, they'd run the intermediate casing, let the cement set up, drilled out, and were drilling deeper. Yesterday, they'd taken another heavy gas kick and ended up shutting in the blowout preventer to control the well. The surface pressure had reached almost nine-thousand pounds, which was near the limit they could control. After bleeding off the gas for several hours, they managed to pump heavy drilling mud down the well and get everything under control. Now, they were drilling ahead cautiously and continuing to mix heavy mud, which was coming back highly cut by gas. This had gone on for nearly a hundred feet. I got out the well-site geologist's log and compared it to Gerri's drilling prognosis.

I turned to Martin. "If I'm correlating this correctly, you're in the main pay zone and it might be a lot thicker than Gerri expected, which means more gas reserves. In addition, you've got several shallower reservoirs where you took the gas kicks last week. I think you've got a real barnburner. It's at least as big as she thought and maybe a lot more. Congratulations."

"What the hell good is it, Cort?" Martin's voice was low and raspy. "This is Gerri's prospect—- everything she'd worked for over the last ten years. It'll make a lot of people rich, me and you included. What the hell good is it if Gerri's gone? What the hell happened? Why is she dead?" Martin's nose began to drip and tears ran down his face.

It hit me that Martin had been in love with Gerri too. His wife had died six or seven years ago and he'd thrown himself into work. He didn't have kids and was several years older than Gerri. I'd always believed he thought of us as the kids he didn't have. I'd been wrong, although he might have seen me that way. He'd been in love with Gerri.

I walked around the desk and put my hand on his shoulder. "I think I know how you felt about Gerri and I understand. We all loved her. Gerri would want us to get through this and make the project work. It's the least we can do for her." It hurt like hell to be the one offering solace and guidance. I was the one who needed it.

Martin slumped in his chair. He put his head in his hands and didn't raise it for several seconds. When he did, his eyes were better and his breathing had eased. "I was attracted to her romantically, you know. I never told her...maybe I should have. I saw how it was with the two of you and couldn't say anything. Now, we've both lost her forever. This prospect meant everything to her and she deserves to get the credit. We need to make sure it works."

He stood and I stepped back. "I need two things, Cort. First, I want you to take over for her on the technical side of things, at least for this one well. And, second, I want you to go after whoever killed her. She told me about your private detective business and thought you had a chance to be good at it. If you're as good as she thought, you can do both things."

"All right, Martin, I'll take over the project—- only this one. I don't want to go back to working 24/7 in the oil and gas business. And, I'll find the bastards who killed her too. I'm already on it—- you didn't have to ask."

We shook hands. He had a strong grip for a guy who'd pushed pencils and colored land maps for forty years.

"Let's go to Gerri's office," I said. "I'm sure she has the prospect maps laid out and some logs to correlate with the well-site report. I'll see if I can come up with a revised well completion plan and where you need to concentrate your leasing for the next few weeks. I'll have the daily reports sent directly to my cell so I can keep up with what's happening at the well."

We walked around the corner to Gerri's office. I had to smile when I saw her drafting table and desk. Maps, reports, and electrical logs were scattered around like a mad woman's shit, as Hedges used to say. Gerri had not been a neat freak. She used to say everything she had was filed under "F" for "File." Luckily, the Green River Basin data was at the top of the pile.

Martin shook his head at the mess. "Good luck. I know you worked with her so if anyone can figure out her system, you can." He walked out and I heard his office door close behind him.

I laid out the drilling time plot next to an electric log graph from the closest abandoned dry hole to Gerri's well. The old well had been drilled thirty years ago and, although it had reported lots of gas shows, had never been completed. In those days, there were no gas pipelines in the area and gas was only worth ten or fifteen cents per thousand cubic feet. Now, it was more like five dollars and pipelines were within a couple of miles in two directions. If my correlation was correct, the old well had stopped just a few feet above the zone Gerri's well had encountered. The shallower zones had similar gas shows. Thirty years ago, they had stopped drilling too soon.

I pulled out her maps and cross-sections of the prospect and it was easy to see how she correlated to the deeper gas pay zones in wells over ten miles away on either side of her drillsite. She'd projected them across her location at exactly the depth they'd reached. She'd been right—- this was a major gas field. It would be measured in trillions of cubic feet of natural gas. It'd be worth billions of dollars to Mountain West and its investors—- including me.

I found a lease map printed on clear acetate and laid it over Gerri's prospect map. The company owned most of the leases around the wellsite and south, but had only scattered coverage to the north. That was where Gerri had been trying to lease new acreage and had discovered LA Warehouse Leasing taking top leases. Anyone searching the lease records could have figured out Mountain West's lease position and could have taken nearby leases—- a strategy called "closeology." Buying leases close to someone else's idea wasn't illegal. When Biggs had burgled Gerri's condo, he'd found the exact leases she thought were prospective. He'd given the descriptions to landmen working for LA Warehouse Leasing. The landmen were just contract guys. They didn't know their instructions were coming from a crooked outfit and based on stolen, proprietary information. They took top leases where Biggs directed them.

I spent another twenty minutes studying the maps and cross sections and wrote some notes for Martin. Finally, I picked up my stuff and went back to his office. "I've got a bunch of information for you," I said. "Let's get Peggy Sue in here so she can take everything down and make copies of my notes so we'll all be working off the same pages."

Martin called Peggy Sue and we gathered around the map I spread out on the desk. "Think about the prospect as looking like Galveston Island down in Texas, except it's filled with gas and buried under fifteen thousand feet of rock. It's twenty or thirty miles long, five miles wide, and a hundred feet thick. Picture the well as located in the southern third of the island. We've got a good lease position around the location and to the south. Our problem is, we're wide open north. That's where we need to concentrate.

"Here's the bad news—- Gerri called me last week and I found a letter from her in my office mail this morning confirming what she'd told me. She found an outfit called LA Warehouse Leasing taking leases north of the well plus they're top leasing us. They're a front for Black Blizzard Petroleum—- where Jerome Biggs works. Biggs broke into Gerri's condo and got her lease outlines. Another guy named Landry sent two killers to Wyoming after Gerri to get revenge on me. The same guys killed a woman here in Colorado. A woman I was helping on a case."

"*Goddamn motherfuckers!*" Peggy Sue's voice was shrill in the quiet office and stunned me. I'd never heard her swear before. She was blinking rapidly. There were no tears in her eyes now.

"Here's what we need to do," I said. "Martin, you need to either go to Wyoming yourself, or send somebody you trust and start retracing Gerri's steps. Green River PD has her papers and she will have written down legal descriptions or taken copies of the top leases she found. The cop heading the investigation is Jim Carstairs. He's a good guy and I'll give him a call. You need to go back to those ranchers and find out if they've cashed the top lease drafts yet. For the ones who haven't, tell them exactly what happened to Gerri and who did it. Tell 'em the people behind LA Warehouse Leasing are going to prison. That should buy us some time to clean up the lease situation which we've got to do before completing the well. It might be several months before we complete. Hopefully, the rumors will die down quickly when we quit drilling and that'll help the lease buyers."

I did a quick, back-of-the-envelope calculation. "Do you guys have any inkling of how big this could be?"

Martin raised his eyebrows, Peggy Sue shook her head.

"It's astounding. This thing could be Mid-East big. I'm talking about *fifty trillion* cubic feet of natural gas worth over two hundred and fifty *billion* dollars. It's bigger than Gerri's wildest dreams—- or anybody else's."

Martin and Peggy Sue stood in stunned silence for several moments.

Peggy Sue said, "Concentrate on getting the killers, Cort."

chapter

THIRTY-ONE

I programmed my cell phone to receive the automated daily drilling reports, gathered up what I needed, and went back across the street. I had a message from Jeff Linfield. "I just got off the phone with George Albins. I can't tell you how sorry I am about your girlfriend. If there's anything I can do, please let me know. I'm staying at the ranch until Mary's services on Friday. They're at the Byers Methodist church at 10:00 a.m. I hope you can make it, we'd all appreciate your being there. Also, I need to make arrangements to drop off your Bronco, so give me a call whenever you can. Take care and I'll speak to you soon."

I got the rest of the things I needed, locked up, and headed for my car. I drove out, circled the block to hit 17th Street, and then south on Broadway. This would be the long way home. It would give me time to think.

By the time I got to I-25, I'd made up my mind. I hadn't lied to Tom, I wouldn't go to New Orleans—- I'd go to LA. I'd call Jeff and see what else he could tell me about Ron Suarez. If I could get to Suarez before the LA cops or his New Orleans bosses put heat on him and he ran, there might be a chance to find the killers. Since my interrogation technique had worked pretty well with Biggs and Landry, maybe I could come up with the same results in LA even if I didn't have a friend in the police department to cover for me.

Traffic was heavy all the way home. I thought about Lindsey when I passed Belleview; the roof of Cool River was barely visible from the highway. I wasn't ready to call her yet. I kept thinking about "closure." I was used to seeing the word whenever anybody was killed who shouldn't have been. Everyone close to the victim needed closure. I wasn't exactly sure how it was supposed to work, although if I could catch the killers, it might help. I didn't know if it would ever allow me to be with Lindsey—- for now, I couldn't be with her anyway.

At home, I went straight to my office and called Jeff. His voice was sincere when he said, "I'm sure sorry about your girlfriend."

"I appreciate that, Jeff. It's tough. You're one of the few who can appreciate how bad it really is."

"I meant what I said about helping. I've behaved about as badly as could be imagined. I'd like to feel I'm helping out some way."

"Some things have changed that might make you feel a little better, although nothing's over yet" I told him about what had happened at Black Blizzard's office and how Landry and Biggs were in custody.

Jeff was quiet during my story. "It sounds like everything might be coming to a head. What did you mean by it not being over?"

"It's not over until I've got the guys who killed Gerri and your sister. And I mean dead or alive. I want to get the New Orleans assholes and Metropolit too."

"I understand. What can I do?"

"I'm going to LA and shake up Ron Suarez. I'm hoping he'll give up the Mexicans who did the killings. I need to know how to find him."

"His office is 35 Harbor View in Long Beach. It's right off the Seaside Freeway just before the toll bridge. You know, don't you, that he's in the same offices with Metropolit? I don't know how often Metropolit is there, I think Ron goes in every day."

"Maybe I'll get lucky, like with Biggs and Landry, and catch them together. From what you've said, it sounds like Metropolit might be the weak link in the chain as far as the New Orleans bunch goes."

"I don't know anything about that, he's the only one I've met. Cort, there's something else you need to know...I've told Maria everything. She wasn't that surprised about Ron. She's already been to Tahoe and packed. We're meeting where nobody will think to look for us. We'll stay away until everything is settled. I'll check in every few days until it's safe to come back."

"She sounds like a good person. Thanks for calling and offering to help. I need to get moving on this. Be careful with what you say and do until I tell you it's safe."

I heard Jeff sigh. "I hope for Maria's sake you don't have to fight it out with Ron. I still feel responsible for Mary, I would hate to see him get killed—- he's still my wife's brother."

"That'll be up to him. I won't make any promises. He's facing some serious prison time regardless of whether he cooperates. It will be better for his health if he does."

Jeff said, "When are you leaving? What about Mary's funeral? And what about your truck?"

"I can't wait, Jeff. As much as I want to be there for Mary and your family, this is more important. You can just park the truck in my driveway and lock the keys inside. I've got another set in the house. I assume Evan or somebody can follow you over and get you back."

"No problem. That's what we'll do. If you need to talk to me, call my home in Tahoe and leave messages. I'll check it as often as I can and return your calls from wherever we end up staying."

I sighed. "Jeff, please give my deepest condolences to Bob, Julie, and Evan. I hope they'll understand why I can't be there."

***

I called Tom intending to leave a message and was surprised when he picked up. "Hey, Tom, I need a favor."

"What the hell else is new? Did you shoot another citizen?"

"Not yet. You'll be the first to know when I do."

He laughed. "I believe that for damn sure," he said. "What's the favor?"

"Don't worry about me going to New Orleans—- I'm going to LA. I wanted to know if you've contacted LAPD."

"I *knew* I couldn't trust you not to do something stupid. Actually, I expected it—- at least LA is better than New Orleans. No, I haven't talked to the cops yet. I was trying to get my notes in order first. What difference does it make?"

"I talked to Jeff Linfield and I know exactly where to find Suarez and maybe Metropolit. I thought I'd have a talk with them before the cops do, try to get them to give me the hitters."

"Why the hell would they do that? You don't have any leverage."

"I do if I'm the one who tells them about Biggs and Landry, that I shot Landry, and that they're both singing like Barbra Streisand. Those guys know Landry can tie them to everything. I'll tell 'em if they cooperate it might go easier for them. If the police go there to question them, they're going to clam up and bring in a lawyer. I'll tell them I don't give a shit about them and I only want the killers. If they don't give 'em up, I've got my Landry story to convince 'em."

"I'll give you this much, Cort, shooting Landry got him and Biggs talking, for sure. When I interrogated Biggs, he was falling all over himself to spill his guts. He's resigned to doing some hard time.

He just doesn't want it to be anywhere around Landry—- and, he's scared shitless of you."

"That's a good thing. I want that bastard to be scared." It felt good to say it out loud.

"I don't know if the same crap will work on the other two... probably worth a try. I'll give you a couple days before I call LAPD. When I do, I'll tell 'em we've got two mugs here talking about murders and they've implicated some guys in LA. I'll tell them you might already be there, you're a loose cannon although on the good guys' team. If you get any info out of Suarez and Metropolit, you need to pass it on to LAPD, in due time, of course."

"What constitutes 'due time?'"

"Just enough to give you a head start. If you catch up with the Mexicans, you'll have to make a decision. I doubt if there's enough evidence to convict them of first degree murder in Colorado—- I can't speak for Wyoming. Chances are they'd go away for a long time. Between you and me, that ain't good enough. If you have absolutely no doubt you've got the right guys, you'll know what to do. If you're lucky, they'll make a fight of it so everything will come down to self-defense. If they just give it up, make it look good. And forget we ever had this conversation."

"I hear you. Thanks, Tom. I'll head for LA as soon as I can get a flight. I understand you've been talking to George Albins. Have you brought him up to date on everything we know?"

"Mostly. It wouldn't hurt for you to give him a call. He really wants to lay hands on whoever did Mary Linfield. He'd known her for a long time. Her murder is at the top of his list."

"I'll do that after I talk to Kirk about flying me to LA." The part about George knowing Mary Linfield "for a long time" seemed different from what he'd said at the ranch.

"Listen to me for once—- be careful out there. We know these guys play rough and they're liable to be suspicious since they haven't heard from Biggs or Landry in a couple days. I asked Biggs about that and he said they hadn't talked to them since the day after Gerri was found."

"Got it, pards. I'll call you from LA if I do any good."

"Call me *however* you're doing. See you when you get back."

I called Kirk Chase at home. "Kirk, I need to get to LA as quickly as possible. Is there any way you guys could get me there first thing in the morning?"

"What about tonight? Is that too soon?"

"Are you serious? Tonight would be even better. What time?"

"Whenever you want to go. We can be wheels up fifteen minutes after you park your car."

"That's great. I need to make a couple more calls. Let's shoot for 7:30."

"You got it."

I decided to call George Albins and let him know what I had planned. "George, it's Cort Scott."

"Good to hear from you. Tom Montgomery called earlier to tell me what's going on. Sounds like you found out some things that might get us headed in the right direction."

"I think they could. I've got a line on Ron Suarez and Metropolit. Suarez is Jeff Linfield's brother-in-law and the guy who got Jeff mixed up in this mess."

"I know who he is, Jeff told me about him. And Metropolit is a bag man for New Orleans, right?"

"That's right. Jeff told me where to find 'em. I'm headed to LA in about an hour. I've got a friend who flies a charter jet. Tom's giving me a couple days' head start before he lets LAPD know what we've found out. I'm hoping I can convince Suarez and Metropolit to give up the Mexicans."

"Do you plan to use the same 'convincing' tactics you did on Landry?" George's tone bothered me a little. I didn't know how much Tom had told him. Obviously, enough to make him ask the question.

"That depends on them. I need to see what they're willing to do and then I'll play it by ear. Why do you ask?"

"I just wondered if you'd like a little company. I can spare a couple of days and maybe my being there would make it a little more, shall we say, 'official.'"

What the hell was George saying? Did he want to make sure I didn't shoot somebody else, or didn't he think I could handle the assholes?

"I don't know how to answer that. I would definitely like the help, though my interrogation style might not be the same as yours."

"I'm not going to get in the way if that's what you're worried about." George's voice was firm. "I want those bastards about as bad as you and how we get it done isn't a huge concern to me. I've got a friend in the LA County Sheriff's department who can give us some off-the-book help if we need it."

"Can you be packed and ready to go in an hour?"

"I'm packed now. I assume you're flying out of Centennial. I can be there in ten minutes."

"I'll be there at 7:30. Meet me at Mountain Man Air Service."

That was a strange conversation. What was motivating Albins to drop everything, go "off-the-book," and fly to California with me?

chapter

THIRTY-TWO

I opened the gun safe, surveyed my small arsenal, and selected the Beretta .38 and the big Colt Army .45 automatic. I put the guns in a hard sided, briefcase sized carry case along with an extra clip for each one. Next, I packed a small travel bag and my shaving kit, checked all the locks, set my alarm system, and took off. As I drove to Centennial, I kept thinking about what Tom had said about George knowing Mary Linfield well.

At Mountain Man Air, I saw George standing beside a Ford F-150 pickup. He had a small carry-on bag and a hard-sided briefcase similar to mine. I knew what was inside.

I parked two spaces away and grabbed my gear. "Thanks for coming. I can use the help."

George stuck out his hand and we shook. He had on Wranglers, boots, and a Stetson. No sign of badges or insignias anywhere. "This thing with Mary has been eating me up and I want a hand in closing it out, one way or another. I appreciate your willingness to bring me along."

"I'm planning on closing it out, one way or another."

We saw the pilots standing near the sliding doors to the tarmac. I started to introduce George but Kirk stopped me and said, "We know George. We've flown him all over Colorado and the Rockies. It looks like you're out of uniform for this one, George?"

"I'd just as soon you guys forget I'm along," George replied.

"You got it—- if you're ready, we are," Clark said.

We hurried to the Falcon, loaded our stuff in the storage area behind the cargo net, and took the same seats Tom and I had for the trip to Green River. Kirk got in the left seat while Clark buttoned up the door and joined him up front. "Make yourself a drink if you want. We'll sit here for a couple minutes while we run through the checklist. Be sure and buckle in when we start to taxi."

I raised an eyebrow at George and he nodded. "What's your pleasure? Scotch, bourbon, vodka, or beer?"

"Just a couple fingers of bourbon over one ice cube."

I found a bottle of Knob Creek whiskey, good stuff by all accounts, poured a generous amount over the ice, and handed it to George. I poured myself a stiff shot of Talisker scotch, neat.

We both took a sip and settled back as the Falcon started to roll out. The take-off was smooth...like being shot out of a slingshot. As soon as we were airborne, Kirk said, "We're going for pure speed tonight, guys. We've got a little bit of a headwind so we're climbing to about forty-one thousand and kicking it in the tail. We should be able to make John Wayne Airport in just a hair over two hours, about 8:30 their time. What are you guys doing for wheels out there?"

Shit, I hadn't even thought about it. "What're my choices?"

"I can take care of it," George said. "Can you get patched through to the sheriff's office in the airport?"

"No problem."

"My friend works the airport detail. He'll arrange an unmarked of some kind. We'll have it when we land."

I gave him an air toast. "I knew I brought you along for something."

We had another drink somewhere over northern Arizona and sketched out a game plan for the next day. George would fill his sheriff buddy in on what was going down. He said we could trust the guy implicitly and he'd give us any kind of help we needed. We'd pick up the car and find a motel near the harbor. We planned to get up early and be at LA Warehouse Leasing's office around 8:30. The idea was to hang out and watch the place for an hour or so to see who was coming and going. Neither of us knew Suarez or Metropolit on sight, although we'd both seen a mug shot of Metropolit. If we were lucky, they'd be together.

I finally had to ask, "Are you all right with this? You sound like you're not that concerned with what goes down—- that you just want to get it over with."

George sipped his whiskey and was silent for a moment. "I don't give a shit about what happens to these guys, Cort. I misled you and the Linfields about Mary. Truth is, I was in love with Mary Linfield for twenty years. I met her when we were both showing horses. I knew her brother, Randy, a little before he married Julie. Bob was always away at school so we never met. Jeff was just a snot-nosed kid running around the ranch. He doesn't remember me.

"We were close to making a go of it when her dad got sick and died. Mary didn't deal with his passing real well and then her mother passed right after. She and Randy got all caught up in running the ranch and holding everything together. We talked some and then finally just sorta drifted apart. I didn't see her for years—- until Randy's funeral and there was no time to talk." He finished the drink and sat in silence for several more seconds.

"I didn't tell Sheriff Weaver about me and Mary. He wouldn't have let me run the case and I wanta be in on nailing the killers. Nothing's gonna bother me about how we get whatever we need from Suarez or Metropolit. The only thing that matters is getting the bastards who killed her. I owe her that much. Maybe I owe myself."

It was the longest speech I'd heard from George. He told the story with a firm, steady voice and looked straight at me. I didn't know what to say so I just reached across the aisle and offered my hand. He took it and we nodded.

We touched down at 8:35 local time at the fixed base operator's ground facility, grabbed our gear, and caught a courtesy car to the main terminal. As we were getting in the car, I pulled Kirk to the side. "I don't have a clue how long this'll take. It might be over tomorrow, it could be three or four days. I don't know what to tell you."

"I don't have any charters until Tuesday so I'm content to leave the plane on the ground for a couple, three days. Clark and I'll get a car and drive down to San Diego and play Torrey Pines or something. You've got my cell number—- if you get what you need, give me a call and we'll haul you back. If you don't finish up, we need to leave around noon on Monday."

"Sounds like a plan. I'll be in touch. Thanks, again."

"Just make sure you tag those guys."

***

We found the sheriff's office next to Airport Security and went in. A big uniform stood up and grabbed George's hand. "I saw your plane was in. How the hell are you? Thanks for all the advance notice, buddy."

"Good to see you too, Buck. Long time. Meet Cort Scott. Cort, this is Buck Welks. We go back a long way. We were MPs in the Corps and ended up doing a tour in Desert Storm." George pointed at me. "He's a PI in Denver and one of his clients was murdered in my county, someone I knew. We started working together on the case and now it looks like the same assholes killed his girlfriend. Both murders are tied to a scam financed with drug money coming out of LA. We've got a lead on two players here who can point us toward the killers."

Welks and I shook hands. He motioned to the other officer who strolled over to join us. "This is Tim Burgess. You guys can say

anything in front of him you'd say to me. He's my brother-in-law."
George and I shook hands with Burgess.

We all sat. Welks said, "Tell us what we need to know and how
we can help. We've got a set of wheels for you when you're ready."
George told the story to the deputies. He didn't flinch when he told
them we intended to do whatever it took to get information out of
Suarez and Metropolit. They didn't seem to care and said they'd like
a shot at them for running dope if it worked out.

We'd talked for forty-five minutes when Buck said, "All right,
we've got it. Let's go get your rig. I checked out an unmarked Dodge
Durango for you. It doesn't look anything like a cop car, the new
undersheriff treats it like his private vehicle. Try not to get it shot up
or anything."

George grinned and said, "We'll be real careful...Say, where
are the entry forms for the Baja Off-Road race?"

Buck and Tim laughed.

***

We decided to cruise the LA Warehouse Leasing office and
find a handy motel. George drove and we rode most of the way in
silence. When we hit the Seaside Freeway, we searched for Harbor
Way as we approached the toll bridge, found it and took a left to
number thirty-five. It was a typical warehouse/office building with a
dozen parking spots out front and four palm trees equally spaced in
small grassy areas. The entrance was in the center of the building up
a short sidewalk from the lot. Flood lights at the top corners of the
building trained down at the sidewalk and entrance. The place was
totally nondescript and resembled a hundred others around the area.

We got back on the freeway, drove a mile to a La Quinta Inn,
and checked in. When we got to the rooms, which were adjoining,
we agreed to meet in the coffee shop at 7:30 a.m.. I dropped my
bags on the bed and turned on the TV. The Dodgers were playing
the Rockies back in Denver. Although I had some interest in hearing Vin Scully call the game, I decided to go for a run on the beach
instead. I needed to clear my head and stretch from the plane ride.

The stretching part worked out, however, it was impossible to clear my mind. Too many traumatic things had happened in quick succession. My first client and my girlfriend had been murdered. I'd shot a guy who was not the killer. Now, I was twelve-hundred miles from home and traveling with a revenge seeking cop who was off-the-clock. I was planning to get information from Suarez and Metropolit by any means including torture or injury. It turned out to be too much to clear out with a run on the beach.

chapter

THIRTY-THREE

I rolled out at 6:10, cleaned up, and pulled on khakis, a golf shirt, and running shoes in case I had to move quickly today. I turned on my phone and checked on Gerri's well. They'd drilled another sixty feet since yesterday and the geologist thought they were through the big gas sand. If he was right, the reservoir sand was almost ninety feet thick. Current operations were circulating mud to clean the drill hole in preparation to run production casing. Martin was following the plan I'd laid out.

As I was reading the report, my cell rang. I didn't recognize the number so answered, "Cort Scott."

It was Jeff Linfield who said, "Morning, I just thought I'd check in."

I said, "Good idea. Did you find someplace safe?"

"I think so. I'm calling on a burn phone, I don't think it can be traced. How about you?"

"I'm here. I'll be going to see your brother-in-law later this morning."

"I hope you find out what you need. Be careful and let me know what happens."

"I'll try."

I hung up and checked my watch: 6:50. Jeff was either an early riser or he was somewhere farther east in a different time zone. The coffee shop was an indoor/outdoor set up with six tables and umbrellas outside. George was sitting at the end of the patio. A middle-aged woman was seated at another table closer to the door. Two couples were inside at separate tables. I stopped at the coffee bar, filled a cup, and joined George.

"Morning. Get any sleep?" I asked as I sat down.

"Two drinks and the flight did the trick. I slept until 5:30, which is about the same time I get up at home. You?"

"Went for a run on the beach trying to get everything straight in my head."

"Did it work?"

"It felt good. I'm not sure about clearing anything up."

George waved his hand through the air in the direction of the ocean. "Fabulous weather, I expected it to be hotter."

"I guess we should count ourselves lucky, particularly if we have to spend much time in the car today. Jeff Linfield called to say he and his wife are someplace safe. He didn't tell me where, which is fine because I don't need to know. We can make contact through his home phone if we need to. He's calling on throwaway cells. We need to make sure Suarez and Metropolit are in jail before we give him the all-clear to go back to Tahoe."

George nodded. "I agree. I'm glad Jeff didn't turn out to be the bad guy in all this. It's too bad it took Mary's murder to scare him straight."

I gazed at the beach. "I hope his wife isn't involved...other than being Ron Suarez's sister."

We drank coffee for a few minutes and went through the breakfast buffet. We both picked up cereal and fruit, although I couldn't resist a big sticky, frosted cinnamon bun. George laughed and said, "There's another five miles."

***

We finished, agreed to meet at the car in five minutes, and went back to the rooms. I opened my gun case, took out the Beretta, and put it in my shoulder holster. I put an extra clip in the pocket of the light jacket I'd brought to cover everything without being hot. I left the .45 and its extra clips in the case, closed it, and prepared to leave. I looked in the mirror and thought, here I go—- I hope I'm tough enough for this. I didn't feel that tough.

George was already in the driver's seat when I got to the Durango. I opened the back door and set the gun case behind the passenger seat; George's case was behind his seat. We drove the short distance to Harbor Way, and stopped half a block from the office. The Durango had high seatbacks with built-in head rests so it was impossible for someone approaching from behind to see us inside. Anyone coming the other way wouldn't bother to look at a rig parked half a block away on the other side of the street. Only a couple of other cars were on the street.

We waited silently for twenty minutes until George said, "Do you have something going on with Lindsey Collins?"

It came as a surprise and I didn't know how to answer. "I'm not going to lie to you, George—- I've been with Lindsey. I was with her when Gerri was in Green River and it's driving me crazy.

"I don't know how to explain about Gerri and me, we'd been together for a long time and were more than friends. We didn't have any arrangements, or rules, or ties that bind. Lindsey made the first move...she called me, said she knew about Gerri, and wasn't trying to get between us, but wanted to get together. I agreed and that's how it started. I know it's absolutely no excuse for the timing...or for anything else. The whole thing is tearing me up and I don't know how to deal with it other than trying to catch the guys who killed Gerri.

"It's extremely rough on Lindsey, too. She called me after Gerri's murder and said she'd stay out of the scene until I told her different—- forever if that's the way it turns out. I don't have an answer for that—- I'm a tunnel vision guy, I need to get this business taken care of before I can think about anything else. What made you ask?"

"Just a shot in the dark." George said. "Lindsey kept coming into my office and asking about you...how you were doing. She said she wanted to help you any way she could and just seemed way too interested. Look, I'm not judging you...either one of you. It is what it is. Fact is...we need to have everything out in the open. We're about to start something that might be hard to finish if we don't trust each other."

"Fair enough." I wished that whatever was going to happen would get started. I didn't have long to wait.

chapter

THIRTY-FOUR

We resumed our silence. It was getting warm in the car, so we cracked the windows hoping for a breeze. A silver Cadillac Escalade passed us from behind and pulled into a slot in front of 35 Harbor Way. The driver leaned over to the passenger seat and seemed to be looking through something for a couple minutes. Finally, the door opened and Myron Metropolit got out. He walked around the car and opened the passenger door. He struggled with lifting a large square-topped briefcase. "That's Metropolit," I said.

"Jesus, he's an old man. I had him pictured a lot younger."

I said, "I wouldn't let his looks fool you. He's been a bagman and numbers guy for organized crime his entire life. I don't know if he's been personally involved in any violence, regardless, he damn sure knows it happens."

"I don't know if that's good or bad. If it's a good thing, he might give up some information without much trouble. If it's bad, he might not threaten too easily. Either way, we probably need to wait and see if Suarez shows."

"I agree."

We didn't have long to wait. A red Jeep Cherokee pulled into the lot and parked next to Metropolit's Cadillac. A medium-build guy with short black hair wearing Levis and a black shirt with a sport coat got out and started up the sidewalk. Although neither of us had seen pictures of Ron Suarez, this guy matched the description Jeff had given me. I looked at George. "Whadda you think? Should we make our play?"

"Good a time as any. Let's go."

We bailed out and started up the sidewalk. George had a light jacket like mine covering his gun. I would have placed a large wager he wasn't packing his sheriff's service piece.

The door was unlocked, we pulled it open, and went in. The tiny entry opened directly to a long hallway with several doors on each side. To the left was an open, two-flight stairway to the upper floors. A plastic chain blocked the stairway entrance with a sign reading *No Admittance*. A computer printed sign posted on the wall outside the hallway said, *LA Warehouse Leasing, Suite* 112 with an arrow pointing down the hall. Under that, another sheet sign said, *M. Metropolit, Suite* 114.

We unsnapped our jackets and took out the guns. George had a 9mm auto in a shoulder rig similar to mine. He gave the index finger-across-the-lips sign for quiet and took the lead down the hallway. The first office was 102 and the next was 104. That made 112 and 114 the last two on the left. Those doors were open with light streaming across the hallway. The other doors were shut. I didn't like that, however, we didn't get a vote. A thin industrial grade carpet over the cement floor made our entrance silent.

Halfway down the hall, George pointed at me, turned and pointed at the first open door, then raised his index finger. He pointed at himself, raised two fingers, and pointed at the second door. I nodded. He wanted me to go into 112 and he'd go into 114 at the same time. We walked silently toward the doors.

We could hear a mix of music playing. George mouthed the word "ready" and raised his eyebrows. I nodded. We got side-by-side and jumped the remaining distance into the doorways.

The office was small, maybe fifteen by fifteen, with two windows on the back wall. The guy I believed to be Ron Suarez was sitting at a desk reading a newspaper. Manila folders lay on the desk next to a monitor. The screen was lit and Latino rock music was coming from the computer speakers.

The guy looked up and stared at the gun in my hand. He didn't say anything. I stepped inside and said, "Ron Suarez?"

He kept staring at the gun. "Who's asking? What's up with the gun? Do I know you?"

"Are you the Ron Suarez whose sister, Maria, is married to Jeff Linfield?" I repeated.

"What if I am? Who the hell are you? Why're you pointing a fucking gun at me?"

"I'm the guy who's going to gut shoot you for killing those women in Colorado and Wyoming." Suarez blinked, swallowed, and started to get up. "Keep your ass in the chair!"

He sat back. "What the hell are you talking about? I didn't kill any women. You've got something fucked up."

"I don't think so, shithead. How the hell do you think we ended up in an office with your name on the door without somebody dropping a dime on you? I just had a long talk with your buddies, Biggs and Landry. Turns out, they had a lot to say after I shot half of Landry's foot off. They told me you and your office mate next door gave the orders to kill two women. They said you didn't like Jeff Linfield backing out of a crooked deal and killed his sister as an example. You fucked up, Suarez—- you had my girlfriend killed to keep me from blowing the whistle on your scam. I'm Cort Scott, you prick, *and I'm going to cancel your fucking ticket!*" I was yelling by now.

"*Wait!* I didn't kill anybody. I've never even heard of you. Jesus Christ, man—- You've got something wrong. Sure, I was pissed off at Linfield. He's my fucking brother-in-law, for chrissakes. I didn't order any killings. I ain't got that kind of juice, man." Suarez jerked his thumb to his left. "Metropolit, though, he's connected. He's got these guys in New Orleans who can order that kinda shit. All I did was go to a meeting, man. I heard 'em talking about putting pressure on Jeff and that's all, I swear."

I knew he was lying. I listened for something from next door. I couldn't make out what was being said, so I backed up to the doorway, keeping my gun trained on Suarez. "George, you doing any good?"

"Maybe a little. It seems old Myron doesn't fancy getting shot or even roughed up. He seems kind of anxious to tell me all about how Suarez found a couple of mopes from down in the barrio to take a trip out to Colorado. Myron keeps talking about how he's just a bagman. He handles money for some guys…he wouldn't hurt a fly let alone a woman."

"*He's a fucking liar!*" Suarez yelled. He started to stand again. I motioned him back down with the Beretta. "He set me up with those guys. He's the one who's been calling the shots all along. I didn't know what was happening. All I did was go to a meeting in New Orleans and another one in Denver. I didn't have anything to do with anybody getting killed. Goddamn Landry did that. He works for those fuckers in New Orleans. They're the ones who gave the orders."

I said over my shoulder, "Why don't you bring Myron in here so these two 'buddies' can see each other while they're pointing fingers."

"Good idea. Move outta the doorway and we'll come for a visit."

I heard a chair scrape and in a couple of seconds Myron Metropolit shuffled into 112. George followed with his 9mm trained on the old man. Metropolit looked even older close up. I knew he was in his seventies; he appeared ancient. "If it isn't the old-timey mobster,

Myron Metropolit. I can't say it's a pleasure to meet you, you old bastard. It *is* going to be a pleasure dropping the hammer on your ass, though. Get over there and sit down."

Metropolit did as he was told. George walked up beside me and checked out Suarez. "This grease-ball have anything useful to say?"

"He's mostly trying to bullshit me——- just telling little dribs and drabs," I said. "Maybe being in the same conversation will help him out a little."

I looked at both men, then said, "Listen up, shitheads. We want the truth, all of it, and we want it right now. Here's something for you to think about before you try lying——- I've taken Landry on twice. The first time I took his gun away, beat the shit out of him, stomped on his hand, and made him crawl to his car. The next time, when he wouldn't tell me what I needed to know, I shot his foot off. He got real talkative then. Don't make the same mistake and think I won't fuck you up too——- because I will, big time."

Suarez squirmed in his chair and shot a glance at Metropolit.

"So, here's where we are…Landry and Biggs say you two are the prime movers in this deal…that you work directly with New Orleans. They said it was Metropolit's idea to rough up Linfield's sister. What've you got to say about that?"

It was Metropolit's turn to glance at Suarez. His wrinkled and lined face was contorted, although he didn't appear particularly worried. He knew I was making it up as I went. He rubbed his stubbly chin and wheezed out, "The guys in New Orleans don't put up with any shit. When Linfield tried to back out, they told Landry to keep on him, and to teach him a lesson. Landry figured if they got rid of the sister, Linfield would end up running the family's money and he'd go along with anything we said. Me and Suarez met Landry and he told us to hook up with some Mexican in San Diego who'd done some work for him."

"What kind of work?" I asked.

"You know what kind of work—- hired muscle work," Metropolit said.

"Go ahead."

"He gave us a name and—-"

"What's the name?" I interrupted.

Metropolit sat back and glanced out the window. He looked at Suarez, but didn't say anything. George quietly said, "You better say something, *Myron*. If you don't, I'm going to find out how it feels to fire a warning shot right through *your* goddamn foot. It worked on Landry and I don't think you're nearly as tough as him."

"Fernando Aquilar," he answered. "He goes by Freddy. We found him and told him what Landry wanted done. He said he wanted us to find someone local to help. It was a two man job. Ron remembered this Benitez guy who used to work with him at a delivery outfit. The guy'd been in the pen for second degree murder and made parole after sixteen years. We got ahold of him and set up a meet with Aquilar. We laid it out and told him there was twenty grand in it for him. He went for it, but that was for taking care of Linfield's sister. We didn't know anything about what happened after that, about another woman. That must have come up after Freddy and Benitez got to Colorado."

"How much did you promise Aquilar?" George's voice shook a little.

"Thirty."

I asked Metropolit, "What happened after you told them what to do?"

"The next thing we knew, Freddy showed up here three days ago and said he needed to talk to Landry. He didn't tell us anything else, he made us leave the office when he called Landry. When he left, he said Landry owed him more money. He said he'd done more than we'd agreed. That's the last thing we heard. We've been wondering what's happening because Landry used to call damn near every day."

I jabbed my gun at Suarez. "Your turn, asshole. I want you to do your share. What do these guys look like and where can we find them?"

Suarez knew it was over. He gave up the tough guy attitude. "Freddy is real dark for a Mexican. He wears his hair in a buzz cut and almost always wears a baseball cap.

"Benitez is a big son-of-a-bitch. He must be as tall as you." Suarez pointed at George. "He used to box. I heard he was the toughest guy in the Pelican Bay pen and that's saying something. That was several years ago and he's put on some fat since then."

Benitez sounded like the guy who came to my house with Landry.

George repeated my question. "Where are they?"

Suarez shifted positions again. "I don't know if they're together, if they are, they're probably at Benitez's place. He's got a place across the bridge over in San Pedro."

George asked, "What kinda place?"

Suarez said, "A junk-pile house out by the end of the jetty road."

I exchanged glances with George. "You got any more questions for these jerks?" George shook his head no.

I said, "Okay, we'll get the cops over here and follow up on what you told us. If it checks out, for what it's worth, we'll tell the cops you cooperated. Either way, you're both looking at stiff jolts in the pen. And Myron, you dumb fuck, you're going to get tagged with being a habitual." I faked a laugh. "If we say you cooperated, maybe you can get into a nice soft can where you'll be a white guy's bitch instead of some big black gangbanger's."

George said, "Keep an eye on 'em for a minute, I'll pull the car up. Buck said there are some cuffs in the back."

"Go ahead. I'm already tired of listening to these assholes."

When George left, I said, "I should just gut shoot both of you right now. You killed one of the best people in the world...a woman I cared about. The only thing keeping me from doing it is I want to do it to the bastards who did the murder. I'm still tempted to put a round in you and tell the cops we had to shoot you to keep you from escaping."

By the time I finished my little speech, George was back. He brought twist-tie restraints, put them around their wrists behind their backs, and around their ankles. They weren't going anywhere.

"Who should we call first?" I asked.

"Call Tom, fill him in, and have him call LAPD. When you're done, I'll call Buck and have him come by for these birds."

I picked up Suarez's desk phone and dialed Tom's direct office number. I checked my watch, which was still on Denver time. It was 9:05 a.m. in Denver.

"Detective Tom Montgomery."

I did a double take until I realized his caller ID was probably showing LA Warehouse Leasing with an LA area code. He would recognize the name and was wondering what the hell was going on.

"Tom, it's Cort. I'm calling from Ron Suarez' office."

"That must mean you're still alive."

"So far so good. I've had a very interesting conversation with Metropolit and Ron Suarez. They've given me a big head start on where to find Benitez and Aquilar, the killers. One thing is particularly interesting—- Landry may be a lot more involved than he's admitted. Gerri might have been killed on his orders alone. New Orleans might not have known about her. Go ahead and call LAPD and tell them what we got out of Biggs and Landry. Tell 'em about me just like you planned. By the time they get up to speed, I should have the rest of it wrapped up. If it all goes down, I'll tell them the rest of the story."

"Okay, I got it. Did they give you any shit? You have to shoot anybody to get the story?" Tom didn't sound too amused.

"It worked out well. I got the drop on them with no problem. Metropolit is older than dirt. He might have been a tough nut to crack twenty years ago, but I think he knew the jig was up. Suarez acted dumb, tried to hold out, and bullshit me. When Metropolit started crying the blues, Suarez came around. He didn't want to take the weight all by his lonesome."

"Good deal. You need to hold down the shooting crap. It's not a good precedent."

"I've gotta go. I've got places to be and people to meet."

"Keep being careful."

I'd decided not to tell Tom that George was with me. It wouldn't change anything and was something Tom didn't need to know. George, who'd listened to my end of the conversation, said, "I see what you're doing and I appreciate it. Tom's a friend, however what he doesn't know won't hurt him and won't come back to bite me in the ass either. Before I call Buck, why don't we toss this place and see if we can find anything that'll give him a good reason to lock these two assholes up? That way, by the time Tom calls LAPD and they start hunting for 'em, they'll be pleasantly surprised to find the sheriff's office has them in custody on dope charges."

"Works for me," I said. George had brought latex gloves along with the cuffs and we each rolled on a pair. We started pulling drawers and files, and poking through the cabinets, most were empty or had a few loose papers. One drawer in Suarez's desk had a bunch of keys with no tags on a board. We took turns checking other offices down the hall. All were empty. Finally, I said, "This isn't working. Got any more ideas?"

"One or two." He walked back to 112 and looked at the sad sacks. "You both know you're fucked, however they're some things that might make it easier on you. You'll be a lot better off in the sheriff's county jail than in LAPD's Central lockup, and if you go in on a dope bust, you won't have a lot of trouble. On the other hand, if you go either place with a snitch collar, you're gonna be in deep shit. If you guys have any dope here or know where to get some real quick-like, we can make sure the sheriff gets you instead of LAPD. What do you say?"

"Fuck off," Suarez said. "I've said all I'm going to. You assholes just want to add drug charges"

Metropolit shook his head. "Shut up, Ron. He's right. It's a hell of lot better to be with a bunch of dopers in county than with the hard cases at Central. If the New Orleans guys get even the slightest hint we've been busted and cooperated, they'll put a contract on us so fast we might not even clear booking."

"Who's going to tell them anything?" Suarez countered.

George chuckled and answered. "We will, you dumbshit. That'd be easy. Hell, we wouldn't even have to call New Orleans. We'd just let it drop that you guys are being booked into Central as material witnesses and are cooperating in a big time investigation. Believe me, tough guy, that's all it'll take."

"You...you can't do something like that." Suarez looked incredulous.

I liked the idea. I hoped Suarez would keep up his newly acquired bravado. I said, "Maybe *he* wouldn't, but *I* would, dipshit. It would save me the trouble of killing you. And I wouldn't have any risk either."

Suarez caved for the second time. "Up on the second floor, it's all container lockers. About halfway back on the right side are a bunch with numbers ending in 998X. If you look at the keyboard in my desk, you'll find some keys with the same numbers on them. There's all kinds of shit up there, coke, speed, oxycontin pills, whatever."

George called Buck and told him we had Metropolit and Suarez and would be waiting for them, although we needed to move—-we'd got a location on the hitters. As he gave him the address and the information about the dope, I could hear Buck laughing through the phone. George asked him to book Metropolit and Suarez into county on drug charges. Because Central was always overflowing, LAPD was usually happy to leave perps in county lockup until bail or trial. In this case, they'd probably end up being extradited to Denver on charges a lot more serious than drugs.

George's tone changed. "Hey, Buck, what kind of firepower do you have sitting around your place? We don't have any idea how loaded up these two creeps we're going after might be. I'd like to have a shock-and-awe strategy."

I couldn't hear what Buck said. George kept nodding. When he got off the phone, he grinned. "Buck's happy as a pig in a mud hole. He'll be right over. They're bringing us a couple of things to give us a little more impact if we need it. Tim's driving his van and Buck's in a cruiser to pick up these two. Let's go out front to meet 'em. We can put the 'package' they're bringing in the Durango and be on our way."

"Are you just going to leave us here like this?" Suarez complained.

George grinned. "That's the plan. Why? You gotta piss or something?"

Metropolit didn't say anything.

chapter

THIRTY-FIVE

Tim and Buck pulled up and parked the van behind the Durango. Tim slid the door back and raised the hatch on the Durango. He checked the street, reached in the van, and took out a couple of shotguns—- a Browning 12-gauge pump and a Beretta Street Sweeper automatic. He quickly transferred them to the Durango, sliding them under the floor matt. Buck grinned and shook hands with George. "They've both got six-shell magazines and are loaded. Here's a couple more boxes of double-ought buckshot just in case. It's been our 'experience' when you start blasting with the Street Sweeper, bad guys sometimes rethink their position."

I shook hands with both of them. "Thanks, fellas, we owe you."

We took the Seaside Freeway, crossed the toll bridge, and entered San Pedro. We had to drive around a little before George spotted the jetty road. The jetty ran about a mile to the harbor entrance. The road only went about half way. There were a few trashy houses along the road, which wasn't paved——- just sand and pea gravel. We couldn't see any bushes or trees to provide cover. Suarez had said Benitez' place was at the end of the road. An open lot sat between his house and the next building. Other than dune grass and trash, there wasn't anything in the lot. Getting close to the house was going to be a chore.

George pushed his hat back and stared over his sunglasses. "Shit. This isn't going to be easy, is it?"

"Nobody promised it would be. We'll have to put off making a move until dark and even then, we'll be out in the open."

George studied the set up. "Let's drive past the house to where those cars are parked. I can see some people out on the jetty. I'll bet they go out there to fish. We can probably get at least that close without attracting much attention. We can check out the house on the way by, I'm guessing it's maybe fifty yards from the cars to the house. We'll have a lot better idea of how things set up."

I said, "Let's switch seats and I'll drive. That'll put me on the other side when we drive past the house. Benitez got a good look at me when I was punching him out on my front porch. When we get to the cars, I'll park sideways and keep the truck between me and the house."

"Good thinking." George nodded and we switched.

I started the truck down the road. We were both pointing and gesturing as if we'd just discovered the road and were looking for a parking spot. That part, at least, was true. Benitez' place was a dump. On the far side, toward the parked cars, it had an attached carport with an older model Chevy Caprice in it. The good news was there were no windows on that side of the house. The house had one small front window and the top half of the door was glass. The curtains were drawn. A couple of cement pavers on blocks formed the porch. The whole place sat on blocks providing a crawl space under the house. We could see the pipes and foundation supports.

I parked and saw George was right about the people on the jetty. Two groups of fishermen about fifty yards apart were perched on the rocks. The closest were a few hundred feet from the cars.

George studied them for a while, sighed, and finally said, "I don't like having civilians here. If this comes down to a gunfight, and I think it will, they're too close. Even if we win, they'll be able to give a good description of our rig, maybe even get the plate number."

"What do you know about jetty fishing? Do they fish after dark?"

"Damned if I know—- it's only about noon and they're already here. I can't believe they'd stay all day and all night too. Maybe we can wait 'em out. Hopefully, no one else shows up to take their place."

"Why don't we join them?"

"You mean go fishing?"

"Yeah. We can go into Wal-Mart and buy some cheap poles, come back out here, and walk out a little ways. We don't really have to fish. We just throw the lines in the water and sit. We outwait the real fishermen and when they clear out, we come back to the truck, get out the guns, and run over to the house from the blind side."

"Could work. I hope we don't have to sit out there too long. These mutts could take off at any time and then we're stuck doing a stake out until they come back."

"I don't think we have a lot of options with that damn house located like it is."

"Let's do it then."

I started the truck and we did a looping turn that took us completely out of sight of the house. We confirmed there were no windows on the side toward the fishermen's cars. I drove back past the house, put my hand and arm up by my face so anyone looking out couldn't get a clear view. We drove toward San Pedro until we spotted a Big 5 Sporting Goods store, went in, and bought two sets of cheap fishing gear.

We grabbed In-and-Out hamburgers, super-sized drinks, and hoped our bladders would hold out.

As we started down the jetty road to the parking area, the Caprice backed out of the carport and headed our way. George muttered, "Ah, shit!"

There wasn't anything to do but keep going. If we stopped and turned around, the dirtballs would notice. When they were fifty feet away, I reached up and made a production of lowering the sun screen so my arm was up and covering most of my face when they passed. Two men were in the car. I got a good look at the driver and there was no doubt—- he was the guy who'd tried to bust into my house. We were in the right place. "Did you get a look at the passenger?" I asked George. "The driver was definitely Benitez, the guy who came to my house."

"Not really, I was trying not to make eye contact."

"That's all right, we know we're in the right place. This might actually work out good. Let's park the truck and bust into the house. We can be all set up when they come back, and we'll be the ones with surprise on our side."

"I like it. Let's hurry. We need to get in there."

We drove to the parking area and pulled in away from the other cars. Just as we started to get out, George said, "Hold it. One bunch of fishermen is coming back."

Three guys were headed our way carrying their gear. We got out the burgers, rolled down the windows, and started eating. The fishermen walked slower than hell, taking forever to get to their car. They never even looked our way, just loaded up, got out a six pack of Coors Light, and took off. The other fishermen were a good three hundred yards away. They couldn't read any license tags from there.

We stuffed the remains of the burgers back in the bag, checked in both directions, and hurried to get the shotguns and ammo out of the back. George opened the sheriff's first aid-kit and got out two pair of latex gloves. "Put these on. If we do what we planned, there's no reason to leave any more evidence than we have to." I took the gloves.

We checked the road again, it was clear. Same thing with the fishermen, no movement from them. We ran across the open space to the back corner of the house near the carport. Everything stayed quiet. George peeked around back and motioned for me to follow. Another set of cement steps led to a weather-beaten backdoor. Although this door didn't have glass, there was a window which we crouched beneath. George took off his hat and slowly straightened until he could see in. He stood still for several seconds before resuming his crouch.

He whispered, "Window's in the kitchen. There's a small table with four chairs right in the center of the room. It looks like a linoleum floor. The fridge is on the far wall, stove is to the right, and the sink is right under the window. I can see down a hall into the front room. I saw a couch under the front window to the left of the door and not much else."

We stepped up on the blocks in front of the door and I tried the knob. It was locked. With no room on the steps to get any leverage, George handed me the shotgun, leaned back, and kicked the door next to the knob. It must have been rotted from the ocean air because the whole damn thing exploded like we'd set off a charge. The door burst in, banged against the wall, and came back fast. George was already inside and stopped it. The wood on the inside of the jamb was completely destroyed with a big chunk lying on the floor.

I got inside as fast as I could and shut the door behind me. We did a quick recon of the rest of the house, which wasn't much. We found two dinky bedrooms with a postage stamp sized bathroom between them off the hall. Both had only enough room for a double bed and a cheap nightstand. The closets were the stand-up kind in the corners. The living room crossed the front of the house and shared a wall with one of the bedrooms and the kitchen. The whole place was about eight hundred square feet.

We went back to the kitchen. George picked up the piece of door jamb, turned it over and said, "This could be a problem if they use this door to come and go." I hadn't had time to think about it. He was right. We should have figured another way to get in the house.

"Let's prop it back together enough that they'll come in the house. There's no way to hide in the kitchen." George held the wood up to the jamb. It was a fairly clean break without too many splinters and fit like a puzzle piece.

"If we can find something to hold it in place, it might last long enough to get the job done." I searched around the kitchen without finding anything, so went to the living room. An old TV was sitting on a beat-up cabinet along the wall. I pulled out the top right drawer and found exactly what I was looking for: duct tape. I took it back to the kitchen and raised it like I'd won first prize.

Putting the jamb back together was a two-man job. We had to put the bolt into the seat at an angle with the door open. Then, we closed the door and fit the jamb back into the wall where it had been knocked off. After a couple of tries, we got it. George held it in place while I taped it all together as securely as I could. We turned the inside bolt lock and it seemed to work. Once the door was unlocked and opened, it would be obvious it had been kicked in and repaired. We'd have to jump them as quickly as possible.

I shook my head. "How should we handle this now? They'll see the tape soon as they get inside. They'll be single file and one of 'em will still be outside when the first guy starts in."

George sounded frustrated. "This screws up our plan some. What about this? One of us will go outside and we'll close and lock the door. The other one waits in the living room where he can see them coming. When they unlock the door and the first one goes in, the inside guy steps into the kitchen with the shotgun on him. The outside guy comes around the corner with a gun on the other one."

I considered his plan for a few seconds. "We don't have time to come up with anything better. I guess we'll have to hope they won't be too damn long and our timing is good when they get here. You want to be Mr. Inside or Mr. Outside?"

George cleared his throat and looked straight in my eyes. "First, we need to decide what we're going to do with these guys."

"What are you talking about?"

"Are we trying to grab 'em, get some answers, and turn them over to the local cops? Are we trying to get them back to Colorado? Or maybe we're just here to kill 'em, you know, put an end to the whole damn thing right now."

That was a shot across the bow. I hadn't thought it through too well. I didn't know what I intended to do. Revenge was high on the list—- but what kind and for whom? What about the assholes in New Orleans who were ultimately behind the whole deal? Weren't they just as guilty as the Mexicans? If we murdered these two, what would we do about New Orleans? How the hell did I get this far without thinking through all this?

I didn't break the gaze between us. "What a time to be asking that. These guys killed two women who meant something, maybe everything, to each of us. They aren't going to give it up easy. I think we should just let it play out. Let's try to grab 'em. If we can get more information out of them and tie it all together, we may be able to make murder cases against everybody from New Orleans to Denver, including Metropolit. The more I think about it, the more I know I want to finish off Landry. The perfect ending would be to have that bastard laying between these two, waiting for the death needle." We both glanced out the front window as we heard a car. It wasn't the Caprice. George leaned against the counter, I pulled out a chair and sat down.

I said, "If this pair winds up dead, we'll have to come up with a story that'll keep us out of jail. If we kill 'em, there'll be lots of loose ends hanging out. Landry, Biggs, Metropolit, and Suarez. Hell, even Buck and Tim—- and Tom when you get right down to it. Nobody but the pilots and Buck and Tim know you're here. Metropolit and Suarez don't know who you are. Let's keep it that way. If the Mexicans end up dead, I'll try to keep you out of it. My story'll be I came looking for them, found 'em in this rat hole, and we got in a gunfight. Even though they started shooting first, I had better equipment and killed 'em both. It'll be my word against two dead felons. It'll work out."

George dropped his head and let his shoulders sag. "I've never planned a murder before. I don't like it much. This doesn't make us much better than them, does it? I guess if it turns out that way, we'll learn to live with it. The bastards killed Mary and your friend Gerri. What's worse, they did it for money. They did it on somebody else's orders. As far as I'm concerned, they signed their own goddamn death warrants."

George straightened up. "I'll go outside. If they make it inside the kitchen, aim the scatter gun right in the middle of whoever comes in and pull the trigger as fast and as many times as you can. Don't let him get a gun out, or turn, or duck, or run. I'll do the same outside. As soon as we're done, we need to pick up all the shells and I mean every damn one of them. Shotguns don't leave forensic evidence and both of 'em use the same ammo. If we kill 'em, we'll put their guns in their hands and squeeze off a couple of rounds each. We'll position the bodies so it looks like whoever shot 'em was inside and there was a shoot-out at the door. Goddamn it, I hope we don't have to do any of this shit!"

I stared at him for a few moments. "That's the way we'll play it."

We took turns using the toilet while the other guy watched the road. Nobody drove in. George stepped out onto the little back porch. We carefully shut the door and I turned the bolt lock. George tried the door from outside and it seemed pretty sturdy. I could see the tape give a little and thought it might allow us enough time.

I went to the living room and glanced up the road. Nothing was happening. I heard a knock on the back window and carefully looked down the hall. George's face was in the window and he was gesturing to come his way. I walked to the window, tried to raise it, and could only get it up about half an inch. George said, "The guys on the jetty are coming back. We might luck out and not have any-body around when this goes down."

"I hope the greasers don't get back while the fishermen are packing up and leaving."

"Yeah, that would be bad timing. I'm going to step around the corner so the fishermen won't see me back here. That'll put me on the street side of the house for a bit."

"It's probably better than being spotted by the fishermen."

I closed the window and hoped like hell Benitez and Aquilar didn't show up in the next few minutes.

We lucked out. In three or four minutes, I saw the old Chero-kee pass the front of the house. I wondered if they'd looked for who-ever left the Durango parked out there. We sure as hell weren't on the jetty.

Time seemed to drag by like geologic epochs, which are mea-sured in tens of millions of years. The first time I checked my watch, it'd only been sixteen minutes; the second was twenty-nine. At least I could sit in a chair and look out to the street. George was prob-ably sitting on the cement steps out back. The day was turning hot and there wouldn't be any shade in back. I started to think this might turn out to be a giant waste of time. What if they'd taken off for good? Probably not—- clothes were hanging in the closets and stacked in the drawers. A couple of duffel bags were at the end of the hall. Still, it could be hours or even days until they came back.

Again, luck was with us. After two hours, I saw the Caprice turn off the pavement onto the dirt road to the house. I ran to the kitchen and hit the wall three times hard. George replied in the same way. I went back to the hallway, picked up the Browning pump and jacked a shell into the chamber. I could see the Caprice through the curtains and watched it turn in the driveway. My pulse start-ed pounding and my hands were sweating inside the damned latex gloves. I took a deep breath, held it, and tried to slow my heart rate.

I heard a noise at the back door, a shout, and then the explosion of George's shotgun.

What the fuck had gone wrong? I charged into the kitchen. The door was still closed. I saw Benitez standing outside the window with his hands in the air. I turned the bolt lock and opened the door. Benitez swiveled his head in my direction. His eyes widened as he recognized me. George was on the other side of the steps with the Street Sweeper at hip level aimed at Benitez. George yelled, "Get in the house, asshole. Cort, keep your gun on him."

chapter

THIRTY-SIX

Benitez took one step into the kitchen, stopped, and stared at my shotgun. I backed away and said, "You heard him. Get your ass in here. Leave room for him behind you."

Benitez moved into the kitchen and stood beside the stove. George followed and said, "Keep him covered while I get the damned door shut."

When George had the door closed and the bolt in place, he turned back to Benitez, patted him down, shook his head at me, and said, "Okay, shithead, pull out one of those chairs, straddle it, and sit on your hands." Benitez did as he was told. George said, "I was around the corner like we planned, only one car door slammed, so I waited until I heard him try the key. I jumped around the corner, put the scatter gun on him, and yelled at him to step off the porch with his hands up. I hoped you would hear and open the door. When you didn't, I fired the shotgun in the air to get you moving."

I started breathing regularly again and felt my pulse subside. "Good catch on the car. My pulse was so damn loud, I couldn't hear anything."

George grinned. "Must be your first try at this kinda shit. It does make your heart beat a little faster, doesn't it?"

I spoke to Benitez. "Where's Aquilar?"

"Who are you talking about? I don't know nobody by that name."

This time I yelled. "*GODDAMN IT!* Last time I saw you, I beat the shit outta both you and Landry. I shoulda shot you both right then and there. This time, you won't get off so easy! Now, where the hell is Aquilar?"

Benitez started to shake his head. "Like I said, I don't know who—-

The blast from George's shotgun was so loud I almost pulled my own trigger when I jumped. I would have cut Benitez in two. George had shot the cabinet next to the stove about a foot from Benitez's left arm. At that distance, there was no room for a pattern to develop. Light streamed through the two inch hole in the cabinet and outside wall . *"The next one is in your left knee, motherfucker! Now answer his question!"* George yelled.

Benitez turned pale yellow and was having trouble catching his breath. He swallowed hard, dropped his head, and muttered, "I took him to the airport."

"Where's he going?" I asked in as loud a voice as I could. I hoped it wouldn't crack.

"New Orleans."

"What's he going there for?" George asked.

Benitez hadn't raised his head and I could barely hear him. "He went to see the bosses. They owe us money and we haven't been able to get ahold of anybody to pay us. We thought Aquilar would fly in, unannounced, and collect. We thought if we tried to call, they'd just blow us off. We want to surprise them, collect what they owe us, and split town for a while."

"Are you collecting for murdering two women?" I snarled.

Benitez raised his head. His eyes started to water. "I didn't kill either of them. I was there when they got killed, but that woman down in Colorado—- the fucking horse knocked her off the rocks when we tried to grab her. Aquilar did the woman up in Wyoming. I was just trying to get ahold of her, she was fighting like hell. She started to scream, and Aquilar hit her in the head with his gun. I guess he hit her too hard 'cause she dropped like a rock."

I turned to the side and silently choked back the puke rising in my throat. I hoped Benitez hadn't seen me. Screw getting anybody else. I wanted to shoot the bastard right now.

I swallowed hard and screamed, *"Did you go up there to kill her?"*

Benitez turned his torso back and forth on his hands, not looking at either of us. "Landry told us to go. He said the woman was in the way, and getting rid of her would fuck you up too. He was so mad about what you did to him, he wanted to get back at you any way he could. He told us to make everything look like a robbery turned bad, take her out to one of the old coal mines west of town, and get rid of her. We hadn't planned on killing her in the motel—- that's how it happened. We thought somebody might've heard something so we didn't take time to grab anything or try to make it look like a robbery. We got the hell out, drove down to Salt Lake City, and got a plane back here that night." Benitez shifted his weight and grimaced.

"When did you let Landry know what happened?" I was still choking back bile. It was hard to talk.

"We called him soon as we got back and told him we wanted the rest of our money."

"What do you mean, 'the rest of your money?'"

"He paid us up front to grab the woman in Colorado. He just gave us part of it for going to Wyoming. He kept making a big deal out of saying it was his own money, and he'd have to get the rest from New Orleans. Freddy said Landry and the guys in New Orleans would be good for it. That was the last we heard from Landry."

George said, "How did Aquilar know who to talk to in New Orleans?"

"He did some other work for those guys a long time ago," Benitez said. "He'd met them and Landry before."

It hit me suddenly. "We gotta go to New Orleans." I turned to Benitez. "What time is Aquilar taking off? When's he supposed to get there?"

"Plane's at 4:15. With the time change, he's supposed to get in around eleven their time."

I checked my watch; it was 3:12. I called Kirk. "Where are you guys? If we can make the airport by four, can you beat a commercial flight taking off from LAX at 4:15 to New Orleans?" I listened to his reply. "We'll see you at the plane. Thanks."

"Okay, we can do this—- call Buck, tell him we're taking off at four, and we're bringing a present. We haven't got time to screw around with this asshole so we'll drop him off with them. Will they be able to hold him if we tell 'em he's wanted for murder in Colorado?"

"Sure. What'd Kirk say?"

"They're on their way back from San Diego, about twenty minutes out. He said it'd be no sweat beating a commercial to New Orleans. We should make it an hour ahead of them. Did you get a good enough look at Aquilar to recognize him when he gets off the plane?"

George shrugged and looked at Benitez. "What was he wearing when you dropped him off?"

"Dark blue pants and a blue-and-white striped shirt."

George nodded, "There won't be many guys matching his description. We shouldn't have any trouble spotting him."

"Let's get a move on," I said. "We need to get this son-of-a-bitch to the truck. We'll call La Quinta on the way, tell them to check us out, and ship our bags."

I told Benitez to get up and we started out the door with him in the lead. No cars were parked by the Durango so we kept the shotguns on Benitez. When we got to the truck, George got out another set of twist-tie handcuffs, pulled Benitez's arms behind his back, and cuffed his wrists. We boosted him into the front passenger seat and shut the door. I got in the back seat.

George found the switch for the inside mounted flashers and lit them up as we tore down the road. We hit the highway and crossed back over the bridge. With the flashers on, we skipped the toll booth. We made good time to the airport and pulled into the police lot at 3:50. Buck was waiting beside the door, stepped over, and dragged Benitez out. "Can we expect some paper on this guy, George?"

"As soon as I can get on a phone with the Arapahoe County DA and get it started."

"The quicker the better. Hang-on, I've got an idea." He opened the trunk of their cruiser, took out a cardboard box, and using his fingernails, extracted a baggie with several colored tablets inside. He walked behind Benitez, dropped the bag into his right hand, and closed his fingers on it. Then he carefully took it back, again with his fingernails, and laid it on the seat. We stared at him.

He laughed at our expressions. "We hadn't marked up the evidence from busting those other jerks. It's just a natural follow-up that we went to this prick's house after they ratted him out and, Lordy, look what we found. Matching dope. Just good police work on our part. Now, we can hold him at County on the drug bust while you're getting us the paper."

George and I grabbed the briefcases for our guns, ran through the door into the police office, down the hall, and into the lobby. Kirk was inside and waved us out the door toward the plane.

***

We flew without talking for several minutes. Finally, I turned to George and said, "I'm glad you stopped Benitez outside. If he'd opened the door and come in, I probably would have cut him half."

George sat in silence for a couple moments. "That's what I was afraid of. Then we wouldn't have known where the other one was."

I thought about everything for a bit. "If we can believe Benitez, Aquilar killed Gerri. Do you believe the story about Mary Linfield's horse?"

George reclined his seat as much as he could. "I don't know. You said you heard the same thing from Landry, although it might just be what they told him. I don't see how it makes any difference."

I sat forward and stared into George's eyes. "The more I hear, the more it sounds like Landry caused both murders...I should've taken him out completely instead of just crippling the son-of-a-bitch. The good news is we might catch Aquilar with the New Orleans bunch. I hope we can control the situation down there because I want to hear what the head assholes have to say."

George nodded slowly. "I'm with you for whatever happens. If they'll talk, things will go easier, though I'm past the point of caring."

"Ya know, George, I gotta say it was kind of a surprise you were willing to let the cards play out."

He bowed his head and mumbled, "I kinda surprised myself. What's your plan for when we get in?"

"I've been thinking about that. First, we're going to need a car. I'll talk to Kirk and see if we can get one at the charter terminal. Next, we need to meet Aquilar's flight. Can you get your gun through security with your badge and ID?"

"Probably, although you can't. Yours will have to stay in the car."

"That's okay, we don't want a shoot-out in the terminal anyway. You can bet Aquilar has one in his checked baggage. When we spot him, we'll follow him. He'll have to get a rental car. What I don't know is whether he plans to see those guys tonight or try to catch up with them tomorrow."

"There's no way he's going after them tonight. It'll be past midnight by the time he gets downtown," George said.

"We just need to make sure we don't let him out of our sight."

"It'll end up being a long night sitting in a car someplace."

I went up front and asked Kirk if he could get us a car. He said he'd check and let us know. I asked Clark for an ETA and he told me another thirty minutes. I hoped we hadn't cut it too close.

Kirk gave me a thumbs up. "The Execu-Jet terminal has a couple of courtesy cars. They'll have a Ford Taurus ready for you as soon as we touch down. We'll start the descent in another five minutes. You should have plenty of time. I checked on the commercial and it's due at 10:53. We made good time and should be on the ground by 10:00. The only problem I see is the Execu-Jet terminal is clear across the airport from the general aviation gates. You'll have to drive around the airport and it's raining like hell."

I shook my head. "Why not? Everything else has gone like clockwork. Might as well have some kind of roadblock now that we're in the home stretch." Kirk shrugged. I went back and updated George. He just raised his eyebrows and sighed.

I felt the jets throttle back and we started our descent. When we dropped into the clouds, the ride got rough and stayed that way. It was eerie falling through the clouds with the landing lights reflecting from them. When we broke through the bottom, the city lights were laid out below us. The Mississippi was a series of black S curves dividing the lights. Lake Pontchartrain was a huge ink splotch in the sea of lights. The landing lights revealed heavy rain on the windows.

We came in hot and the reverse thrusters threw us forward against our seat belts. We taxied for a long way and eventually pulled up to a facility with *Execu-Jet* displayed in a large, rain-washed neon sign. Clark came back through the cabin and said, "Sorry about that one. The window wasn't very big and we had to drop through pretty fast. You guys okay?"

We both nodded.

When he opened the door and dropped the stairs, humidity rushed in and filled the cabin. The rain was coming down in sheets. Two women stood at the bottom of the stairs struggling with golf umbrellas. We grabbed our briefcases and got out, ducking under the umbrellas.

"Welcome to New Orleans, sir." The girl holding the umbrella was getting drowned trying to keep me covered.

"Why don't we make a run for it." I suggested. "I won't melt. See you inside." I took off sprinting and ran the fifty yards to the terminal. The girl tried to run with the umbrella in front of her and didn't have much success. Finally, we were all standing on the red carpet, dripping water everywhere.

"Do you ladies have a set of car keys for us?"

"Yes sir, we do. You 'all surely have picked a wet one to come and visit. Do you need any maps of the city or anything?" She was an attractive brunette even with her hair plastered down from the rain.

I said, "Tell us the quickest way to the main terminal. We need to pick up a passenger coming in from LA."

The other girl spoke up. "That's about the hardest trip you can make around this swamp, gentlemen." She was Creole and had the soft lilting accent common to her people. Her black hair sparkled like it was full of diamonds from the rainwater. "You 'all will need to take this street out front here to the right and go about half a mile to the entrance/exit gate. When you get there, take a left on East Airport Road and keep going until you come to the main terminal entrance. Then it's about another half mile to the parking facility. I suggest you take the Close-In Pickup and Drop-off. It's a right turn."

"Thanks, ladies. We're running a little late so we need to go. I hope you don't have many more inbounds tonight."

The pilots were coming in the door and I yelled, "We gotta hurry. Will you make the car arrangements for us?"

Kirk said, "Okay, good luck. We need to go back to Denver in the morning. Can you guys catch a regular flight when you're done?"

I yelled 'yes' over my shoulder as we ran out the front door.

chapter

THIRTY-SEVEN

It was still pouring buckets as I ran to the driver's side and jerked the handle. Luckily, the doors were unlocked and we piled in. The clock display indicated 10:20 local time. I followed the girl's directions to East Airport Road. The wipers barely put a dent in the rain. The first puddle I hit with speed caused the car to hydroplane and we almost went in the ditch so I slowed down. We made it to the main entrance at 10:35 and found a parking spot in a row close to the sliding doors. We had eighteen minutes to get inside and set up.

George slipped his gun into his shoulder holster, stepped out of the car and put on his jacket. He checked his wallet badge and ID and we hurried to the entrance. Inside, we checked the flight information boards and found the LAX inbound. It was now scheduled for an 11:05 arrival at Gate 47B. George said, "I'll check in with TSA and the airport security detail and meet you at the entrance to the baggage claim."

We split up and I headed for the baggage area. I saw George inside a small office talking to a huge black woman with a TSA shirt and insignia and a short, white guy in a New Orleans PD uniform. Everybody was nodding. George shook hands with the cop and the woman let him out the back door of the office. He walked over to where I was standing. "Man, that was way too easy. If we were in Denver, I'd still be cooling my heels. They took one look at my badge and ID, asked to see my weapon, and what I was planning to do, and let me through."

"What'd you tell them you were doing?"

"The truth. I said I've been tailing a murder suspect from Denver to LA and on to here. I said he's coming in on a commercial at 11:05. They said I shoulda called them in to help and then wished me luck."

We checked out the LAX flight for the baggage carousel... number three. Unfortunately, three was in the center of five carousels, opposite the main concourse entrance, so Aquilar would be coming in along with passengers from two or three other flights. I checked it out. "Let's split up. I'll hang out by the exits and try to spot him when he's picking up his bags. You go over by the rental car counters in case I miss him. When I spot him, I'll fall in behind after he passes and call your cell. Everybody in here's on a damn cell. Do you know whether the rental cars are in the terminal or remote?"

"No...I'll ask."

"Go ahead. We've got time."

After a minute, George came back and said, "Everybody except Alamo has their cars directly outside that doorway. Alamo's counter closed at 10:30, so we don't have to worry about them anyway."

"Perfect. Since we've got a few minutes, I'm going to check all the traffic lanes and exits. I don't wanta get hung up in the toll booth and lose him on the way out."

I headed toward the end of the building and the rental car exits. The exit for our parking area was separated from the rental car exits by a chain-link fence. We'd have to take a left and go up six aisles to the ticket booth. After exiting, we'd be on the same road as the rental cars. I took a minute to watch for traffic and didn't see a single car come out. I could see each of the rental car aisles from where I was standing, so we could wait inside long enough to see which counter he approached, go to our car, and pull up to the aisle before the ticket booth. We could see the door from there and watch him get in a car. As soon as he did, we'd pull through the ticket booth and be ready to follow him out.

I went back in and explained the set up to George. The displays over the baggage carousels changed and indicated his flight was on the ground. George took his position by the rental car counters. Unfortunately, there weren't many people in the terminal to blend in with. The flight schedule was light after about 9:00 p.m.

The buzzer on the carousel to the left went off and a few bags started to spit out. At the same time, twenty or thirty people entered the area from the concourse. The display said the plane was from Chicago. A few minutes later, the buzzer sounded on three. I looked at George and we exchanged nods. This time there was more of a delay until passengers started showing up.

There were seventy or eighty passengers, more than I'd expected. I spotted Aquilar immediately. He was wearing blue pants and a blue-and-white striped shirt like Benitez had said. He was a little older than I'd imagined, maybe fifty, medium height, under six feet, and stocky, probably around one-eighty. He had a dark complexion and a pock-marked face with a cookie-duster moustache. He wore a Dodgers cap so I couldn't see his hair. There wasn't anything particularly distinctive about his appearance. I was glad he didn't know either of us. It should make this a little easier. As he stood by the carousel, I nodded at George to make sure he'd seen him too.

I watched as most of the other passengers found their bags and left. Not many headed to the rental car counters so the area was almost deserted. Aquilar must have been one of the first guys to check-in because his bag was one of the last ones off. He had a large soft-sided duffel with a slide-out handle and wheels. He glanced around and headed directly for the rental car counters. So far, so good.

I stayed a little behind him and stopped when I reached George. We made a big show of shaking hands. Nothing registered with Aquilar. He bee-lined to the Budget counter and queued behind a fat woman with three kids who'd obviously had a long day. There was only one agent, a young black girl, who must have been good at her job as she was rapidly moving the fat woman through the process.

I handed George the car keys and said, "It's Budget. Let's head for the car. You drive, you've probably had practice at tailing people in a car. When we get in, pull up to the aisle right before the toll booth and wait. We should be able to see him come out and get his car. The Budget aisle is the second one in."

We got in the Taurus and George pulled into the aisle we wanted. It seemed like forever though it was only five minutes until Aquilar came out, walked down the line to a dark blue Chevy Impala, and put his bag in the trunk. George eased out, drove to the pay booth, and handed the attendant our ticket. The guy stared at it a minute and said, "Too bad, mister, you just missed the complimentary pickup parking by a couple of minutes. It'll be twelve dollars." As George reached back for his wallet, I saw Aquilar driving for the exit.

"We need to go."

George fumbled around a little, finally handing some cash to the attendant who took his time ringing it up. The gate arm went up as the register recorded the payment and George hit the gas. We spotted Aquilar's tail lights through the rain. As soon as we pulled out of the garage, the rain hit us full blast and George fumbled around finding the wiper switch. We were damn lucky there wasn't any traffic. After half a mile, the road merged with the exits from long-term parking and the drop-off lines. There still weren't a lot of cars, although enough that we needed to be closer to the Impala. George cut off a merging car and dropped in two cars behind Aquilar.

At the main airport entrance, the Impala turned onto Airline Highway toward downtown. We followed, staying two or three cars back and usually in another lane. Aquilar turned right on Clearview Parkway, dropped down to the Jefferson Highway, and pulled into a Super 8 motel. George went past the motel to the McDonald's next door and turned into the parking lot. We watched the Impala stop under the covered roof at the entrance. Aquilar got out and went in. He must have had to wake up a desk clerk because he was inside almost fifteen minutes. I checked the dashboard clock: 12:18 a.m.——- an hour and thirteen minutes from landing. The prick had made good time.

Aquilar returned to his car, drove back through the entrance, and around the side. From McDonald's, we could see the back parking area and the rear of the motel. He drove halfway down and took a spot next to the rear entrance. We watched him go inside and a couple minutes later, a light went on in a ground floor room three windows from the door. We watched for another five minutes, circled the McDonald's, and went back toward the motel from the other direction. We turned into the Super 8, drove around back past the Impala and Aquilar's room to the far corner of the lot. George parked, facing out, in the back row between a pickup with Texas plates and a beat up Cadillac Sedan de Ville. The rain had slowed but hadn't quit.

George unbuckled his seat belt and pushed the seat back as far as it would go. I did the same. "Not much legroom for a guy like me," he said. "He's in for the night. We're stuck here till he makes a move tomorrow. Would you go over to the McDonald's and get a couple of coffees? We can put a plan together for tomorrow."

Just as he said it, the lights went off at McDonald's. "Shit. So much for that idea," George snorted. "Wasn't there a Lamar's Doughnuts back a mile or so? They stay open twenty-four seven. Aquilar just shut off his light. He's not going anyplace. We'll get some coffee and a doughnut, use their restroom, and be back in less than half an hour."

"Okay by me if you don't think he's going anywhere." Coffee sounded good.

"He's in to stay."

We found the doughnut shop, although it was more than a mile. We went in, ordered, and took turns using the can. Walking back to the car, George said, "Hey, it quit raining."

"That'll make it a lot less depressing sitting in a car all night."

We drove back to the motel and parked in the same spot. "What's our plan, George? How do you think tomorrow will play out?"

"Aquilar knows where these local mutts hang out. He's gonna make a run at surprising them in the morning. I figure he'll go in hot and try to jack 'em up for some cash right on the spot. If they've got enough around, he'll take it and run. If they don't, he'll hold a gun on one of 'em and send the others to get more cash."

I thought about that for a minute while I sipped coffee. "When's our best shot at getting all of 'em?"

George pulled the lid off the coffee cup and took a big gulp. "Hard to say...everything could go to shit the second he walks in, especially if they've got muscle standing around. Or it might go easy if he gets the drop on them, they pay up, and he takes off.

"If they're in a restaurant or bar, anything open to the public, we can probably get inside and see what's happening. If it's an office or house, we'll be blind. We need to decide whether to try to take them all at the same time or pick 'em off one-by-one."

I finished my coffee and said, "I'd vote for trying to get them all at once if we're not totally outmanned."

"I thought you'd say that. Let's go this way—- if it's a place where we can see what's happening, we'll walk into the middle of it like a couple of dumb tourists. If we're blind, we'll wait and see what happens. If he pulls it off, we'll grab Aquilar by himself. Then, I'd say we get some help from NOPD to go after the locals."

I nodded. "That sounds good. And this time, I *really* don't care if Aquilar ends up dead."

George nodded back. "No argument from me."

We sat silently for a while. Finally, near two o'clock, George said, "There's no reason we couldn't catch a couple of hours of sleep. Why don't you climb in the back and try to grab a few Zs. I'll wake you about four, then I'll sleep till six. The McDs will probably open at six and we can get some more coffee. I doubt if anything much will happen before eight or nine."

"George, I'm so jacked up on coffee and adrenaline, I feel like a tree full of owls. Why don't we switch the shifts?"

George laughed. "A tree full of owls? Where the hell did you hear that?"

"An old-time friend of mine, long dead, used to say it all the time."

"That's funny as hell. Okay, sure, we can switch, just don't forget to wake me around four. Don't try to Ironman it. You need to be sharp tomorrow."

"I'll play it straight."

George unwound himself from under the wheel, closed the door quietly, and climbed in the back. I glanced in the back and said, "You'll have to be a contortionist to fit on that seat. Good luck on getting to sleep."

"I've done it before and in a lot smaller rigs than this." Ten minutes later, I heard his breathing slow and become deeper. I guess he was right.

Half an hour later, the light in Aquilar's room flipped on.

chapter

THIRTY-EIGHT

I made a quick decision not to wake George unless Aquilar came outside. After a couple minutes, the light shut off. He must have had to use the can.

I sat in the darkened car thinking about all that had happened since last fall—- the Linfields, Biggs, Landry and LA...all of it. The thoughts of Gerri and Lindsey filled my conscience. My life was totally different from a few months earlier and I would never go back to being a retired geologist.

Gerri's death and the success of her well were game changers in several ways. If I was even close to right about the size of the field she'd discovered, my share of Mountain West would be worth millions. Yet, what difference would it make? Martin Gear was right—- she was dead and all the money in the world wouldn't change that.

I thought about the things Gerri had cared about, the things she might have spent her fortune on. I realized I didn't know Gerri as well as I'd thought. Although I knew the things she liked, I didn't know what she was passionate about. I didn't even know if she had a will. If she did, it might provide some answers. With her folks dead and being estranged from her free-spirited brother, I couldn't imagine she would want him to inherit her fortune. I had a lot of loose ends to take care of when I got back to Denver, "if" I got back to Denver.

George stirred and I checked my watch: 4:05. I'd hardly noticed the time go by. "You're supposed to wake me up now. Are you going to do it?"

He unwound and climbed back in the driver's seat. "Anything happening?"

"Not much. His light came on for a couple minutes a half hour after you went to sleep. He must've had to piss. I would've awakened you if he came outside or something. There's been one car drive back here. A guy got out and went to the end room on the top floor. That was about 3:15. You were sawing logs pretty good."

"I don't snore." George acted like it concerned him.

I smiled at him. "No, George, you didn't snore. I'm not making any promises about myself."

I got in the back and tried to get comfortable on the bench seat. I wondered how George had managed. He was at least four or five inches taller than me. I tried different positions thinking this wasn't working...

***

"Cort, wake up. Something's happening." George's loud whisper brought me around. I bolted upright.

"What time is it?" I had to come back from another world.

"About 5:45. The light came on in Aquilar's room five minutes ago."

I rubbed the sleep out of my eyes and blinked a few times. The sky showed ribbons of pink and orange. I quickly slipped back into the front seat. I couldn't see much through the condensation on the windshield, however I could make out the light glow from Aquilar's window. His Impala was parked where he had left it.

"What do you think?" I asked.

"I don't know. All we can do is wait and watch. Unless he looks right at us, he won't see us with these fogged up windows. Better yet, let's move back over to the McDonald's and be in position to tail him when he comes out."

"Let's do it. I'd feel better with clean windows and a clear view of what he's doing."

George used his arm to wipe the driver's side windshield, started the car, and drove to the McDonald's lot. We cracked the windows an inch and turned the defroster fan to high. I couldn't see much until the heat kicked in and the window cleared. The McDonald's sign flared into golden arches and the inside lights came on behind us. I craved a bathroom and a cup of fresh coffee, but we couldn't risk missing our tail on Aquilar.

It was a good thing we hadn't taken a rest stop because a minute later he came out of the motel carrying his bag. He got behind the wheel and we saw a puff of steam as the engine started. He waited while the windows cleared, drove around the motel, turned right onto Claiborne, and headed downtown.

We circled Mickey D's and came out a block behind him. With no other cars on the street, we had to hope he hadn't noticed our white Taurus last night. He headed straight down Claiborne, dropped down to St. Charles, and pulled over to the curb between Louisiana and Jackson streets. Only two other cars were parked on the block. We drove past, took a right on Jackson, and pulled over. I could still see his car but at a bad angle and only the passenger side.

George said, "What's he doing?"

"I don't know. I can't see him. What should we to do?"

"*Shit!* This position is no good! What kinds of places are on the street?"

"Looks like a mixed bag, cafes and bars mixed in with houses."

"There's no telling which ones are open. Christ. It's only 6:30. He's either waiting for someone to show, meeting somebody, or maybe even thinking about breakfast. Either way, we're hung out here like goddamn laundry. Let me think a second." After a moment, George said, "We gotta take a chance. We'll drive to the end of this block, double back on the first street, then come back up to St. Charles. We can stop a block or so behind him. If we're lucky, we can duck in behind another car. At least we can see where he goes if he gets out... assuming he doesn't make his move while we're fucking around."

"Let's go for it." I didn't know what else to try although I hated letting him out of our sight long enough to get into a new position. I didn't have any better ideas though.

We took a right at the end of the block. By now, we were close to the river and the street curved around and jogged every couple hundred feet. Finally, we got on Tchoupitpulas Street and had to take it all the way to Audubon Park before we could turn back north to St. Charles. We were probably a mile east of where Aquilar had parked. With no traffic yet, George drove as fast as he could until we spotted the Impala. A block behind it, we pulled to the curb behind two other cars. With the curve in the street, we could clearly see the back and passenger side of the car.

A café in the front of a long, narrow two-story building was across the street from Aquilar's car. The buildings were closely packed storefronts and apartments except for a weed-filled vacant lot next to the café on the side toward us. Some buildings had the second story balconies and iron railings prevalent in this part of New Orleans. Most of the storefronts were lit and the café, in particular, looked open. I checked my watch: 6:53.

Finally, some good news. We both exhaled in relief when we saw smoke coming from the driver's side window. Aquilar hadn't gotten out while we were driving around, he was sitting in the car having a cigarette—- and waiting for someone. I wondered who he was waiting for...was this going to be the end of the line for Gerri's killers?

chapter

THIRTY-NINE

Although we were both stiff from our night in the car, we couldn't risk getting out to stretch. Twice, cars pulled up in front of the café. Both times they came from the other way. Each time a single driver got out and walked in. The first guy stayed only long enough to order, came out with a large foam cup, and drove away. The second one took a seat inside. We didn't know yet if the cafe was Aquilar's target.

At 8:10, a silver Lincoln Town Car passed us, drove ahead a few yards, and pulled up four or five spaces behind Aquilar. Two guys exited, crossed the street, and went into the café. One was fairly tall and heavily built; the other was short and fat. We kept watching. Three minutes later, Aquilar started across the street.

I said, "If that's who he's after, he must not have known their schedule. We've been here over an hour. How do we play it?"

George pulled his gun, jacked a round into the chamber, and opened the door. "We go *right now*. Get your gun ready and tuck it under your jacket when we cross the street. We'll cross right here and walk down the other side to the café. When we go in, we keep our guns out of sight until we can see what's going on and where everyone is situated.

"If the two outta the Lincoln and Aquilar are together out front, we walk right up to them with our guns up, and sort their asses out. If we can't see 'em, we have to assume they're in a room in the back or upstairs. In that case, we put the guns away, order coffee, and grab a table close to the door. We'll have to wait it out."

I put a round in the chamber and followed George. We crossed the street, walked down the sidewalk toward the café, opened the door, and went in. We were hit by the strong aroma of French roast coffee and chicory. One guy was sitting out front reading a folded-over paper. He didn't even glance up when we came in. Neither the Town Car guys nor Aquilar were anywhere in sight. We'd caught a break because the counter person had gone into the kitchen. We quickly holstered the guns and closed our windbreakers. As we approached the counter, a huge black woman came through the saloon style swinging doors from the kitchen.

"Marnin', gennelmuns! How're you all doin' dis marnin'? You all wan' some cawfee and beignets?"

"That sounds real good," George said.

I smiled. "You just made a sale, Sadie." I'd spotted the name plate above her monstrous bosom. "Make mine café au lait."

She boomed out a laugh. "Hoo-wee, Yankees! How on eart' did you Yankees find my l'il ol' place?"

George answered. "We were driving by, saw your lights on, and thought we saw a couple of guys come in. Must have been wrong though, I don't see anyone except that fellow."

"Nah, suh, you was right 'bout seeing some otha gennelmuns come in. Dey own dis here buildin'. Dey gots a little bit of an office way down to the back. Now, you fellas go on over dere and sit down and I'll be bringin' out yore cawfee and beignets in jus' a minute."

George asked, "Do you have a restroom here? We've been driving for quite a while and would like to wash up."

"It's right on down dat hall toward da office. It's da white doh' on da left."

As she turned back to the kitchen, George jerked his head toward the hallway. I glanced back at the customer. He was absorbed in his paper. We turned at the end of the counter, took out our guns, and walked down the hall. As we approached the lavatory door, we heard low voices coming from behind the door at the end of the hall. George opened and closed the bathroom door and took two long strides to the office. I did the same.

George counted to three with his fingers, kicked the door in, and we banged into the room. Aquilar had made a mistake when he'd forced the two mobsters into their office at gunpoint. He'd remained in front of the door after shutting it behind him. When George kicked it, the door smashed into Aquilar's left shoulder and hip. It knocked him to the right and completely off balance.

As he stumbled, Aquilar tried to shoot across his body. The bullet went wildly into the wall to our left. George's gun barked and Aquilar pitched forward and went down hard. He dropped the gun as he fell and it slid across the floor toward two desks in the back of the room.

The desks faced each other with just enough room behind each for chairs. The thugs from the Town Car were seated in the desk chairs.

The fat one leaned to reach for Aquilar's gun. George yelled, *"Hold it, shithead. Sit up or I'll blow your head off!"* The fat guy straightened back up. George said, "Both of you, put your hands on the desk and scoot your chairs up as far as they'll go." They did what he said. George stepped forward and kicked the gun back toward the door.

Aquilar was sprawled out on his back. A bullet hole was obvious high on his left hip. Blood started to leak out of the entry wound and began pooling next to his thigh. I couldn't tell whether the slug had gone through and into his guts or had lodged in his side. He was growing pale, his teeth were clenched, and his eyes were tightly closed. I stepped over and kicked him in the shoulder. *"Open your goddamn eyes!"*

His lids fluttered as he tried to open them. A tear ran out of the left one and trickled down into his ear. I yelled at him again, *"Goddamn it...I said open your fucking eyes!"*

As I pulled back to kick him again, he managed to get his eyes open. I leaned over and put the barrel of the .45 against his forehead. I watched the full gamut of emotions register in his flickering gaze. Fear, pain, hate—— they were all there. "I want to pull this trigger, you bastard! Except, that'd be the easy way out. I want you to hurt like hell for a while before I decide whether to let you live or not. You can stay alive a little longer if you answer some questions. Do you understand that, you grease-ball son-of-a-bitch?"

He grimaced and gave a nod. The fear and pain were crowding out the hate in his eyes. Tears flowed out of his left eye and dripped on the floor.

"Why'd you kill that woman in Denver? Who sent you to her place?"

He swallowed hard and tried to take a deep breath. It went in jagged. Finally, he managed a weak cough and whispered, "Landry. He send us. He say to grab woman an' keel her. He say make eet look like accident." He spoke with a heavy Spanish accent, although he obviously understood English.

"Say that again. Landry *told* you to kill her?"

"Si, he say to keel her."

"How did you kill her?" I knew George needed to hear the answer.

"When we try to grab woman, her horse knock her off rock first."

"Did Landry tell you to kill the woman in Wyoming too?"

Aquilar coughed and kept trying to catch his breath. He finally nodded. "Si."

"One more time, asshole. Landry *told* you to kill the woman?" Now, I needed to hear the answer.

"Si, he say grab woman, take her away, and keel her. He say throw her in mine. He say steal her papers, make look like she robbed."

"Did you get paid for killing them?"

"Landry pay some. He say he have to get money from dese guys."

I turned to the two thugs in their chairs. "You two are next. As soon as I'm finished here, I'm starting on you." They stared back with hard, black eyes.

I turned my gaze back to Aquilar. "How come you're here?"

"Landry no pay. Benitez and me call heem, but he no answer. He no call back. He owe us feefty thousand. I been New Orleans so come back to get money. Landry work for dese guys." That speech must have taken all his strength. His eyes rolled up as he lost consciousness. I felt his throat for a pulse; he still had one.

One more time I wished I'd shot Landry in the guts instead of the foot. The guy who killed Gerri was laying on the floor with my gun to his head. Landry was the one who'd ordered it. At that moment, I wanted both of them to suffer, and then die.

I needed one more thing. "Which one of you is DiPaulo and which one is Marcello? How 'bout you, fatty? What's your name?" I pointed my gun at the fat guy.

"I'm Marcello, who da fuck are you?" Marcello had a wheezy fat man's voice. He didn't look or sound scared. I wanted to change that.

"Are you thinking about where you wanta get shot, John? How about taking it in the balls? You're too damn fat for them to do you any good anyway. Push back from your desk a little and swing your chair around toward me. I can't get a clear shot at your nuts where you are."

Marcello stared. "Who da fuck you think you are, huh? You got any idea of da shit we can rain on you? You better drag dat dead Mex outta here and take da fuckin' cowboy with you."

I shifted my gaze from one to the other and settled back on Marcello. "You're in no position to be dictating terms, fatso. I told you to move your goddamn chair."

He shuffled his feet to back up the chair. When he had room, he swung his knees and turned the chair toward me. I lowered my aim a little, pointing the gun at his crotch. He shut up but didn't quit staring.

My gun sounded like a cannon going off. Marcello yelled and looked down at the bullet hole in the floor between his feet and then back at me.

I began wondering what was happening with Sadie and the customer. They were either scared as hell or should be calling the cops by now. I wasn't too surprised that neither had come down the hall. They might want to know what was happening, but gunshots had a way of stifling curiosity.

I made my voice as hard as I could. "I've got a question for you, fatty. Did you order those women killed? Think carefully how you answer. I'm going to keep pumping shots between your legs until I decide you're telling the truth. Who knows when my arm might get a little tired or I might flinch."

Marcello glanced at DiPaulo, then turned his gaze back to me, "You still ain't said who da hell you are." These guys were a big step up from Landry and Metropolit. The fat bastard had barely flinched when George shot Aquilar and he still didn't seem inclined to answer any questions. It occurred to me to pull a Landry on him, shoot him in the foot, and see if that bothered him. Maybe if he saw how *I* was connected to the questions I was asking, he would change his mind.

"I'm Cort Scott, lard-ass. I was working for the Linfields and it was my girlfriend you sent that pile of shit over there to kill."

A flicker of recognition showed in his eyes. "We didn't order 'em killed. We told Landry to rough up the woman in Colorado, you know, send a message to her and her weasel-ass brother. What the hell good would it do to kill her? She had the fucking purse strings."

DiPaulo nodded. I walked over to his side of the desk. He had remained sitting with his palms on the desk. I smashed my pistol grip on the fingers of his right hand at the second knuckle. He let out a loud gasp, groaned, and grabbed his right hand in his left.

"You agree with that, do you, Mo?"

Through clenched teeth, he said, "That's what happened."

"One or two more and we'll figure out how to finish this. Consider your answers carefully, the first one to answer gets a prize. The prize is I won't shoot the winner or break anymore fingers right now. No promises for the future. Did you order the hit on the woman in Wyoming?"

They both yelled at once. "*No!*"

"Good answer, shitheads. Now, the most important question of the day. Who did?"

Again, they answered simultaneously. "Landry."

I raised my eyebrows and gestured with the pistol for them to expand their answer. Marcello said, "We didn't even know about the woman in Wyoming until after it was done. Landry called two or three days after the deal in Colorado and told us what happened. He wanted us to pay another fifty grand to Aquilar and the other Mex. We told him to get fucked, we didn't have any part of that...it was on him. We told him he overpaid for Colorado. The Linfield woman wasn't supposed to get killed and this was his problem. That was the last we heard from him. We've been calling his cell and the Black Blizzard office for a couple of days, but nobody answers. We couldn't find out what had gone bad."

DiPaulo added, "It's like John says, everything's on Landry. We screwed up sending him to Denver. We needed somebody to keep an eye on that dip-wad, Biggs, and thought Landry could handle it. I think the little bastard got greedy. He planned on skimming off a bunch when the money started coming in. He thought the Linfield deal was his ticket. He got paranoid when it started falling apart.

Killing people is bad for business. No repeat customers, you know what I mean?"

I saw Sadie standing at the head of the hallway. I motioned for her to come down the hall and she waddled to the doorway. "What you be doin' in dere? You ain't killin' and robbin' Mistah Mo and Mistah John is you?" Her voice was shaky.

"We're definitely not robbing them, Sadie. We're still trying to figure out whether to kill them or not."

If Sadie was capable of turning pale, she did. "Oh, man, doan be sayin' shit like dat, mistah."

"Your landlords are mixed up in killing two women. One of them was my girlfriend. Where's your other customer, the guy reading the newspaper out front?"

"He done took off, mistah, soon as we heer'd dat door get busted in an' dem gunshots."

"Do you know him?"

"Yas, suh. Dat's Mistah Rene. He come in ever' marnin' for his cawfee and beignet, read dat paper, and den he go home."

"Is he going to call the police?" George spoke softly to the scared waitress.

"Doan rightly know, suh. Mister Rene, he doan hardly never say nothin'."

George raised his eyebrows at me. "I'm betting that guy will call the cops. You wanta wait around till they show up? We're going to have to tell the whole story."

I was thinking of a short cut. "I'm going to call Tom and tell him what's going on. He's got a friend in NOPD, a woman detective. If he'll give me her name, and she'll help us, maybe we can cut this deal off at the pass."

George said, "That's a lot of maybes. Probably worth a try, though."

Sadie seemed transfixed by Aquilar laying on the floor. Nothing registered on her broad face when I told her not to bother with the coffees we'd ordered. She slowly backed up to the doorway, turned, and started back up the hallway toward the cafe.

"You got these assholes, George?"

"Yeah, go ahead, make the call."

Aquilar groaned and started coming around. He wasn't going to be a threat. The bleeding had slowed down or quit. I didn't care, I wanted him to suffer.

I got out my cell, punched the speed dial, and waited. Tom answered and I could hear car noises and traffic so assumed he was driving to work. "Where the hell are you?" Tom was his normal affectionate self.

"I'm in New Orleans and I need help."

"How come every time I pick up a call from you, you need help? What is it this time?"

"I'm standing here with a gun on Fat John Marcello, his buddy, DiPaulo, and their hitter, Aquilar. He's the one who killed Gerri. I need to talk to your friend in the cop shop here."

"You shoot anybody yet?"

"Just Aquilar."

"*No shit!* Is he dead?"

"Not yet. I don't think he will be unless I let him bleed out."

"Too bad. Why didn't you kill the son-of-bitch?"

"I needed a couple of answers. We wanted to know who had ordered the killings."

"Who's 'we?'"

Shit. I 'd slipped up. I'd been carefully avoiding telling Tom that George was with me. I looked at George and mouthed, "I'm sorry." He shrugged.

"I wasn't planning on telling you for a while, but George Albins came with me. Kirk flew us to LA and we ran down Metropolit and Suarez. They folded like laundered sheets and spilled their guts on the hitters. It was Benitez and Aquilar, just like Landry said. Benitez was the one who came to my house with Landry. Aquilar's imported talent for these mopes in New Orleans. Aquilar split to come here before we could grab him. We got Benitez without much trouble. Suarez, Metropolit and Benitez are all in LA County jail.

"Here's the problem. We beat Aquilar to New Orleans and tailed him to DiPaulo's and Marcello's place. We busted in on them about twenty minutes ago. There was a little bit of a gunfight and Aquilar got shot. There 'may' be some witnesses who saw us come in. We don't know if he'll call the cops or not though we're betting he will. It would be great if your friend in NOPD could head that off. The hard part will be explaining how two of these bastards ended up dead. Aquilar for sure and whichever one of the others tries to escape." I looked at the two wise guys and winked.

Tom heaved a huge sigh. "You really are a fucking idiot, Cort. You should've called me when you took off for New Orleans. I could have gotten NOPD to help. I'm not sure we can clean this up after the fact. All I can do is give it a try.

"My friend is Therese Hebert. She's a detective sergeant in Central Homicide Division. She's a tough nut, likes to do things by the book—- I'm not sure if she'll help you. Give her a call and tell her you're a friend of mine. Tell her you've got a Colorado sheriff's investigator with you, and you've got three guys who are wanted for murder in Colorado and Wyoming. Admit you screwed up by not contacting NOPD as soon as you hit town. Here's where you might get lucky—- the Arapahoe DA issued arrest warrants yesterday on Mary Linfield's murder. I gave the DA's office the names Landry gave us. Call Therese right now. Good luck."

My pulse was pounding as I punched in the number Tom gave me for Therese Hebert. Although the adrenaline rush from the confrontation had subsided, anticipating dealing with an unfamiliar police department was jacking me up.

"Detective Hebert, Homicide. What can I do for you?" Therese Hebert had a lovely Louisiana accent.

"Good morning, Detective. My name's Cort Scott. I'm a friend of Tom Montgomery up in Denver."

"Yeah, Tom's mentioned you. Didn't I look up some information on some local scumbags for you a few months back?"

"That's the reason for my call. I'm standing here with a Colorado cop who's holding a gun on two of them——- DiPaulo and John Marcello. When we busted in, one of their button-men got shot. All of them are mixed up in the killings of two women, one in Colorado and the other in Wyoming. They were contract killings. The rest of the bastards are in jail in Denver and LA.

"I know we screwed up by not contacting you as soon as we hit town last night. We were tailing the hitter, didn't want to take a chance on losing him, and, well, we screwed up. We're asking you to cut us a little slack and help us out. There's paper on all these bastards, unfortunately, we're ahead of it."

Therese Hebert's accent wasn't as lovely at the new volume. *"Jesus Christ!* What kinda goddamn, rinky-dink outfit do you all think we're runnin' here? You can't come cowboyin' into New Orleans and start shooting people. I don't give a damn how good a friend of Tom's you are. *Shit!* Stay right where you are until I get there. I'll be in an unmarked, but I'll bring a prowl car and some uniforms. As soon as we walk in, lower your guns and let me and the uniforms take over the scene. You got all of that? Now give me the address, goddammit!"

"2987 St. Charles." She disconnected on her end. That hadn't gone as I had hoped. I looked at George. "I think we're in deep shit. That is one pissed off lady detective heading our way."

George shrugged again. "We're volunteers here. We weren't drafted into this deal."

I looked at DiPaulo who was holding his smashed hand. "Where's Davidoff? Are you guys planning to take the whole rap by yourselves?"

"He's in the fucking hospital. You ain't getting him. He's almost dead from cancer."

"I hope he's in pain." I also hoped Detective Sergeant Therese Hebert was going to extend some professional courtesy——- at least to George.

chapter

FORTY

Five minutes later we heard police sirens. I saw the flashers reflecting in the front door glass and watched Sadie waddle toward the door. It flew open before she got there. Two uniforms raced in with their service pistols out. They yelled at Sadie to get back and go sit down. As they started down the hall, a tall woman followed them down the hall. She also had a gun out. When they got to the door, the woman said, "Hold it, guys." She stepped between them into the office, looked at me, and said, "You Scott?"

I nodded. "Yes, I'm Cort Scott."

She surveyed the scene quickly. "Both of you lay your guns on the floor and step back here. Who's your partner?"

George answered, "Sheriff George Albins of the Arapahoe County Sheriff's department in Colorado." We laid our guns down carefully and stepped backward to the doorway. I felt cuffs go over my wrists and snap into place. They were cold, hard, and tight. I didn't like the feeling. Therese Hebert was taking no chances. She was doing things by the book, just like Tom said. I heard cuffs snap into place on George.

Hebert walked farther into the room to look around more carefully. She was a large woman, well proportioned, and reasonably attractive. Her clothes fit her well. No one would've been mistaken about who was in charge. She took the two steps over to Aquilar, squatted beside him, and put her left index finger on his throat above the carotid artery.

Aquilar stirred slightly and moaned. His eyes were open but not focused.

Hebert stood and said, "Looks like he'll make it if we get him moved pretty soon...that's probably a good thing for you two."

Marcello started to stand. Hebert told him to stay down and her tone didn't accommodate any argument. He started talking in his wheezy voice. "I don't know what the hell is happening here. Me and my partner were just coming in this in this morning when this Mex---"

Hebert cut him off. "You two assholes get up, come around, and stand facing the desk. Put your hands behind your backs. Patrolman, cuff 'em, then get the paramedics in here for the guy on the floor."

Four more officers crowded into the hall. Hebert said, "Put the gumbahs in different patrol cars and haul them down to the station house. I want 'em in separate interview rooms and don't let them talk to each other. I want the second team to go with the medics to Mercy Hospital. Make sure the guy on the floor is secured in a police ward when he comes out of surgery."

As the uniforms filed out with the mobsters, the EMT team arrived, wheeled in a stretcher gurney, loaded Aquilar on it, and took him to the ambulance.

Hebert looked at George and me, shook her head, and said, "You two are a couple of sorry looking fuck-ups. I oughta haul both your asses in and lock you up. *Goddamn it!* All you had to do was give me a call when you got in. I could've given you a hand with all this shit.

"We've had an undercover guy, Rene Marchand, sitting out front in this place for weeks now just waiting for an excuse to bust their asses. He called in about two minutes before you to say shots were fired. Now, I've got to make it look good in front of the uniforms plus explain everything to my boss...and maybe even the DA. You and that goddamn Montgomery owe me big time." She unlocked the cuffs. "Let's see if that big-assed waitress has some coffee. You two cowboys have a bunch of *'splainin'* to do. Don't forget to pick up your cannons."

chapter

FORTY-ONE

On the Wednesday after Labor Day a year later, I packed the ornate wooden case holding Gerri's urn and a bottle of '77 Jordan cabernet in the Corvette. I drove to Salida the long way through Colorado Springs, Canon City, and the Royal Gorge. It gave me three hours to think.

The past months had been a whirlwind of preliminaries, trials, verdicts, and sentencing hearings. I attended all of them. In the process, I learned more than I'd ever wanted to know about money laundering, racketeer influenced and criminal organizations...the RICO act, assault, assault with a deadly weapon, fraud, habitual criminal acts, conspiracy to commit murder, attempted murder, and the jackpot...first degree murder. The judges and juries had lengthy lists of charges to consider for the assemblage of assholes connected to Mary Linfield's and Gerri's murders.

Throughout all the trials, I'd been nervously awaiting one of the defense attorneys to raise the question of coerced confessions. I'd even retained my lawyer, Jason Masters, to monitor Biggs' and Landry's trials in case it came up and I would have to face some charges. Inexplicably, it never surfaced.

I still had lingering regrets about not killing Landry. He got twenty-five to life in Colorado plus another twenty-five to life in Wyoming—- to be served consecutively. That meant he'd never get out. Benitez testified against both Landry and Aquilar, and ended up with a life sentence because of his priors in California. He was going to serve it in the Super Max pen Colorado. Biggs got five to fifteen for RICO act crimes, fraud, and conspiracy to commit murder. When I attended his sentencing, he was a broken man and sobbed through the hearing. I caught his eye as the marshals marched him out. I gave him the finger and laughed out loud. That cost me five hundred dollars for contempt. It was worth every penny.

Maurice DiPaulo and John Marcello got the same sentences as Biggs. They both ended up in the federal pen in Lakewood, Colorado, although their lawyers, Renoir and Mondragon, were already appealing. I was extremely interested in the stated basis for the appeal...lack of jurisdiction. I would have bet they'd raise the coercion charge.

DiPaulo had been right about Davidoff. He never left the hospital in New Orleans, dying of stomach cancer two weeks after our shoot-out in the back of Sadie's café.

The old bag man, Myron Metropolit, caught a habitual criminal collar along with everything else and was doing life in Vacaville, California.

Ron Suarez came around early in the process and his testimony was instrumental in bringing down the entire drug operation. The feds were being quiet on his whereabouts and what kind of deal he'd cut. I suspected he may have gotten into the federal witness protection program. In some ways, I hoped he was smart enough to disappear forever. In other ways, I hoped he would screw up and end up doing some hard time.

Jeff Linfield testified at several trials and was never charged with any crimes. I was happy for him, Maria, and the reconciled Linfield family.

I was surprised, thrilled, and happy when Wyoming sentenced Aquilar to death. It would be years before they could stick a needle in his arm and he would suffer every day of it. The bullet George put in him had done a lot of damage. He would never walk and was in constant pain. I hoped the medical staff at the Wyoming state prison in Rawlins would cut his meds and keep him that way. Tom Montgomery, Jack Carstairs, and I attended Aquilar's death sentence hearing and celebrated long into the night afterward. It cost me another five hundred dollar contempt of court citation for loudly applauding when the judge told Aquilar he was going to die. Tom and Jack insisted on paying it for me.

I'd been on an emotional roller coaster through it all because Gerri's Green River Basin prospect turned out better than even I'd dreamed. Mountain West's stock had soared on news the well was completed for the largest gas flow rate in Wyoming history. It was unusual, although not unprecedented, when Martin Gear and I prevailed on the Wyoming oil and gas commission to name the giant gas field that resulted Gerri's Dream. It would be a fitting memorial.

***

I passed through downtown Salida, took US 285 north toward Buena Vista, then turned onto a paved county road paralleling the Arkansas River. I parked in a pull-off next to the river where the water shot between huge granite boulders and plunged into a slow, deep pool. I opened the wine, removed the urn from the box, walked down a path, and stepped onto a boulder where the water chute entered a long, deep pool. I sat on the edge of the boulder and balanced the urn next to me. I took a long drink of the Jordan, savoring the intensity of the cabernet, and remembering how it had been Gerri's favorite. I studied the water for a while and spotted a big German Brown trout working the riffle at the downstream end of the pool. After a couple of deep breaths, I removed the lid from the urn, averted my eyes, and tipped it upside down. The volume of ash was surprisingly small. Such a tiny residue for a life well lived. I focused on the rocks on the other side of the river. I couldn't watch Gerri's ashes swirl away in the current. I'd promised myself—- and her, I'd be strong for this.

When enough time had elapsed, I looked down. The water was clear with no trace of ashes. I stayed another few minutes and listened to the murmur and splash of the river. After a final drink, a toast, I emptied the rest of the bottle into the river and said, "Good bye, Gerri. It was a great ride and I'm sorry it ended like it did. I'll miss you forever. I'm moving on with life. I know that's what you would want for me."

Made in the USA
Charleston, SC
25 November 2012